Damn Yankees
By Cherie Claire

Damn Yankees (The Cajun Embassy series, Book Two)
© 2016 Cheré Dastugue Coen

For more information, visit www.cherieclaire.net
Printed in the United States of America

Cover Design and Interior Format

DAMN *Yankees*

CHERIE
AWARD-WINNING AUTHOR
CLAIRE

Dedication

This book is dedicated to the "Damn Yankee" in my life, my husband Bruce. He graciously followed me back to Cajun Country where he now makes a mean gumbo and I've even caught him saying y'all, although he denies it. I couldn't have asked for a better partner.

He lucked out as well. The Sox gained a new fan.

The gluten-free recipe included goes out to my good friend and awesome novelist Lauren Royal.

Chapter One

MAGGIE KNEW SHE WAS IN trouble the moment she spotted the crawfish pie. When she found two pairs of eyes staring at her from behind a table stocked with every cholesterol-ridden Cajun specialty, her mind raced. Surely in all her depressed state some important event hadn't arrived. Lizzy's wedding was not until the fall, Dewey's birthday had passed and the next Cajun Embassy event was a holiday family reunion months away in Louisiana.

Her best friends from college, now living across the country, sat before her in the living room of her meager Atlanta apartment, staring at her with anticipation.

"What's the occasion?"

Maggie's roommate Stacy Walker, who hailed from northern Alabama, joined the others carrying something more typically Southern, a plate of her mother's famous deviled eggs. "Maggie," she stated firmly, her face flushing.

Maggie let out the air she had been holding hostage, dropping her keys and purse on to the coffee table. She didn't like the looks of things. "What's going on?"

Suddenly, her friends bolted into action. Lizzy and Dewey slipped behind her to the door, blocking her exit. Then Lizzy grabbed her elbow and led her down on to the couch. Dewey and Stacy planted themselves on opposite chairs, folding their arms and offering such stern looks that an intense shiver ran up Maggie's spine.

Dewey leaned forward, her hair teased in a hip new hairstyle and her designer outfit snug about her curvaceous figure. She stood the queen among them, Southern perfection in all its glory dressed up in Hollywood flair.

"Maggie," she began as if talking to a child, hands planted firmly on her hips. "We need to talk to you."

If she hadn't felt so inadequate in her ripped jeans and unironed denim shirt, hair two days from washing and in need of a good cut, Maggie might have laughed. But, like so many times before, her professional friends reminded her of her many shortcomings and she felt like a child among goddesses.

Still, she wasn't going down easy. She leaned back against the couch and extended an arm along its top, trying to appear nonplussed. "What is this, an AA consultation?"

Stacy crossed her legs, tapping her Toms against the coffee table. "Well, now that you mention it, honey pie, it is."

"Right." Maggie glanced at the myriad bottles peeking over the edge of the couch. "That's why there's so much alcohol in this room."

"What's a Cajun Embassy meeting without alcohol?" Lizzy said in her subdued Cajun accent, a smile peeking out from beneath her erratic brown trellises. "What kind of friends do you think we are?"

Dewey leaned forward, her gaze now stern with worry. "You haven't returned our phone calls since the convention. Stacy said you've barely left your room, sometimes sleeping all day. We're worried about you."

Whatever hope Maggie carried disappeared. If she hadn't been surrounded, she would have charged for the door. "That's so sweet of you all but I'm fine, really."

"Hardly," Stacy said. "You haven't said a word since you came back home."

"Whatever's the problem," Lizzy wrapped an arm about her

shoulders and Dewey took her hand, "the Cajun Embassy is here."

Maggie quickly glanced toward the bedroom door, but there was no escape. She was trapped like a coon up a tree with hounds at its heels. "I love you all but I really don't want to talk about this."

"No kidding, sweetpea." Stacy descended on to the edge of the coffee table so they sat eye to eye. She folded a lazy leg over another and leaned an elbow on her knee. Maggie leaned back to avoid her stare, wondering where the air in her lungs had gone.

Dewey lightly touched her hand. "Please, Maggie. We're really worried."

Gazing around at the best friends a girl could have, Maggie felt remorse. No doubt their imaginations were soaring inside those intelligent journalistic brains. Maggie knew she had to clear the air, at least ease their worries.

"Nothing horrible happened to me at the journalism conference in Vegas." She ran a nervous hand through her hair that became stuck in the tangles. Pulling her hand free, Maggie realized she must look a sight. "I just did something really stupid."

All three women exhaled, then took long sips from their drinks, and in that instant Maggie felt insulted. So they worried she might have been raped or robed but doing something stupid, well that was something they were used to.

"Let me guess," Dewey began. "You didn't get a job and you're feeling low about it, especially since you've been laid off — what, three times now? It's nothing to feel bad about, Maggie. The job market for journalists is abysmal at best."

"And if it's about the money," Lizzy inserted, "I told you it was a gift sending you to Vegas in hopes of getting a job. If you didn't, no worries. You don't have to pay me back. You know I'm loaded these days since I won the California Lottery."

Only Stacy wasn't convinced it was that simple. She had witnessed Maggie's overindulgent sleeping patterns, days spent on the couch watching Hallmark movies, her refusal to talk to her friends who kept calling. "I don't think that's it," she whispered.

It was all eyes on deck again, staring at Maggie, waiting for answers. And just what was she going to say?

"It's really stupid." All three women took another sip of their drinks, then looked at each other for want of something to say. Maggie felt the hairs on the back of her neck rise. "I know I do stupid often but you could act a little more surprised."

Finally, Dewey put down her glass. "It's not that and you know it. We're waiting for you to tell us more."

"Right." Maggie smirked. "You're an editor at the top entertainment magazine in the world. What was it you did last month? Cannes?"

Dewey frowned. "It's not as glamorous as all that."

"I'm sure the south of France in May is a difficult pill to swallow."

Maggie turned to Lizzy. "And you won the lottery all right, plus married a millionaire and you both now live in this paradise outside Santa Barbara."

Both women attempted an argument, but Maggie held up her hands. "And my dear roommate, who is waiting anxiously for me to continue my rent payments, used to own her own newspaper."

"Don't get me into this," Stacy said in the middle of woofing down a deviled egg. "I'm not part of the Cajun Embassy."

Maggie picked up Dewey's glass of wine and downed in one gulp. "And I'm the laid-off queen who can't find a job. Who married a perfect stranger in Vegas on a whim."

She hadn't meant to blurt it out, but there it was, her ridiculous night in Vegas hanging before them all like the odor of a burnt gumbo roux.

"You did what?" Stacy began.

"Married?" Lizzy said.

"To whom?" said Dewey, always the grammatician among them.

Maggie closed her eyes, not knowing where to begin. How had it happened? To this day, she was never sure. Amazingly, as she exhaled deeply knowing that a full explanation was evident, it felt good to get the experience off her chest.

"I didn't have much luck at the convention," she began, sending Lizzy an apologetic look. "I was so low after losing my job at Georgia Roadways magazine that my heart wasn't in it. Or maybe the publishers interviewing me weren't interested."

"Doubtful," Dewey said with sincerity. "The job market sucks."

Maggie offered her a thankful smile. "Right, but I've had like what, three layoffs."

A silence followed that almost swallowed Maggie whole. She knew her friends supported and believed in her but three jobs in seven years? She saved them the embarrassment and plowed on. "Anyway, the last night of the conference I went to the lobby mixer and decided to take advantage of the free drinks. And that's when I met him."

"Who, *chèr*?" Lizzy asked.

"Jake Webster," Maggie remembered, and shivered at the deliciousness of his name, not to mention the rest of his being. "He walked by my table, looked at my nametag and reacted like we were old friends. To this day, I don't remember ever meeting him before. We talked for a long time, and then he asked me to dinner. We had martinis, wine with the meal and then champagne with dessert and the next thing I knew I was married."

Questions starting swirling around Maggie's head like swallows returning at sunset. All the same questions she had asked herself over and over again. How could she have fallen in love with a man after one night on the town, at a journalism convention no less where she was trying to find a job, not a husband? And how had she been so convinced of his character that she had agreed to marriage? She was a logical, intelligent woman who prided herself on not acting impulsively. So why had she succumbed to such primal desires, even if she was a few sheets to the wind at the time? More like ten thousand sheets but still…

The truth was Jake Webster was gorgeous. Not handsome, nor cute, nor simply charming. He was all of those things yet absolutely, no doubt, one hundred percent magnificent. Every time Jake had gazed into her eyes, she ceased breathing. Every word from his lips stilled her heart. He could have asked for her soul and she would have offered it to him without question.

He was the first man to show her such devoted attention, and most definitely the first handsome man to ever look her way. Perhaps if she had been seasoned in the realm of dating and men, Maggie might have seen through his charming veneer, if that's what it was. But she hadn't. And now she was married to Jake Webster of New England, a man she knew nothing about, including his whereabouts.

"Why don't you start from the beginning," Lizzy suggested. "Start from the moment you first laid eyes on this man."

Now that they all had drinks and were delving into the food, all three women made themselves comfortable and waited for Maggie to begin, like an audience anticipating the rise of the curtain. Maggie took a gulp of her wine that Dewey had thankfully replenished, pausing to let the alcohol take effect. How many times had she replayed the events in her mind, looking for clues? There were none that led to answers. She had been talked into marriage, then deserted, of that she was sure. And she doubted her friends would make any more sense of her predicament than she had.

"Like I said, I had failed miserably in my interviews so I was being a wallflower at the mixer, feeling really sorry for myself and then this dreamboat appeared."

"What did he say exactly?"

Maggie recalled spotting Jake across the room, mainly because every female had set their eyes on him and she was curious to see what the buzz was about. Only the blonde flirting at his side hadn't impressed him. Jake had been all charm and politeness to the long-legged beauty, but it was clear he was bored with the conversation.

Or something else was going on. He appeared tired, as if he, too, had been job-hunting for three days. When he finally made some excuse to the blonde, he headed in Maggie's direction, his countenance suddenly devoid of energy. It was only when he had reached Maggie's side and examined her nametag did the light return to his vividly blue eyes.

"I know you," he had said.

"That's it?" Dewey interrupted her thoughts and Maggie was

ashamed to find herself falling in lust all over again remembering those sensual eyes. "That's the oldest pick-up line in the book."

"It wasn't a line. He said he knew me, although I hardly see how." Maggie couldn't help feeling defensive of her so-called husband, who had seemed honest in his attentions. Besides, if he hadn't been sincere toward her, she was the biggest fool in the world. And that was a difficult thought to bear.

"Then what happened?" Stacy asked.

What had happened? A night of such intense bliss that Maggie had difficulty remembering it all, although she wondered if the details had disappeared with her sanity. "We got along famously. He went to the Strip for dinner. I told him all about my career troubles and he was genuinely concerned, said he would help me find another job. We danced. We drank. We drank some more."

She felt Lizzy squeeze her hand gently. "Is this when he asked you to marry him?"

Maggie closed her eyes to ward off the tears. She was done crying over the man and the whole insane situation, but with her friends assembled around her, dragging up the painful emotions, she found the effort fruitless as she recalled that night.

"He kept telling me I was perfect although for the life of me I can't imagine why."

"Of course you're perfect," Stacy insisted, but Maggie glanced her way and rolled her eyes.

"When did you get married?" Lizzy prodded.

Maggie tossed back her wine, emptying the entire glass. "I don't remember much else except a hazy scene at the Viva Las Vegas Chapel saying our vows."

"The what?" Lizzy asked.

"Was it for real?" Dewey asked, with a smile. "Maybe it's all a joke."

Maggie had traveled down that road already, especially since they had been married by Elvis with *Blue Hawaii* playing in the background. With the last of her severance checks, she had paid a private investigator to research the quickie Nevada license and found it to be an unfortunate reality.

"It's for real," Maggie said.

"And then what happened?" Lizzy asked. "Hopefully something romantic."

If only, Maggie thought. "Jake dropped me off at my room, said something about something, kissed my hand and left."

"What?" Dewey asked incredulously. "He left you?"

"It didn't matter. I passed out. Woke up the next morning and had a lovely relationship with my toilet which, thankfully, I didn't share with my so-called husband."

"And no word from the cad?"

"While I was lying on the tile — you know how it makes you feel better to have your face on cool tile when you're sick to your stomach."

"Oh my yes," Dewey said.

"Uh, back to the story," Lizzy demanded.

"From my position on the floor, I saw a note in the hallway. Jake must have slipped it under the door in the night."

Stacy leaned forward, her brow furrowed. "He did explain himself, didn't he?"

Maggie pulled out Jake's note from her sweater pocket, its pages wrinkled and torn in spots after hours of reading and re-reading. " 'Sweet Maggie,' it says. 'Business has come up and I must leave Vegas immediately. My lawyer will contact you and make sure you are well taken care of. Good luck in all your adventures and please give my family my best. Love, Jake.' "

A silence fell upon the group of women, a rare quiet among such strong personalities. The mystery seemed to hover above them, zapping their energy, stilling their tongues. Maggie swore she heard her heart beating.

"That's the craziest thing I've every heard," Dewey finally announced.

"What did the lawyer say?" Lizzy asked.

"Never heard from him." Maggie poured herself another glass.

"And this family, have you tried to contact them?"

Maggie sighed. She was a top-notch journalist and few things eluded her but Jake Webster was an enigma. "I only have money

for the private investigator to check out the marriage certificate. On my own I Googled him, naturally, and found dozens of
entries for Jake Webster in New England. I was going to call every
last one of them but I haven't had the heart — or nerve. I mean,
really, what was I going to say? 'I just married someone named
Jake Webster in front of Elvis while drunk in Vegas, is that you?'"

Again, silence, until Lizzy wrapped up the scenario with one
perfect word. "Wow."

Finally, Stacy straightened, her confidence renewed. "He's gay."

"Or an immigrant wanting papers," Dewey suggested.

Maggie's shoulders dropped and she released a heavy breath. "I
don't think so."

"Makes sense to me," Dewey said, reloading her mouth with
a boudin ball. "Couldn't be for money." Maggie grimaced and
Dewey gave her a tight squeeze. "Just kidding."

"Definitely smells of either one," Lizzy agreed. "He might need
a visa to work here. Or he might have married you to prove to
his family or friends that he's straight, then took off before he had
to perform."

"He's American," Maggie insisted. "I saw his driver's license
when we got married. I think it was Vermont or Maine or one of
those Yankee states. And he's definitely not gay."

"You slept with him during this night of bliss?" Lizzy asked, one
eyebrow lifted.

Maggie winced.

"He's gay," Stacy pronounced again like a scolding mother.

"He's not gay."

Maggie placed her glass on the coffee table and rose, walking to
the living room window and gazing out on to the street where
normal people went about their business. People with spouses
and children and jobs.

"Honey pie," she heard Stacy say behind her, "if you never slept
with the man, why won't you fathom that he might be gay?"

Because Jake embodied masculinity, Maggie thought. Every
inch of him exuded male virility. Whenever he entered a room,
all female heads turned and sighed.

And then there were his kisses. No man uninterested in women could kiss that good.

Maggie leaned her head against the window, tracing the humidity on the sill with her fingertips as she recalled the sensual way Jake had kissed. Even if they never consummated the relationship, they had done enough to prove the man was totally straight.

"You all are going to have to take my word for it." She slide her fingers up the curtain, enjoying the feel of late summer sun on her face. "Jake Webster was not gay."

Another lengthy silence filled the room until Dewey rose and straightened her skirt. "Well, *chèr*, regardless of your troubles, we, the Cajun Embassy, are here to help."

Maggie looked over and found everyone grinning as if they shared a big secret. "What now?"

Lizzy rose from the couch, pulled an envelope out of her jacket pocket and ceremoniously handed it to Maggie. "Maggie Delta Mallory, the Cajun Embassy is going to find this Jake Webster. But today, you are being treated to a day of beauty at the Four Seasons. And we won't take no for an answer."

The scissors kept clipping away, but Maggie refused to open her eyes.

"Oh quit being such a ninny," Stacy admonished her. "It's about time you got yourself a fashionable haircut."

"I've never done more than trim my hair," Maggie uttered as the hairdresser kept combing and cutting. Clip, clip, then the fall of something heavy. "What's wrong with long hair anyway?"

"That's your father talking."

Maggie could hear Dewey turning pages of a magazine, Vogue most likely, the fat September edition. Dewey loved the fashion rags, but then she bought clothes to attend Hollywood events like the Oscars. "What's my daddy got to do with my hair?"

"Your daddy has to do with a lot of things," Dewey continued. "I wouldn't be surprised if he was the reason you ran off with that Yankee."

At this, Maggie bolted upright in her chair. She started to retort until she caught the shoulder-length bob in the mirror's reflection. "Oh. My. God."

"It's adorable," yelled Lizzy from across the room, where she was having her nails painted a bright shade of pink.

"Shoulder length is perfect for you," the hairdresser said, shaping the locks around her ears. "With your shape of face, you need something to…"

"De-emphasize the fat?"

"Accentuate your high cheek bones," the hairdresser finished, giving her a friendly nudge on the arm.

Dewey leaned in close, taking Maggie's hand as she gazed at the new woman in the mirror. "Maggie, you were never fat. Stocky, perhaps, but never fat."

Maggie felt the back of her neck, exposed for the first time in her life. "That's not what the boys used to say in high school. Pudgesicle I believe was the word. And being 'stocky' sure hasn't gotten me any dates."

"Darlin'." Dewey squeezed her hand tighter. "Have you not noticed all the weight you've lost in the past few months?"

Now that Maggie thought about it, her new hairstyle did complement her high cheek bones, ones not as full as they used to be. Her neck appeared longer, thinner somehow, and her denim shirt a size too big. She leaned in close to make sure the woman starring back at her was the same one who had left for Vegas a month earlier.

"Why did he marry me?" she whispered. "He could have had any woman in the world and he chose stocky, unfashionable me."

Dewey leaned her fashionably teased head against hers. "I don't know, sweetpea."

"I've gone over and over inside my mind why I did such an impulsive, ridiculous thing. But the big question is why did Jake Webster marry me?"

Dewey straightened, then took both of Maggie's hands. "I don't know what that man was thinking, but I do know this. He got the better end of the deal, and don't you ever forget it."

Lizzy rushed up and gushed over Maggie's haircut. "I can't believe it. Ah *chèr*, that is the cutest thing I've ever seen."

"Okay," Stacy said, breaking into the circle. "What's with all these *'chèrs'*? And just what is the Cajun Embassy anyway?" The three women laughed, and Maggie relished in how good that felt. How long had it been since she laughed, was happy? It seemed ages.

"We met at Columbia," Dewey began. "I was homesick for Louisiana so I decided to make a roux in the journalism department's kitchen. A roux is a mixture of oil and flour that's the basis for gumbo."

"I know what a roux is," Stacy said. "I have a roommate who makes one quite nicely."

Maggie grinned. She did make a great gumbo.

"Anyway," Lizzy continued. "I smelled this delectable thing cooking and I knew exactly what it was so I came into the kitchen to check it out."

"She was homesick too," Maggie said. "And that's how I found both of them, crying their eyes out over a pot of gumbo."

The threesome smiled at the memory, but Lizzy tilted her head up in Maggie's direction. "If I remember correctly, you were crying too."

The laughter long gone, replaced by a tightness in her chest, Maggie could only nod. Her Cajun mother used to make a damn good gumbo and that was who she was remembering.

Lizzy must have noticed for she squeezed Maggie's shoulder and continued. "We called ourselves the Cajun Embassy because the whole department started filing through the doors wanting some of that delectable gumbo. And we had to explain what it was we were making and why."

"It was during Carnival so we had king cake too," Dewey added.

"You know most people in America haven't a clue why we do the things we do in Louisiana so we figured we would be the ambassadors," Lizzy concluded proudly.

"Okay, but you two have the accent," Stacy said. "At least Lizzy does and every once and a while I hear it in Dewey. But Maggie sounds like she stepped out of *Gone With the Wind*."

"I'm half Cajun," Maggie explained. "And even though I was an army brat I spent most of my formative years in Georgia. Plus my dad's family hails from LaGrange and he has a thick Georgia accent. Oh hell, I don't know."

All four women laughed, with Dewey offering Stacy a membership into the group, even though she was born and raised in Alabama and was suspicious of spicy foods. Maggie was finally relaxing and starting to feel half human when the spa assistant arrived.

"It's time for your nails."

Maggie cringed. She disliked nail polish and hated long nails even worse. They got in the way of her writing. But she knew she had to appease the Cajun Embassy and her accommodating roommate and all their kindness. "Something conservative, pa-lease."

Stacy rolled her eyes. "Can we at least talk you into some clothes that aren't from the L.L. Bean catalog?"

"What's wrong with L.L. Bean?"

At this, Dewey and Stacy moaned.

"I like the classics," Maggie said in her defense.

"Fine," Lizzy interjected. "How about Liz Claiborne and Ralph Lauren?"

Being the fashion flunky, Maggie had heard of these people but doubted she could pick their clothes out in a closet. She wasn't up to fighting the three of the most clothes-conscious, hardheaded women in Atlanta so she simply nodded and let them lead her off to a corner that reeked of ammonia.

Truth be told, she loved her new bob and perhaps she'd enjoy the manicure as well. For the first time in months, Maggie felt alive and well. Whatever mistakes had occurred, there was a light beginning to shine at the end of the Vegas tunnel. Things were turning around, she could feel it. With the help of her journalist friends who could find a cotton ball in a snowstorm, she would locate this elusive Jake Webster who beguiled her of her sanity.

She'd get some answers.

Not to mention a divorce.

Maggie shook her head, enjoying the feel of her thick brown hair caressing her neck, then leaned back in her chair, watching the dark-haired woman before her apply a rich shade of magenta on to her nails. Maybe she would buy new clothes, something more fashionable than her conservative wardrobe, most of it purchased at Goodwill since for the past seven years she was either laid off or working jobs that paid little money.

"Time to move on," she whispered to no one.

Just then, her cell phone rang out the Georgia fight song that sounded like the *Battle Hymn of the Republic.* With her unfinished hand, she reached down and brought the phone to her ear.

"The new Maggie Mallory," she answered with a grin.

A pause ensued, then the sound of a deep male voice. "Mrs. Webster?"

Her newfound joy faded instantly. "Who is this?"

"Charles Riley. I'm Jake Webster's lawyer."

Fending off the dark side she had known all too well during the past few weeks, Maggie drew in a breath and straightened her shoulders. "I'm glad you called, Mr. Riley. We need to talk. I need some answers and I need them now."

"Yes, Mrs. Webster, I can well imagine and I'm sure they will all be answered in time but…"

"But nothing. Do you have any idea what I've been through?"

The lawyer sighed. "It *is* an unusual situation."

Maggie couldn't believe the man. "Unusual is an understatement."

She began to rattle off all the frustrations, anger and confusion of the past few weeks, never given the lawyer time to respond. All the while the Cajun Embassy — now a foursome — starred at her in bewilderment.

Her energy spent, Maggie took a deep breath and exhaled. "So what do you say to all that?"

The lawyer sighed once more. "Mrs. Webster, I'm afraid I have bad news."

Maggie's heart stilled, so anxious and so curious at the same time. "And that is?"

The lawyer fell silent and Maggie could hear his light breathing across the airwaves. "I'm afraid it's not good. Your husband, Jake Webster, has passed away."

Chapter Two

TWO HOURS. AS IF TRAVELING to Portland, Maine, to meet in-laws she never set eyes upon was bad enough, Maggie had two hours to waste in the busy terminal of Pittsburgh. Two hours to think about what was before her. Two hours to drive herself crazy.

"What am I doing here?" she wondered aloud, casting her eyes back across the aisle where a plane lay waiting to carry its passengers to New Orleans. All she had to do was cross over the hundred feet of carpet and change her ticket, take the opportunity to visit her Louisiana cousins. It would be so easy to send her regrets to the Webster family, sign the lawyer's papers through an intermediary and pretend Vegas never happened.

Maggie shut her eyes to clear her mind, but the gold ring on her left hand kept bringing her back, a simple band Jake had purchased; she had been wearing it the morning after their so-called marriage so it was the only explanation. She pulled it out of her jewelry box for the trip, but it felt as intrusive as her actions. Rolling the ring around and around her finger, she convinced herself she needed to play the perfect daughter-in-law and lie through her teeth, if only to ease the suffering of Jake's mother. She owed Bonnie Webster that much.

Poor Mrs. Webster, Maggie thought, knowing that a mother's grief was the toughest.

Poor Jake. The lawyer hadn't gone into details about his death except that he had been fighting a disease for some time. It explained his fatigue that night, maybe even why he left her on their wedding night.

"Wedding night," Maggie said with a huff. "Who am I kidding?"

Jake's death offered more mystery than answers. If he had been as ill as she imagined him to be, why on earth would he want to marry a perfect stranger?

Maggie watched as happy travelers eagerly boarded the plane to America's most fun-filled city. She wanted to join them, rejoice in their revelry, do anything but fly to Portland. She didn't know this man, his family. It wasn't her place to be there.

The man next to her began to snore, waking Maggie from her thoughts. A weatherworn fellow with deep, waving lines etched about his eyes, Maggie wondered if the sea winds had carved them, if he caught lobsters for a living. The woman next to him reading the latest Tess Gerritsen novel appeared equally hardened, her jaw set tight while her lips maintained a stiff straight line like a disciplinarian.

Maggie gazed around at the other passengers, searching their faces for clues. Being an army brat, Maggie had lived many places, noticing subtle differences between the nation's populations. But Yankees? She had never been further north than Washington, D.C. Were they as unfriendly and reserved as her Southern-bred mother had once claimed?

Just then the novel reader looked up and noticed Maggie staring. Maggie offered a discreet smile. "Real shame it's going to be delayed two hours, isn't it?"

Oh, why didn't she keep her big mouth shut? Just like a Southerner, always talking to anyone who would listen.

Surprisingly, the novel reader smiled, albeit a tiny one. "I take it you're not a Mainer."

Maggie cringed inwardly. Only people back home failed to mention her Southern accent, even if it had been watered down considerably since her childhood in Georgia. Maggie always dreaded conversations that began with "You must be from…," for she suspected most people didn't find her accent as cute as they claimed, that the moment her words took air her IQ dropped in their estimation.

"No ma'am," Maggie replied, trying to keep the twang from her voice. "I'm not from Maine."

"First time?"

"Yes, ma'am."

The woman genuinely warmed up, which surprised Maggie more. "You're in for a treat. It's close to autumn, you know."

Maggie had forgotten that fall approached, mainly because September in Atlanta was the hottest month of the year, humidity reaching epic levels and hurricanes blowing in from the Gulf. She forgot that the rest of the world had autumn.

"Is it as pretty as everyone says?"

The novel reader grinned and nodded, then returned to her book and Maggie resumed surveying the second call for the flight to New Orleans, a city devoid of color in fall, unless you included Mardi Gras beads and slow gin fizzes. A hundred yards and she would be safely back toward familiar territory. And heaven knew she needed a drink.

It might be best for everyone involved, Maggie justified, as she watched the passengers in rows eighteen through twenty-six line up before the gate. The lawyer had said Jake's family would be greeting her at the airport, so they at least knew she existed. But, would they welcome her into their homes? Would they be happy to meet the unemployed Southern girl who married their beloved son after mere hours of courtship?

Guilt replaced desire for flight when she remembered Jake's letter. For some reason, he wanted her to meet his family. And Bonnie Webster had lost a son, the ultimate grief, and she needed to find comfort in his bride.

But I'm not his bride, Maggie wanted to shout. Maggie had been seduced by a bewitching pair of aquamarine eyes and a man far too gorgeous for the likes of her.

The flight attendant announced last calls for Flight 288 to Louis

Armstrong Airport. Without letting her mind interfere and grabbing her carry-on, Maggie leaped from her seat and headed across the aisle. It was one thing to play the grieving wife to his family, but in truth she still reeled with anger at his deception and desertion. And that fact reiterated that Maggie was an impostor, not worthy of attending Jake's funeral and comforting his family.

Maggie pulled her purse strap across her shoulder, determined to make the New Orleans flight before they closed the gate. Halfway across the aisle, something large, hard and smelling of Old Spice blindsided her, throwing her carryon one way and her purse and jacket the other. As Maggie felt her legs give way, two strong hands gripped her forearms and held her steady.

"I beg your pardon," an accented voice told her.

When Maggie regained her balance, she found herself staring into enormous brown eyes as serious as a preacher at Sunday noon. Once she resumed her senses, she realized everything about this man was large, including the strong grip on her arms.

"No problem," she assured him, although for some reason she dreaded those enormous warm hands leaving her body or those intense eyes heading down the corridor.

"Forgive me," the man said breathlessly, "but I'm late for a plane."

With those final words, Old Spice headed for his gate, dropping his garment bag noisily on the floor and calling for a flight attendant.

"It's been delayed." For some insane reason, Maggie found herself glad his flight was her own. For a moment, she forgot all about New Orleans.

The man turned back toward her, both to grasp her meaning and catch his breath, but it was Maggie who found her air catching as those deep eyes, so full of longing and pain, met hers.

"Thunderstorms," she mumbled. "They're estimating a two-hour delay."

Surprisingly, the man brightened, if only a little. He grinned but Maggie still sensed his anguish.

"Alabama?"

Seconds ticked away and Maggie's mind raced to figure out what the man implied. Then it dawned on her. Her dang accent. "Georgia," she replied.

He grinned broader this time, sending slight, attractive laugh lines about his face. He stood tall in his boots, about six feet something, dressed in jeans and a corduroy jacket that hugged his fit frame and sported leather on the elbows. His brown hair was tousled from the dash to the gate, and the ruggedness of him seemed to demand such a look. But it was those expressive eyes, so gentle and warm. Eyes that were now sparkling with acknowledgement.

"I was close," the man said.

"Hardly," Maggie answered, wrapping her arms about her chest in a playful fashion. "Alabama is an entirely different story. You couldn't pay me enough to wear Bama red."

This time, whatever pain lingered in those chocolate eyes disappeared and the man laughed. "Let me guess," he said, drawing out his words like the novel-reading woman had done. "You're a Bulldog."

Maggie equally brightened and relaxed, as if she had opened a door and found relatives inside. She grinned slyly. "Got my masters there. Now, what do you know about the University of Georgia, being a 'Mainer' and all."

The man leaned close, offering up another whiff of Old Spice that made Maggie's head reel. Heavens, but the tall drink of water was as cute as a hound dog at birth. "My best friend went to Georgia Tech, and if I'm not mistaken, they hate the University of Georgia."

Something about this man put Maggie at ease, including the fact that he pronounced it Jaw-ja. Her natural teasing nature emerged and she had a hard time resuming a normal composure more suitable to meeting strangers in an airport.

"Georrrgia Tech?" she said with a snicker of her college's arch rival. "They couldn't catch a football if they wore Velcro."

The Mainer laughed again, seemingly pleased with her silly remarks. For a moment, Maggie feared he found her accent humorous, waiting to board the plane and tell his friends about the ditzy Southerner he had met at the gate. But, something about those eyes made her doubt he was that kind of a man.

Then, within a heartbeat, Old Spice sobered. "They really said two hours?"

Maggie nodded. "'Fraid so. You in a hurry to get home?"

The anxiety returned and he frowned, casting a glance toward the opposite gate, where flight attendants were closing the doors to a plane full of passengers heading to New Orleans. Maggie wondered if he longed for the same escape.

The Mainer appeared lost in thought watching the attendants lock the gate, then his gaze moved slowly back to Maggie as if he finally remembered they were having a conversation. As his eyes locked on hers, he stared intently. Maggie shivered, and that small movement brought the Mainer back to life. "Are you cold?" he asked, picking up her jacket from the floor, the one Maggie had forgotten all about.

"No," Maggie replied, knowing it was male hormones that sent goosebumps up her arms. "Just a skunk crawling over my grave."

The Mainer stared in puzzlement and Maggie mentally kicked herself for repeating such a backwards comment, one of her mother's favorites. "It's an expression."

He smiled again, which replaced whatever anxiety lingered between them. She wished they could return to talk of football so she could hear that delicious laugh again.

"I have an idea," the Mainer said. "I'm having a day from hell and I sure could use a drink. Would you like to join me in that lounge across the aisle?"

Maggie wanted to yell "Hell yes" and leap into the bar, but she remembered her reason for being in Pittsburgh that day, the fact that she was a widow heading to her husband's funeral, even if he was a faux husband. She started to politely turn him down, but for some reason the words refused to emerge from her throat.

The Mainer leaned close, one side of his generous lips curled up in a grin. "It's only a drink, nothing more. We don't even have to tell each other our names."

Suddenly, Maggie felt ashamed for imagining there was anything more to his invitation. She ran a nervous hand through her new haircut, her fingers falling awkwardly at her shoulders, still not used to the lack of hair. "Yeah, I know."

The man straightened. "Then you will?"

"Sure." Maggie shot a quick glance at the lounge. It appeared harmless enough. "But no names."

The Mainer picked up her carryon and effortlessly draped it over one shoulder, while grabbing his garment bag and heading across the aisle. Maggie followed in silence, mentally berating herself for being so rude. What harm would telling this cute stranger her name be? It wasn't like she was interested, would even consider this man attractive on her way to her husband's funeral. Even if he did own the finest legs she had ever seen in jeans, topped by the cutest set of...

The Mainer paused and turned, waiting for Maggie to catch up. A rush of fire stung her cheeks.

"There's a seat in the back."

Maggie nodded, then followed him to the back of the lounge, staring at the various travelers this time, searching for equally handsome men to prove her point that it was natural for a woman to find a man attractive. But when she reached their booth and found herself staring into those seductive eyes again, she swallowed hard, knowing it was this man that set her heart aflutter. And she didn't like it one bit.

The Mainer sensed her discomfort. "No names," he whispered conspiratorially with that slight upturned grin she was beginning to adore.

Maggie fell into her seat. "I have to call you something. My mother taught me better than that."

The Mainer propped the luggage against the side of the booth and sat down. "My middle name is Theodore. How's that?"

"Theodore?" Images of a Rough Rider president came to mind, but then the Mainer did own a rugged look. Wasn't Theodore Roosevelt from up New England way? Still, the name made her smile.

"My nephew calls me Uncle Teddy." His sly grin returned. "But if you call me either one of those names, I'll say bad things about the University of Georgia."

Maggie sent him a daring look and crossed her arms playfully. "Then what will I call you? I can't call you Mainer forever."

"Mainer?" The smile disappeared, replaced by a dead pan. "What makes you think I'm from Maine?"

For a startling moment, Maggie feared she had misread his accent. After all, he could be from Boston or Vermont or any of those maple-producing states that lacked the letter r in their speech. Then she realized he was pulling her leg. "Couldn't be that accent of yours, no sir."

"What accent?" Again, Theodore refused to break a smile.

The waitress approached and asked for drink orders, but all Maggie comprehended were two teasing brown eyes egging her on. She liked this man; he was a hoot. Even if he was a Yankee.

"What do you desire, Miss Georgia?" Theodore asked.

A double scotch straight up, she thought, anything to relieve the pain of the upcoming weekend and the traitorous thoughts running through her mind. But, she was too shy to order such an unladylike drink. It was one thing to drink hard liquor at home, her mother had instructed her, but a proper lady drank wine in public. Too bad wine didn't interest Maggie, never did. "I'll have what you're having."

"Glenlivit then," Theodore told the waitress. "Straight up. And how about some nuts or something to munch on."

Theodore and the waitress talked appetizers while Maggie studied the Mainer's face, hoping to find something that marked him ordinary so she could spend the time in conversation and not wondering how those lips could kiss or how those enormous hands would feel against her bare skin. Rough Rider seemed so perfect, the kind of man Maggie dreamed about meeting, but wasn't this how she had fallen for Jake, a handsome face looks her way and all common sense fades?

Maggie forced her gaze to her hands. She was losing her mind, plain and simple. She had spent way too much time building her career and not enough dating, not experiencing enough of men to know that a gorgeous pair of eyes were just that and nothing more. Her father had been right. She lacked a rational mind when it came to men.

Yet, that realization didn't stop her from pulling the wedding ring off her left hand.

"I hope you like scotch," Theodore said.

Maggie looked up, feeling the heat play her cheeks again as she dropped the ring inside her pants' pocket. "Love scotch."

This time, however, the Mainer wasn't smiling. "I'm confused," he said, placing his elbows on the table and leaning forward, allowing Maggie another whiff of the Old Spice. Images of Stacy flitted through her mind, laughing at how Maggie always preferred the outdoorsy type, the kind who wore colognes of her father's generation.

Maggie swallowed hard at the nearness of him. "How come?"

"You won't tell me your name, but you're hiding the fact that you're married."

For some strange reason, knowing she had been caught forced her to relax. She let out a breath she had been holding and pulled the ring out of her pocket, placing it back on her finger. "I don't know why I did that. I don't know why I do anything these days."

"Want to talk about it?"

At this, Maggie laughed. Sure, she thought, I married a gorgeous man in Vegas because I was starved for attention after spending years alternating between working seventy hours a week at dot-coms and magazines and being laid off and constantly hitting the pavement for work. Because I grew up homely and an army brat who didn't get properly kissed until her freshman year at college. And sex, well, there was Jimmy Rodgers in grad school, a friend who agreed to do her a favor by stealing her virginity, and a couple of short-lived relationships that only existed because, again, she was hungry for a human's touch, but none of which lasted longer than two weeks because of her demanding career. Not to mention they were not the right men.

"No," Maggie finally said. "I really don't."

Surprisingly, the Mainer smiled. "Good. Neither do I."

She laughed again, comfortable in this man's presence, although she couldn't explain why. She felt drawn to him, sure, but he was different than Jake, more personable, less intimidating. Now that she thought of it, being with Jake she had felt nervous and self-conscious, like a beauty queen in a bathing suit, sucking it in.

"I am married," she found herself admitting, "but he passed away. I'm a widow now."

Theodore showed true remorse, as if grief was close at hand for him as well. "I'm sorry."

Maggie straightened and cocked her head. "Don't be. It's not a happy tale. Truth me told, I'm dying to rip this ring from my finger."

Brown eyes continued to stare, his gaze offering solace. "Then I'm twice as sorry, for you and the sod for being so blind."

"Thank you." Maggie twisted the ring around and around her finger until it caught skin and pinched. Shut up, she commanded herself, but she couldn't help herself. Weeks of wallowing in self-pity and now, armed with a sassy haircut and a new outfit, Mr. Rough Rider found her attractive, was taking her side against Jake.

And it felt good.

"How about you?" Maggie asked. "You married? Or close to it?"

He paused for a moment, which made Maggie's heart skip. "No," he replied firmly.

Yep, her mother was right. Yankee women were stupid. "How come?"

Theodore offered that lazy smile. "Never found the right woman."

"Guess you've never been below the Mason-Dixon Line."

He smiled broader that time, perfect set of teeth showing. Lord have mercy he was a looker, and she found herself grinning seductively back.

"Are all Southern women so…?"

"Forward? Only in airports." Heavens, but she had to stop flirting.

"Lucky me."

There it was again, that irresistible grin, that inviting sparkle. And she gave hers right back at him, throwing her cares to the wind, not caring about Jake or Yankee relatives or the fact that she had fallen for a handsome set of blue eyes only a month before.

"Two Scotch, straight up."

The waitress named Carol who Theodore called "Cal" placed the drinks and assorted nuts on the table, breaking the spell, but electricity lingered between them. Theodore rose his glass in a salute. "To Southern women in airports."

"To Rough Rider Mainers."

He didn't grasp her meaning, but they tipped glasses and sipped their scotch, his gaze never leaving her face. "Why are you going to Maine?" he finally asked. "Vacation? Fall foliage?"

Maggie took a large gulp from her drink, enjoying the warm, smooth burn down her throat. "Family business."

"Portland?"

"I think so." Heck, she wasn't even sure where Jake lived. All the lawyer had said was that Jake lived outside Portland, had a mother named Bonnie and a cousin and business partner named Colin who Jake thought a royal pain in the ass. His words exactly. Now that she thought of it, she knew nothing of her deceased husband. Nothing at all.

"You think so? Don't you know where your family lives?"

Maggie swirled the contents of her scotch. "They're my in-laws, never met them before."

"I see."

"And you?"

"Near Portland." He sipped his scotch, his gaze turning serious. "I was in New York today on business."

"Bad day at the office?"

Theodore straightened. "Why do you say that?"

Maggie shrugged. "You said this was a day from hell."

"Nothing like that." He gazed into his scotch and the pain she had witnessed in his eyes earlier returned.

"Sure you don't want to talk about it?"

"No." He smiled sadly, leaning back into the booth, then sighed. "I got some bad news. A family member died."

"I'm so sorry." Maggie instinctively reached out and touched his hand.

"Don't be." He gazed down at her hand on his. "We weren't close. He left me and the family a long time ago."

Still staring at their hands, Theodore slid his thumb over hers and held tight, then moved it back and forth ever so slightly. Both gestures were innocent enough, but a shiver ran through Maggie again.

Theodore released her hand and looked up. "Are you sure you're not cold? I can give you my jacket."

"No. Thank you though." Maggie gulped down the rest of her scotch, hoping it would still her rapidly beating pulse. Theodore signaled to the waitress for another round.

"No," Maggie insisted, thinking of her mother's annoying lady lessons about women and alcohol. "One is fine with me."

"I practically rolled you over. It's the least I can do."

"I should be going."

The Mainer grabbed her hand this time. "Please. Like I said, my cousin and I had our differences but he was still family. I really could use the company."

Was it the pleading gaze of those seductive eyes, the fact that they shared a horrid day or the feel of his large, strong hand over hers? Maggie found herself nodding, knowing that she was plunging again into dangerous waters, yet somehow she didn't care. She had another hour before the flight left for Portland. Surely, one hour with this interesting man wouldn't harm anyone. Tonight she would meet Jake's family, perform the dutiful wife role and bury him the next day. Didn't she deserve a respite before taking on such a duty? Especially considering the past horrendous weeks.

"Okay, one more drink."

"Great." Theodore relaxed. "Now tell me, Miss Georgia, what's your middle name?"

"I think I prefer Miss Georgia. Particularly the way you say it."

"There you go again, accusing me of having an accent."

"Well, I'm glad someone has one," Maggie said, throwing in a Scarlett O'Hara tone and placing a delicate, flat hand upon her chest. "I've never been accused of such a thing."

The waitress brought two more drinks and they tipped their glasses once again. "I'm waiting, Miss Georgia," Theodore said.

"Delta."

"Excuse me?"

"My middle name. It's Delta."

The Mainer stifled a snicker. "Named after the region or the actress?

"Neither. The airlines."

This sobered him up, she thought with a laugh. The teasing sparkle in his eyes disappeared while his mind raced to figure it out.

"My father is in the army," Maggie explained. "His first assignment was in New Jersey, much to my mother's chagrin. She hated it. Too many Yankees."

The sparkle returned and he crossed his arms, making his jacket pull tight across his shoulders. Heavens to Betsy, her mother would say, the man was hotter than the inside of a Hurst in a Macon August.

"She was barely nine months pregnant when my dad got transferred back to Atlanta, but the doctor wouldn't let my Mama travel. Naturally, she wasn't going to stay behind in New Jersey, especially with the prospect of having her first child born on red clay. So, against the wishes of everyone, Mama boarded a plane and headed home."

"Let me guess," Theodore said, enchanted by the story. "You were born in the air."

"At the gate at the Atlanta airport, actually. Mama went into labor in the air, something to do with air pressure I think, and didn't quite make it to the hospital. She was lucky, though, there was a doctor on board and one of the flight attendants was a nurse and I was born in Concourse B, Gate 32."

"Amazing."

"Yeah, like they used to say, Delta is ready when you are."

That throaty laugh emerged again, and Maggie swore she could hear the New England cadence in it.

"Wow," Theodore finally said. "Are all Southerners full of such stories?"

"'Fraid so."

"Can't say the same about my name."

"Well, I doubt your mother named you Theodore for popularity sake. There has to be a story behind that one."

Theodore shook his head. "Named after my uncle, who was named after an ancestor."

"There you go. What's your ancestor's story?"

"Some general. Was decorated for serving in the…"

Theodore halted mid-sentence and Maggie bit her lower lip to keep from laughing. "Civil War?"

They both laughed then. "Served with Sherman too," he added, which made them laugh harder. "Sorry."

Maggie sipped her scotch. "Actually, my father is one of a long line of Georgia military men. But none fought in the War of the Rebellion, if you can believe it."

"War of the Rebellion?" Theodore nearly choked on his scotch.

"How about the War of Northern Aggression? The fight for state rights? The latest unpleasantness?"

The scotch warming her veins, Maggie smiled broadly, enjoying their silly banter. She couldn't remember the last time she felt so relaxed, so comfortable with a man. And Rough Rider seemed to be feeling the same way, eyes watching her intently.

Then the intercom interrupted her bliss. They both jumped at the news. "That's us, isn't it?" Maggie asked.

"'Fraid so."

Theodore signaled Carol and pulled out his wallet. "We still have time. They have to board the coach passengers first."

Maggie's heart sank as she realized it was time to leave this temporary warm cocoon and head toward Portland and a family of strangers. And that Theodore would not be sitting in the same part of the plane and their time was at an end. "I'm in coach."

Theodore absorbed this information silently, most likely thinking the same thing, then reached into his jacket pocket and
removed his glasses to read the Visa receipt Carol was handing
him.

The Cajun Embassy would have laughed at this sight as well.
Not only did he sit before Maggie clothed in what appeared to be
L.L. Bean attire, he wore glasses too. Only they didn't add a vul-
nerable aspect to his rugged face. They emphasized his emphatic
eyes, softened his features. To Maggie, he appeared like a professor
of English at some ancient Maine university or a man who alter-
nated between harvesting cranberries and researching material
for *Poor Richard's Almanac*. Or maybe Maggie had read too many
books on New England.

"Ready?"

She really wasn't, but she had her duty to fulfill. Maggie nodded
and they headed for the gate.

By the time they reached the desk, all the passengers had been
boarded. They handed their flight attendants their boarding passes,
then showed their IDs, and moved down the long corridor to the
plane.

"Can I see you?"

At first, Maggie wasn't sure she heard right, but when she
looked up at Rough Rider she knew he had enjoyed her company as much as she had his. If only they had met under better
circumstances. "I can't."

Theodore nodded hearing the news, expecting it. "I shouldn't
have asked. I have family obligations as well."

That summed it up, Maggie thought, as Theodore paused at his
seat in first class. She couldn't help stopping to take one last look
at her handsome cranberry professor. "Thanks for the drink." She
offered her hand. "It was fun."

Theodore grasped her hand and held it tightly. "Can I at least
know your name?"

She wanted so badly to tell him everything, to call him in Portland, to have him show her around his cranberry farm. But this
was how she had gotten into trouble in Vegas. Besides, she was

unemployed and widowed. It was time to start over and she preferred to do it alone, sans a gorgeous pair of male eyes who could only complicate things. "It's best that you don't."

Theodore nodded again, but quick as a whistle slid his hand into his jacket pocket, removed a card and placed it into her palm. "This is my card. Call me if you like, if you need anything in Maine or just want to talk. Or if you get back to Georgia and want to harass a Yankee in the future, my email address is there."

Holding his card in her hand initiated so many possibilities and Maggie realized she had been holding her breath during his little speech. Forcing herself to exhale, she nodded, and then headed toward coach, clutching his card like a lifeline. Theodore watched her all the way to her seat, his burning gaze sending goosebumps skittering across her skin.

As soon as she squeezed across two men and locked her seat belt, the plane began to taxi, the pilot speaking of making up for lost time and hoping to arrive only one hour and fifteen minutes late. Some of the information registered, but mostly Maggie focused on the card still clutched in her fingers.

Slowly, carefully, she opened her palm and gazed inside.

"Oh. My. God."

Her mind exploded and her heart raced, causing both male passengers to her left to gaze in alarm. She wanted to race from the plane but the engines were roaring in preparation of takeoff. As the noise grew louder and the plane accelerated, finally lifting off the ground, Maggie looked down into her hand one more time.

"Colin Theodore Parnell."

Heaven help her, but she had just spent two hours flirting with Jake's cousin and partner.

Chapter Three

COLIN WATCHED THE SETTING SUN paint Portland with a golden glow as the plane touched down. He dreaded the events before him, the funeral, the questions, the enormous hole Jake would leave behind. Sitting in the lounge, enjoying scotch with Miss Georgia offered a pleasant interruption to his grief, allowed him to think of an enchanting heart-shaped face and delightful conservation, anything but the pain pressing on his heart. For two hours he had forgotten the years of disappointments and betrayals, forgotten that he had to face his family and play the grieving cousin when he still longed to ring his cousin's neck.

It had only been a month since Jake had left for the National Association of Magazine Editors convention in Vegas, mere weeks since his cocky grin assured Colin that everything would be taken care of, that Colin's dream of working in architecture would finally come true. After years of heart-wrenching disloyalty, Colin had been skeptical. But, Jake had been insistent.

"I'll make it up to you and more," his cousin had said, looking every bit the worst for wear from his usual hangover. "This time I won't let you down."

But, of course, he did.

Only this time, Jake had left for good, married some woman he had met on the sly, and refused to come home when Colin needed him most. Jake had destroyed many of Colin's plans throughout the years, including stealing Kathy away, but this one topped them all. This one dashed all of Colin's hopes.

The pilot announced their arrival and passengers jumped into the aisle, anxious to leave the plane. Colin wished he could retrieve Miss Georgia in coach and go back to discussing football, but it was time to face the family and bury his cousin and family partner, although partner was hardly the word. Partners didn't repeatedly stab you in the back.

Colin ran an anxious hand through his tousled hair, knowing he must look a sight. He had spent the good part of the journey tossing in his seat, examining his feelings over and over again, wondering how his family had taken the news. Then, he would remember Delta and her engaging laugh, thinking how God had sent an angel down in his time of need. If only he could see her again, listen to the sweet cadence of her voice, watch her eyes sparkle when she smiled. But, that was impossible now.

Sighing in defeat, he rose and exited the plane, only to find three familiar faces waiting on the other side.

"Colin?" his sister Edith proclaimed in surprise.

Colin dropped his garment bag and outstretched his arms, welcoming the small tyke that wasted no time rushing into them.

"Uncle Teddy!" Frederick cried and Colin nearly crushed him with affection. God, but he loved his nephew and the feel of him in his arms made him forget the pain.

Still, holding tight to Frederick, Colin rose and wrapped his available arm about his oldest sister. "How are you taking the news?" he whispered into the hug.

Edith released him, always one to shy away from emotion, but the youngest sibling, Jude, let lose a stream of tears and rushed into his embrace. Colin tried to keep upright as he balanced the two, his nephew's lower lip now twitching with emotion as he watched his mom cry into Colin's neck.

"What are you doing here, Colin?" Edith asked, visibly uncomfortable with the emotional public display.

Relaxing his embrace, but still wrapping an arm about Jude's shoulder, Colin turned back toward the matriarch of the siblings. Edith was born one year younger than Colin but she always tried to prove that that one year never mattered. "Actually, I was going to ask you the same thing. I drove to the airport yesterday. I don't need to be picked up." He looked at Frederick. "But I'm glad you did. What an amazing surprise."

"We didn't know you were on this flight." Jude pulled out a handkerchief and blew her nose soundly, eliciting a censorious look from Edith.

"I was supposed to be back tomorrow, but I came as soon as I could."

An eerie silence descended upon the group and Colin gazed back at the exiting passengers, hoping to spot Delta and relieve, if only for a moment, that light-hearted feeling. But the line filing past didn't contain Miss Georgia.

"Uncle Teddy," Frederick called out, pulling on his shirt. "We're not here for you."

"Oh?" Where was she? Delta couldn't have passed them; he would have spotted her.

"We're here for Jake's widow," Edith explained, rolling her eyes. "We came to pick her up."

Jake's widow. The woman who had interrupted Colin's plans, who had distracted Jake and ruined Colin's life. Not only did he have to face a grieving family when he still raged from Jake's injustice, but he had to be nice to some woman Jake had picked up in Vegas. No doubt a long-legged beauty with bleached blond hair, super model type, the kind Jake always had wrapped around his arm.

"I guess she won't be difficult to spot." Colin looked back toward the gate door. Still no hint of Delta and now the flight attendants were filing out the gate, their rolling suitcases trailing behind them.

"You probably have that right," Edith mumbled. "In any case, I brought a sign."

Just then, a skunk ran over Colin's grave. Thinking back to the lounge conversation in Pittsburgh, pieces began to fall in place.

Delta was a widow. In-laws in Portland she never met.

"No." Colin shook his head. Delta didn't fit the M.O. Jake would never fall for a short, dark-haired woman who could actually carry on an intelligent conversation. Unless he was having a laugh beyond the grave at Colin's expense.

Still, she had Colin's card. She knew who he was.

"No." He shook his head harder this time, gazing back toward his sisters, who were staring in puzzlement. "She can't be."

"What are you talking about?" Edith asked.

"Jake's widow." This mystery would be easy enough to dispel. "What's the woman's name again?"

Frederick picked up the cardboard and turned it upwards so Colin could read the sign he held in both hands. Colin gazed down at the hand-written letters: "Maggie Delta Webster."

Colin never thought it possible, but he swore he heard Jake laughing.

"You're going to have to exit the plane."

Maggie heard the flight attendant speaking, but no matter how hard her brain demanded it, her legs would not let her stand.

"Can't I stay on the plane?" She flashed the attendant her finest smile. "It's going back to Pittsburgh."

"Tomorrow morning." The attendant crossed her arms, tapping a manicured nail against her elbow.

"I can wait."

The attendant was through being nice; Maggie read it in her furrowed brow and sucked-in cheeks. Maggie began to plead, anything to keep her on that plane, but something caught the stewardess's attention. Maggie gazed down the aisle to find brown suede Oxfords traveling her way. She closed her eyes, knowing the Rough Rider had discovered her secret.

"I'll take it from here," she heard him tell the stewardess in that charming accent. An accent she had grown to adore during the two hours she shamelessly flirted with him in an airport lounge! Heavens, but she wished the ground would open up and swallow her whole.

Maggie heard them exchange words, and then the attendant moved toward the back exit. Still, she refused to open her eyes, refused to look at the man who knew her for the imposter she was.

"Maggie."

He knew her name. And the sound of it spoken with a Maine accent beckoned her heart. Stubbornly, she shook her head, squeezing her lids tighter. She had humiliated herself, removed her wedding ring, no less. She should have run out the back exit when she had the chance.

"Maggie."

She felt two fingers at her chin, raising her head. Slowly, she opened her eyes, hoping to find some semblance of sympathy in his gaze. Instead, he stared at her in confusion and accusation, devoid of all friendliness. Not that she blamed him.

Colin straightened stiffly, then grabbed her carryon. "Let's go. My sisters are waiting."

Something in his tone made Maggie believe he was the oldest of those sisters because, despite her fear and humiliation, she followed him. When she spotted the two women at the gate starring with equally distrusting looks, a child gazing up at her with her name drawn on a piece of cardboard, her legs began to buckle once more. She was thankful for Colin's strong grip on her elbow when he pushed her forward, for she feared the ground was eating her up for sure.

"Judith, Edith, this is Maggie."

The two women displayed a faint smile, then offered their hands. It was all so formal, like greeting people on the street. She knew she wasn't family, really, but didn't Yankees hug their relatives?

"It's a pleasure to meet you, but please call me Maggie."

Colin moved the boy in front, placing both hands protectively on his shoulders. "This is my nephew."

Maggie was sure her heart stopped beating gazing down at the replica of Colin, adorable brown eyes blazing with that trademark glint. "Pleasure to meet you too," she whispered.

The group stared intently for what seemed an eternity and Maggie felt the hairs on the back of her neck rise. Finally, the woman who looked like she might be a school hall monitor, smiled while her eyes narrowed. "You're not what we expected."

"Oh?"

Another uncomfortable silence ensued until the little boy pulled on her pant leg. "Jake usually dates girls like those in the magazines. The skinny ones who are really beautiful."

A tightness formed in Maggie's chest and stole her breath as she contemplated that news. The one named Jude smiled nervously. "Jake used to have a thing for blondes. We were expecting you to be blond, I suppose."

The little boy looked up. "No. Uncle Teddy always said Jake liked them gorgeous. Long legs and big…"

Colin placed a hand over the boy's mouth. "Why don't we go get Maggie's bags?"

"Good idea," Edith said, grabbing Maggie's carryon. She placed a hand on Maggie's back and pushed them lightly in the direction of the baggage claim.

"What did I say?" the boy asked.

"Mom is waiting for us." Edith's step picked up speed. Dressed in tight corduroys and a denim jacket, she really had a take-charge air about her. "The Bradleys are here and Walter is expected later tonight, so we should get a move on."

As the child's words still gripped Maggie's heart, the boy refused to let his comments go as he struggled to keep up with Aunt Edith. "What did I say?"

"We're a little tight on accommodations," Jude told her brother. "But we'll talk about that later."

"What did I…?"

Maggie had had enough of the rushed walk. She halted and bent down to the boy's level. "What's your name, sweetpea?"

The boy moved half of his body behind Colin's leg, but he appeared eager to make her acquaintance. "Frederick."

"Are you named after a Civil War general too?" Maggie stole a sly glance at Colin and swore she say a semblance of merriment in his eyes. For an instant.

"Huh?"

"Never mind." Maggie smoothed out the boy's rumpled shirt and pulled his sweater forward. "I'm Maggie and I'm pleased to meet you, even if I'm not blonde and beautiful."

Something lodged in her throat, an emotion weeks in the making, but she fought it down. She wasn't going to cry in front of these people.

But Frederick surprised her. He leaned forward and kissed her cheek. "I think you're pretty," he whispered, and suddenly the tears rushed forward.

Maggie bolted up and gazed skyward to fight off the emotion. Then, like Edith, the drill sergeant, she headed down toward the baggage claim in a trot.

"She's nice enough," Jude whispered to Colin as they watched Maggie head down the airport corridor. "A little odd, perhaps."

Edith turned and snarled, as if Jude was blind. "She's crying. We've upset her."

Frederick's lips began to tremble. "I didn't mean anything."

Colin reached down and effortlessly picked up his nephew. He squeezed Frederick tight, always so grateful for the small tyke's unconditional loving hugs. "It wasn't you, Frederick. Maggie just lost her husband. She's sad."

Now, if only that were true, Colin thought.

What was the truth, he wondered, as they followed the petite woman to the baggage claim. She wasn't anything like Jake's typical woman, wasn't Jake's type at all. Truth be told, Maggie was the kind of woman Colin enjoyed: fun, intelligent and simple as far as feminine attributes go. The kind of woman Jake always laughed at him about.

"You're going to end up with some mousy woman who writes book reviews for *The New Yorker* and quilts," Jake used to say.

"And you're going to end up with a huge alimony bill," Colin always replied.

So where were the two of them now? Jake had married the mousy woman and died, his death a mystery, and heaven help him, Colin was lusting after his non-grieving widow.

He watched Maggie pause at the baggage claim, gazing down at the three suitcases waiting for them. Her back was to the group, but he could tell she was wiping away tears, struggling to regain composure.

Edith was the first to reach her side and Maggie's back immediately straightened and she offered his sister a faint smile. "Are those your bags?" Edith asked.

"Yes." Maggie picked up the garment bag and placed it on a shoulder. "Sorry there are so many, but I didn't know what weather to expect or what to wear. Where I come from we dress up for funerals, but I don't know if you all do. My mother used to say you can never be too prepared, especially when you're traveling to places you've never been before, and she knew. She lived just about everywhere." She paused and inhaled. "Am I talking too much?"

"No."

Colin almost laughed; they had all answered in unison, but she was rambling on. Something no one in his family ever did, except Frederick.

"Let me take your bags." Colin reached for her garment bag and threw it over a shoulder, then grabbed the two on the floor, both incredibly heavy.

"Let me take one," Maggie insisted.

Colin settled the weight between his arms. What did she have in here, her entire wardrobe? "I've got it."

They headed toward Colin's SUV, while Jude asked how long Maggie was staying. Considering the weight of her baggage, Colin was wondering the same thing.

"Just until Monday morning."

"Great." Frederick ran up and took Maggie's hand. "Where are you from? You talk funny?"

Frederick and the mystery widow began a long conversation about Georgia and whether they had bullfrogs where Maggie came from, some town outside of Atlanta. When she asked him about his week at preschool, Frederick began hopping up and down spewing forth his latest adventures.

"Why don't Frederick and Edith go in your car," Jude offered. "I'll follow you there."

Frederick began to cheer, still holding tight to Maggie's hand. "Will you play with me at Nana Bonnie's house?"

Maggie smiled, the same charming gesture that had seized Colin's heart at the airport when he had teased her about her alma mater. The wave of pleasure that had washed on him then returned, and he wanted nothing more than to kiss those engaging lips, over and over again.

Colin threw the bags into the trunk harshly, making everyone turn and stare. How in the hell did the one woman he find attractive turn out to be Jake's wife?

He finished loading the bags and headed toward the driver's seat, while Maggie and Edith argued over who would sit in the back, Edith winning, of course. Colin had mixed feelings about sitting across from Maggie; he longed to be next to her but dreaded the feelings that produced.

"So, where are we going?" Maggie asked as they pulled on to the highway.

"We live in four houses all set next to each other in Madison," Edith explained.

Maggie contemplated this. "The whole family altogether? Wow, kinda like the Kennedys, huh?"

Colin spotted Edith frowning in the back seat. They had been called that on more than one occasion — the Kennedys of Madison — even though they lived several miles outside of the quaint tourist town. The family intermingled on several levels, including living next door to one another. Edith managed the property that supported all of their houses, even occasionally working the farmable lands, and Jude worked in the printing aspects of the magazine. Colin's mother proofread the magazine galleys and supervised the House Beautiful shoots and watched Frederick on the days when he wasn't in preschool, while Colin oversaw the entire production of the publication and, sometimes, the entire doings of the clan. Only Jake had escaped the family entrapment, even though he had inherited the title of editor.

Jake. His betrayal burned fire up Colin's spine and he stole a look at the woman behind it all. Maggie squirmed in her seat, nervously smoothing out her clothes. Was she in on this? Colin wondered. Did she help Jake destroy Colin's life?

"So how is your father's business?"

Give it to Edith to go right to the jugular.

Maggie didn't even flinch. "Excuse me?"

Edith leaned forward between the two front seats. "Jake wrote us that he'd gotten married in Vegas. He said he couldn't come home because he had to go to Mexico and help your father in his failing oil business. Is it still in trouble?"

A lengthy pause ensued and Colin peered over to gauge Maggie's reaction. She said she had been an army brat. Was her father still in the military? Or was this all some giant hoax she and Jake had shared?

Maggie appeared genuinely shocked, placing a hand over her mouth and staring out the windshield blindly.

"Are you okay?" Edith asked.

Maggie shook her head lightly. "I'm not feeling very well. Must have been the flight."

Edith shot Colin a knowing look but he kept his eyes on the highway, hoping the beauty of the coastline at twilight would distract his myriad feelings raging through him.

"He did tell you about our business…?"

"Shall I pull over?" Colin quickly interrupted. He wasn't ready to discuss that.

"How long before we arrive?" Maggie asked.

"Forever," Frederick said from the back seat.

"About twenty minutes," Colin said. "We live outside of Portland, in a small coastal town."

"Madison." Edith's voice was laced with sarcasm. "Didn't Jake tell you that much?"

Maggie's eyebrows furrowed. "Jake only talked about some

national park he used to love to hike in."

"Bar Harbor."

Those adorable eyes looked at him straight then, a sad grin stealing at the corners of Maggie's lips. "Pardon?"

Colin realized she hadn't understood because of his New England pronunciation and he fought back a smile. "Barrr Harrrborrr."

For an instant, they were back in Pittsburgh, laughing over the differences in their speech. For one blessed moment, they smiled at each other.

Then Maggie's gaze turned back to the windshield, where something distracted her attention as they turned on to Madison's Main Street. Her face lit up with recognition and she appeared almost as excited as Frederick.

"Madison, of course." She pointed out the windshield. "This is where *Yankee Living* magazine is located."

No one said a word as they approached the old colonial building almost as famous as its century-old publication, its line of American flags floating on the breeze in front. A tightness formed in Colin's chest as he remembered the last conversation he had with Jake in that very building.

Maggie turned toward Colin, her eyes ablaze. "I love this magazine. I have had a subscription to it since high school, ever since my grandparents came up here on a foliage tour and brought me back a copy." Her smile encompassed her face as she related this experience, both hands gesturing as she spoke. "I wrote my master's thesis on regionalism in mass media and used *Yankee Living* as an example. The man who runs this magazine was my mentor in journalism school, gave me the most wonderful tools, things I've never forgotten."

A deafening silence fell upon the group; amazingly even Edith was dumbstruck. Her mentor in journalism school?

Maggie's excitement shifted and Colin knew she could sense the tension that had developed as she gazed from one to the other. But, for the life of him, he couldn't speak. Was she kidding?

"Am I talking too much?" she finally asked. "I always talk too much when I get nervous. Just tell me and I'll shut up. Really."

Again, neither he nor Edith could find the words.

Frederick, on the other hand, failed to notice any discomfort among them. He leaned forward proudly. "That's Uncle Teddy's magazine."

At this, Maggie smirked as if being teased, and then her smile vanished when no one disputed that fact. "Are you serious?"

Edith sent her a patronizing glare. "Did Jake not tell you that either?" All color gracing Maggie's cheeks vanished. It was the first time Colin had seen someone turn so pale. He almost thought she might faint.

"Are you okay?" Frederick asked. "Uncle Teddy, she looks like she's going to throw up. Remember that time Sally turned white and puked all over the car…"

They halted at the traffic light, but before Colin could inquire, Maggie turned her head and stared out the window. As she gazed up at the family legacy, Colin could see her shocked and pained reflection in the side window. Watching her profile, Colin noticed the petite, slightly turned-up nose, the way her dark hair framed a sweet, innocent-looking face. She raised a hand to brush loose strands off her forehead and missed when her fingers reached her neck, as if she was pushing back hair that wasn't there, which only increased her discomfort.

He wanted to be angry — he deserved to be furious — but something about her appearance, her distress, the way she bit the inside of her lip to keep from crying, made him wonder if she had been duped as much as he.

When the car behind them blew its horn, Maggie met his gaze, a rush of color filling her cheeks, her eyes brimming with unshed tears. "Was Jake involved in the magazine too?" she asked softly.

Colin heard the car horn again, but he ignored it. "He was my partner."

Again, the color evaporated as she absorbed this news. Perhaps she was going to be sick.

"Would you like me to pull over?" Colin asked again.

Maggie shook her head, bit her lower lip and returned to staring out the window. They turned on to Buccaneer Lane in silence, leaving the lights of Madison, *Yankee Living* and the highway behind. A darkness settled upon the car's interior as they followed the country road, and even Frederick turned quiet.

So many thoughts raged through Colin. Maggie had said Jake was a sad tale. She hadn't known where they lived or that Jake owned part of a magazine she supposedly held dear. How had that piece of information fail to come her way? And this business in Mexico with her father, was that some scheme she and Jake dreamed up to get him out of his obligation? More than likely he paid this Southern belle to be his wife so he could finally be rid of the small town and the family he once called a "giant noose around his neck." But if that were the case, why did he marry a woman who supposedly loved his family business, claimed his father as her mentor?

Perhaps it was all a joke at Colin's expense. Jake's way to skip responsibility, to finally be free of them all.

Only Jake didn't have a chance to enjoy his freedom. One month and his cousin was dead.

Suddenly, a different kind of pain filled Colin's heart, realizing he would never see his cousin again. He longed to feel sad at Jake's passing, but he was too angry, too bitter over years of betrayal. And that hurt more than grief.

"We're going to Bonnie's house?"

Maggie's voice, once so vibrant and laughing, emerged meek and fearful.

"Yes," Colin answered. "The funeral's tomorrow."

Through the occasional moonlight filtering through the trees, Colin made out Maggie smoothing out her shirt with a nervous hand. "How is she taking her son's passing?"

At this, Edith shot up and leaned between the two front seats. "Son?"

Maggie jumped, no doubt worried she had committed another faux pas. Did she know nothing about Jake?

"Bonnie is our mother," Colin said, watching for her reaction as the moonlight danced shadows on her face. Even in the semi-darkness of that lonely country road, Colin made out two enormous brown eyes staring at him with alarm.

"You didn't know that either?" Sarcasm was long gone. Edith's tone was almost hostile.

"The lawyer said Bonnie was his mother."

Colin pulled on to the long driveway leading up to the nineteenth century home. As they approached the old Victorian, the light from the wraparound porch shone into the front seat. "Jake's parents died a couple years ago. In a car accident that also claimed our father."

Maggie's eyes filled with tears and she gazed heavenward. "Gavin Parnell?"

Colin found himself gripping the steering wheel so tight his knuckles ached. After all this time, he still missed his father terribly, wished he were present at times like these. "My father and uncle ran the magazine. My grandfather founded it."

A lone tear fell down Maggie's cheek but she smiled slightly. "In 1902."

In the darkness of the back seat, Colin heard Edith huff. "Well, you know a lot about some things."

He parked the car beside a host of others, but paused as he gazed into the house full of family and sympathetic friends and neighbors. No doubt all of Madison had descended upon Bonnie's house; it was a tight-knit community that looked after each other in times of need. The camaraderie would be welcomed and he longed for a drink, but something held him to his seat. Neither Maggie nor Edith seemed eager to leave as well.

"What are you guys waiting for?" Frederick wailed. "I'm hungry."

This brought Maggie back to life. She straightened her shoulders, wiped away the tears and turned toward Frederick. "Will you introduce me to everyone?"

"Yeah, but can we eat first?"

A smile broke out, despite the tears still lingering on her lashes. "You bet."

Edith unbuckled the boy and he leaped from the car, rushing

toward the house. The rest followed suit in silence, until Maggie stopped dead in her tracks.

"On no," she whispered. "I didn't think it was possible this day could get any worse."

Colin followed her gaze into the living room window, where a man in uniform stood talking to his mother. "Your father?"

Maggie nodded anxiously. So, that was it, Colin thought. She and Jake had lied about the marriage, about the father's oil business, and now her secret would be out. Edith shot him a knowing look, the kind she sent when a deer was in her line of fire. Whatever game those two had played on him, her number was up.

"I'm sure he'll be glad to see you in your time of sorrow," Edith said as she headed up the porch steps. "Aren't you glad to see him?"

Maggie swallowed resignedly as if she knew a gun was pointed at her head and she didn't care. "Not exactly." She paused at the threshold, took a deep breath and sighed. "You see, I never told him I got married."

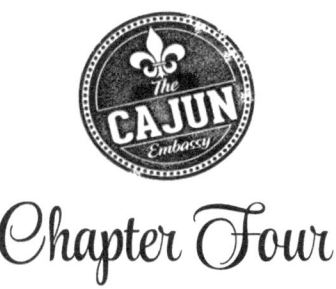

Chapter Four

MAGGIE GAZED AT THE ROOM full of well-dressed strangers all staring back at her, and wondered for not the first time since arriving in Maine why she hadn't jumped on that flight to New Orleans. What was she doing here? She knew nothing about these people, nothing about Jake and his life. And if all the horrid revelations about her deceased husband weren't enough, her father stood talking to the woman who should have been her mother-in-law.

Nothing made sense. Nothing.

"Maggie," she heard Colin say to her right. "This is my mother, Bonnie Parnell."

Surprisingly, the petite, dark-haired woman who embodied what Maggie saw as a traditional New England matriarch, preppy clothes and short string of pearls at her throat, reached out and gave her a warm hug. Maggie leaned into the embrace and found they were both of the same height.

"Welcome to Madison," Bonnie whispered and gave her a squeeze.

Maggie reluctantly broke away, finding Bonnie's hospitality welcome. She longed to cling to the one person who appeared happy to greet her, but her father was soon at her side, his tall, imposing form casting a shadow over her. Maggie could feel the tension emanating from his starchy ironed persona.

"You have a lot of explaining to do," he whispered in her left ear.

Maggie met his stern eyes and nodded. An understatement. But surprisingly it was Colin's stare that unnerved her the most. What did he think of her now? The frown gracing his forehead made her wonder if he thought she had devised some dubious plan, concocting a grand story about her father, Jake and an imaginary oil company.

"Colin, this is my father, Colonel Stewart Mallory."

The two men shook hands, eyeing each other skeptically. "A pleasure to meet you," Maggie's father said in his rich Georgian accent.

"Stewart, this is my son, Colin. My oldest who publishes the magazine."

Strange, Maggie thought as she watched Bonnie offer up polite introductions with a gracious smile, but she didn't seem shocked by the sudden death of her nephew. Jude had been close to tears at the airport and Colin had used scotch to ease the pain, but Bonnie appeared to be at peace with the news.

She didn't seem all that surprised to meet Maggie either.

"Let me introduce you to the rest of the family," Bonnie said, graciously taking Maggie's elbow. "And don't worry," she added with a warm smile, "there will be no test later if you don't remember all of the names."

Maggie shot a glance back at her father, still lingering at the door where Edith seemed eager to make his acquaintance. "We'll talk later," he said, and a shiver ran up Maggie's backbone.

"Are you cold dear?" Bonnie asked. "It's nippy tonight. Can I get you a sweater?"

Maggie was sure it was her nerves causing the chills, but she did wish for something warm about her shoulders. Colin's arms preferably. She swallowed hard, forcing that traitorous thought away. At Jake's wake, no less. She was going to hell for that image, pure and simple.

"I'm fine," she stuttered, hoping Bonnie couldn't read minds. As they made their way across the crowded room, Maggie glanced back and spotted Colin pouring a drink by a side table. Their eyes met for a second, and she shivered again.

"Judith," Bonnie said, pulling Colin's sister aside. "I'm going to get this poor child a sweater. Introduce her around."

Jude attempted a smile but Maggie found Bonnie's absence more chilling than the weather.

"Wow," she heard an accented voice to her rear. "You're not what I expected."

"This is my husband, Mark." Jude pulled the mystery voice to her side and a man dressed in jeans, sweatshirt and a half-grown beard appeared. Mark, pronounced "Mawk," appeared out of place among the Kennedys, like a gardener at an upscale garden party. They shook hands.

"You're not what I expected either," Maggie answered.

His infectious smile disappeared. "I came from work."

"Mark's a pre-school teacher while he's writing his novel," Jude inserted proudly while Mark bristled. Maggie wondered if she had touched a nerve.

"So, what did you expect?" Maggie asked to change the subject.

At this, Mark's grin returned. "You know Jake, always after the long, tall blondes."

Jude elbowed him in the ribs and Mark instantly realized his mistake. "Well, most of the time."

"Tell me Maggie," Jude interrupted, "how is your father's oil company."

She needed a drink. A long, tall drink.

As if reading her mind, a cold, moist glass was placed in her right palm. She looked down at the welcomed scotch and up to find Colin moving back toward the guests. She wanted to voice her thanks but he didn't look back. Her audience, however, was still waiting for an answer. Maggie downed the scotch in one gulp.

Renewed with the warm liquor entering her veins, she focused on Mawk. "Your accent's different from the rest. Why is that?"

Again, the smile returned, this time with pride. "I'm from Boston."

That made sense, Maggie reasoned. He sounded like Matt Damon in *Good Will Hunting*. Or was it Ben Afleck?

"Of course, your accent's different from all of us," Mark added. "Jake said you were from somewhere down South."

"Georgia." She sucked the scotch from the remaining ice cubes, hoping to put the breaks on her own accent but knowing damn well that alcohol only made it worse. "LaGrange to be exact."

Mark moved in close conspiratorially and Maggie wondered if he was going to press her about the oil company. "Tell me," he practically whispered, "what is grits?"

Maggie bit the inside of her lip to keep from laughing. "It's hominy."

Mark frowned. "Hominy?"

Bonnie placed a sweater about Maggie's shoulders. "Let me introduce you around."

"Excuse me," Maggie said.

"Hominy?" Mark repeated as she moved away. "Like four-part hominy?"

"This is Kathy Buchanon," Bonnie said, introducing Maggie to an elegantly dressed blonde who stood inches above Maggie and who seemed to be using that as an advantage. Or maybe Maggie was imagining things. "She was a childhood friend of both Colin and Jake."

"Nice to meet you." Maggie extended her hand but Kathy took the moment to wipe her eyes with a handkerchief, making Maggie feel even more uncomfortable for not crying.

"We were very close," Kathy finally said, her voice breaking.

An awkward silence fell and Maggie couldn't help wondering what that meant. If she wasn't mistaken, Kathy appeared eager to let her know, but Bonnie led her away to a couple she introduced as cousins, a great uncle on her mother's side, a neighbor who remembered changing Jake's diapers and the tall, lean maid who recalled a story about Jake, a bottle of cheap whiskey and a fast car. Maggie couldn't help wondering if the blonde maid had actually been there.

All the while, Maggie's father kept meeting her eyes from across the room where he was busy making small talk, his questioning gaze unnerving. And twice, Colin refilled her drink, silently replacing the glasses in her palms while he made his rounds. Thankful for the reinforcements, she mouthed him a thanks, but he didn't respond, gazing at her as solemnly as her father.

Thank God for the scotch. She downed them as soon as they arrived, anything to make the pain of the night pass easier.

"You're not what I expected."

Maggie turned to find a breathtaking blonde, clearly three inches taller, standing at her side. If she lived to be one hundred, she never wanted to hear those words again.

"Yes, I know."

The woman attempted to say something, then tears choked her words. She pressed a napkin to her mouth and hurried off.

"Wow, am I that startling?" she said to no one.

"I'm afraid Jake broke a few hearts." Bonnie took her elbow and led her to a group of stern-looking people. "Don't let it bother you. They meant nothing."

Unlike me, Maggie wondered. She sucked at her ice cubes again, while Bonnie made introductions to members of the board of *Yankee Living* magazine. It occurred to her who they were as an ice cube fell into the glass with a loud ring.

"Please to meet you," she said, licking her lip to catch the remaining scotch she hoped wasn't trickling down her face. Damn, the one group of people in the world she would most like to impress and she was half-drunk and emotionally unstable.

Just then, she remembered Gavin Parnell and the time they had talked and laughed while she interviewed him for her master's thesis. She gazed at Bonnie, realizing this woman was the husband of her beloved mentor, the man who used to send her encouraging letters and Christmas cards. The man who had thought Maggie would conquer the world, not get laid off three times by the time she was twenty-nine.

An intense sadness threatened to devour her on the spot. Until she remembered what Mark had said.

"You must be reeling from all this?" one of the board members asked.

Maggie heard the question too late. She was busy thinking about grits. She laughed out loud. A little too loud.

The board members stared and a few people nearby turned and looked as well.

Shit, Maggie thought, someone bury me now.

"I'm sorry," she uttered, hoping the drunken slur was her imagination. "I just realized Mark thought I said harmony. As in people singing together well."

No one said a word.

"Harmony. We were talking about grits. He thought I said harrrrmony."

She felt Colin place another glass in her hand, but this time she wondered if he was a foe instead of a friend. Damn Yankees, she thought. Her mother was right. You really can't trust 'em.

"Grits are made from hominy, the white part of the corn." Again, no one spoke, just endless stares aimed in her direction.

"Excuse me," she said as sober as she could manage, and headed for the back door that she hoped would lead to the kitchen and a large knife to slit her wrists.

Maggie saw her father heading in that direction so she immediately turned and headed down a hallway instead. Unfortunately it led to the dining room where Edith was eager to strike up a conversation, no doubt about oil companies. Maggie mumbled something about finding the bathroom and detoured back to the hallway, which appeared to empty out on to the back porch. She slipped out the door into the quiet night air, pressed her back against the wall of the house and sighed.

"Heaven help me," she whispered to the night.

"Having a hard time?"

At first, Maggie thought she was hearing things, but then she spied the orange glow of a cigarette. "Just needed some air."

The orange tip flew across the lawn and Kathy appeared. "I gave up smoking, but the divorce and now this. It's too much of God to ask of me."

Maggie didn't know what to say. For one thing, breathing the clear air made her realize she was indeed drunk, and history had proven that it was best to keep her mouth shut in such situations. Second, this woman intimidated her and she wasn't sure why.

"Is that an Alberta Ferretti?" Kathy asked, scanning her outfit.

That's why, Maggie thought. This woman knew the secret feminine code, something she had failed to discern all her life.

"I think so."

"You think so?" Kathy crossed her arms and huffed. "You're not sure if you bought an Alberta Ferretti?"

If this had been a test, Maggie would have guessed Alberta Ferretti was a sports car maker. "The outfit was a gift from a friend."

Kathy smirked. "Jake always gave the best presents. He had the finest taste."

Maggie wondered if Jake had bestowed many presents on Kathy. She wanted to inquire further, but her inner voice, the one that housed her common sense, told her to remain quiet. Especially since that slur was becoming a regular visitor.

"Oh, and the bag matches." Kathy pulled Maggie's purse forward over her shoulder. "Cute, Mitzi Baker, right?"

The bag was all hers, purchased from her favorite super store that Lizzy loved to mispronounce in her Cajun accent as Tar-jé.

"How did you know Jake?" Damn, she didn't want to know, but she certainly didn't want to talk fashion.

Kathy inhaled, pulling her shoulders back and towering over Maggie. "We dated in high school."

Maggie swallowed. It wasn't as bad as she thought.

"Among other times."

Maggie's mind reeled. That could have meant last week for all she knew.

Kathy pulled another cigarette out of her bag, one that looked ten times as expensive as her own, and lit up. She held the cigarette between her fingers like Katherine Hepburn, all grace and sophistication. Even the smoke failed to bother Maggie as she watched this amazing woman in action.

"So, I understand Jake was helping your father with his failing oil company."

Maggie verbally groaned. This horrid night simply would not end. She ran a hand through her hair, again surprised to find half of it gone, and stumbled to the edge of the porch. Somewhere in the distance a train sounded and a dog barked in a neighbor's yard. In an instant she thought of home. LaGrange. Where cousins and aunts and uncles existed and some things, like annual parades and the taste of black-eyed peas simmered in ham, never changed. Would she ever find a place like that for herself?

"There's no oil company," Maggie said to the darkness.

Kathy huffed behind her. "We all know that, darling. I was being polite."

Maggie turned and leaned against the screen for support. She took a good look at Kathy, wondering what her story was, why this woman held a grudge. The tension emanating from the tall blonde could have killed every mosquito on that porch.

Now that Maggie knew Kathy's objective, she decided to change to the offensive. "So what do you know, darling?"

Kathy took a long drag off her cigarette and exhaled upwards. "That Parnell men will be the death of me."

Join the club, Maggie thought, although she hardly shared the physical requirements of this elite group of gorgeous women.

"Now that Jake is gone, I don't see how Colin would expect me to live here again," Kathy said, removing imaginary lint from her sleeve. "I can't bear to live with the memories."

Maggie sucked the ice dry. She dreaded hearing what that meant, but she couldn't help herself. "Why would Colin expect you to live in Madison?"

Kathy straightened now that the conservation shifted to the living. "Oh, didn't you know? Colin and I are engaged?"

It might have been the culmination of a night of dreadful revelations. Or perhaps the fact that Kathy was the last person she hoped to see on the arm of her handsome cranberry professor. It could have been the scotch. Whatever the cause, Maggie's jaw dropped open and she practically let out a yell.

"His financé?"

Kathy was clearly taken aback, for the first time appearing on the defensive. "Yes."

"As in marriage?"

"Yes."

"Colin Parnell? The one with the leather circles on his elbows?"

"Yes, and not for much longer if I have anything to do with it."

Maggie's mind swirled. She didn't know which angered her more — this fashion witch teaming up with such a kind-hearted, witty man or the fact that Colin lied to her in Pittsburgh.

"Wait, he's not kind-hearted," she said, her slur and accent completely evident. "He's a cad!"

"What are you talking about?" Kathy stared at her as if she had lost her mind, which Maggie wondered herself.

"Nothing. I know nothing about nothing."

"Right." Kathy took a drag on her cigarette and narrowed her eyes. "I guess now you're going to tell me you knew nothing about Jake marrying you to get out of his obligation to Colin."

The night had been one continuous descent into darkness, but Kathy's last comment pushed Maggie's into the abyss. "What?"

"Don't tell me you don't know."

Her stomach tightened and the liquor pounded at her temple. She wanted to run screaming from this place, but she had to know. "What obligation to Colin?"

Now, that Kathy was back as the prowler, she moved forward, blowing smoke in Maggie's direction. "Jake's parents and Colin's father were killed in an auto accident a few years ago. You do know that?"

Maggie nodded. One of the many aunts had explained about the driver of the eighteen-wheeler who had fallen asleep at the wheel. And that Bonnie had been spared because she was home with the flu that night and unable to attend the theater with the others.

"The two families ran the magazine so naturally it was left to Bonnie, Colin and Jake."

Kathy took a drag and then threw the butt on the porch and snubbed it with the toe of her high-heeled shoe. "Jake was out of college and working in Boston at the time, as an editor at the

Globe. Colin had just graduated from architecture school and had been offered a prestigious job in New York City. But he passed it up to become publisher. They were both supposed to run the magazine together, with Jake as editor and Bonnie doing the home shots. But you know Jake."

She really didn't, but Maggie nodded anyway.

"Colin carried the brunt of the magazine on his shoulders during all those years while Jake came and went, always leaving for some fool reason. A few months ago, Colin was offered a job in New York with a major architecture firm. He asked Jake to take over the business and Jake agreed."

"Let me guess," Maggie inserted, "he went to Vegas and got married and gave my father's oil company as an excuse."

Kathy raised a finger as if to take another drag but realized there was no cigarette. For a moment, Maggie dreaded that the horrid woman would bring out another and remain on the porch. She desperately wanted Kathy to leave so she could have her long-overdue nervous breakdown in solitude.

"Last we heard from Jake was a postcard saying he met the girl of his dreams and he was headed to Mexico." Kathy studied Maggie hard, as if gazing directly into her soul. "Only you know the rest of that story."

If only. "But if Jake was to take over the magazine for Colin, what was he doing in Vegas at a journalism convention?"

Kathy offered up her now legendary smirk. "Don't you know?"

Despite the darkness threatening to swallow her whole, Maggie wasn't going down without a fight. "We didn't talk much business in Vegas, if you know what I mean?"

Her shot hit home; Kathy faltered slightly. "He was in charge of all the hiring at *Yankee Living*. He was there to recruit new staff."

All the news of that day suddenly palled in comparison to that piece of information. *He was there to recruit new staff.* The words echoed in Maggie's brain, producing an intense knot in the center of her chest. Dear God, she thought, I needed a job, not a disappearing husband.

"Are you all right?" The words were spoken but Maggie

doubted Kathy truly cared.

"I need some air," Maggie managed.

"I'm going to get a drink, should I get you one?"

Maggie fingers touched the cold metal of the porch railing and she shook her head. "I'm fine, just going to make a quick call on my cell phone."

Somewhere inside the house, Maggie heard Colin call Kathy's name. Kathy turned toward the house and Maggie took the opportunity to exit the porch. She fell upon the back steps of the house and began rummaging through her purse for the cell. Her breath was uneven and her heart racing but she had to call Stacy, had to hear a comforting voice or she'd unravel for sure.

Maggie could barely make out the numbers through her haze of heartbreak and tears, but she finally found Stacy's number and managed to hit the talk button.

"Maggie," Stacy announced on the other end. "How are you, honey?"

Where had her breath disappeared? She couldn't think, couldn't breathe. "Jake…," Maggie whispered.

"What about that damn Yankee?" Stacy asked, concern evident in her voice.

An enormous block of pain constricted upon her chest and Maggie fought to keep the emotions at bay. "He married me to get out of a family obligation, Stacy. He married me and deserted me on my wedding night just to keep from working in his family business."

"Shit," came an accented voice on the other end, pronounced long and slow in three syllables.

"I'm the only woman at this wake who didn't sleep with him." The block was beginning to rise, constricting her throat. "And he could have given me a job. At my favorite magazine." She swallowed hard, gathering all her strength left to utter the next sentence. "He was part owner of *Yankee Living*."

The last thought did her in. The emotions burst through and she began to shake. She couldn't talk, even though Stacy was asking a million questions, demanding to know what was going on and what the hell was *Yankee Living*? The tears rose up and burst free and it was all Maggie could do but cradle her head in her hands and weep uncontrollably.

"Maggie," Stacy kept shouting, but she was helpless to answer. And then someone gently took the cell phone from her hands.

Chapter Five

COLIN SPENT THE ENTIRE EVENING chasing his mother, trying to obtain answers. She had failed to explain the details of Jake's death when she had phoned him in New York and seemed in no hurry to do so now, always carefully eluding him, pushing him to some task like greeting relatives or filling drinks.

And along the way Colin made sure Miss Starlet's glass was refilled.

He watched her making the rounds, blanching at the sight of Jake's old girlfriends, struggling with Mark's heavy Boston accent, avoiding Edith and her endless questions. She was having a tough time of it all, by the rate of the Scotch evaporating. Either that or nervous over her deception being discovered. He watched her carefully, hoping to discern which was the truth.

Then Maggie disappeared. He had spotted her meeting the magazine's board members, a look of pure fright crossing her features as his mother made the introductions. Either the ex-girl-friends or the Scotch — or both — were getting the best of her, for her face paled considerably. To his surprise, she had laughed at something being said, rather loudly too. Only the others hadn't seen the humor.

Colin drifted down the main hallway, peering into first the din-ing room, then the kitchen. No doubt Jezebel was hiding out, either collapsing under the impact of it all or preening herself for her next victim.

He still couldn't fathom if she was innocent of the whole mess or was a partner to Jake's cruel joke. Only Jake wasn't here to enjoy the joke's conclusion and Miss Daisy had been caught in the lie.

It was midnight and he still didn't know what happened.

Colin paused at the kitchen sink and sighed, then turned and leaned against the counter to enjoy the last of his drink. He gazed back inside the dining room hoping to find his mother. He had to get some answers.

Then he heard Kathy on the back porch explaining a sad story about a job in New York City.

"Kathy!" Colin yelled, and slammed his drink hard into the sink. Damn, but it was no one's business but his own. "Kathy."

He exited the back door to the darkened porch and found Kathy still expelling her story to a stunned Maggie on the porch steps. Maggie mumbled something about making a phone call and Kathy turned back toward the house.

"What?" she asked as she approached him.

He grabbed her arm and tried to keep his anger at bay. "What I do with my magazine and my life is my business."

"She's Jake widow, she should know." Like always, Kathy pulled away. The woman was both stubbornly independent and devoid of affection. "Besides, she's probably fool enough to think that Jake fell in love with her. As if."

"She's not the only one." Colin hated to be cruel, but if he knew Kathy, she had inflicted worse on Maggie.

Kathy winced, but quickly recovered. "I'm going to get a drink. Want one?"

He thought he did. He'd spent the evening wallowing in scotch and small talk, anything to ease the pain. But he needed to clear his mind and find out what happened to Jake. And just what the hell was the story of Jake's flirtatious widow who was now sitting on the back porch struggling with her cell phone.

He shook his head.

"Suit yourself." Kathy paused and ran a finger up his lapel, which wasn't like her. "Want me to come over later?"

The damned evening's surprises wouldn't end. Colin gently took Kathy's hand and squeezed. "It's been a long day. And we have a funeral tomorrow."

Kathy sobered and slipped her fingers free. The haughtiness disappeared and her trademark sadness returned. Colin regretted not letting her down easier; the day must have sent her emotions plummeting. She was such a roller coaster these days.

"Come over for breakfast," Colin said, touching her cheek. "Let's talk later."

Kathy nodded, spied someone in the dining room, lit up with a large smile and hurried off. Colin watched the transformation with amazement. Manic-depressive, Bonnie had told him. She had always been that way, but crises seemed to bring out the worst. He made a mental note to pay special attention to her at the funeral, wondering, too, if he would ever relinquish his big brother role of the family and all their close acquaintances.

At the moment, however, all his thoughts were on a brown-eyed cutie who had been born at the Atlanta airport.

"Stacy," he heard Maggie's emotional cry from the back porch.

Colin headed for the stoop, overhearing the worst. He didn't know which was more stunning, the fact that Maggie knew of his predicament or that she might not have slept with his cousin. Of course he knew. The latter gave him hope.

Maggie tried to finish her conversation but tears consumed her. Her shoulders began to shake from the sobbing and she wept into her cradle of hands. Whatever doubts Colin had over who was at fault here disappeared. Jake had used her, he was sure.

He sat down on the step beside her and took the cell phone from her hands. "Stacy?"

"Who's this?" sounded a heavily accented woman.

"Colin Parnell. I'm Jake's cousin."

"What's wrong with my Maggie?" Stacy's voice, twang and all, rose to an authoritative level.

"She's upset right now. Why don't I have her call you back in the morning?"

"You listen here," Stacy demanded. "That girl has been through a lot because of that no-good Jake. Talks her into marriage when she's drunk and then not one word from that cad since Vegas."

Colin paused, soaking in this news.

Stacy paused as well. "She did tell you that, didn't she?"

"Stacy, we're all pretty emotional here. Why don't we talk tomorrow?"

"That's fine, you have her call me in the morning."

"Okay."

"But you listen here, Mr. Colin Parnell." The drill sergeant returned. "That's a very special, sweet girl you have there. If you hurt one hair of her head, I'm going to come up there and kick your Yankee…"

"Got it, Stacy."

Another paused ensued and Colin wondered what was next, but Stacy's next comment surprised him even more. "Thanks Colin" was all she uttered, and then hung up.

Colin ended the call and gazed down at Maggie, who still hadn't taken control of her emotions. He knew he shouldn't touch her, considering how much he really wanted to touch her, but he slid an arm about her shoulders and guided her head into his chest. She gladly accepted the offer and cried into his shirt, while he placed a cheek upon the top of her head.

She smelled old-fashioned, like roses perhaps. She certainly didn't have that sharp, overpowering smell of perfumes Kathy and many of Jake's girlfriends used. Gazing down on to her face, he noticed little make-up as well, although the lack of it only brought out her God-given features of freckles and a button nose. No, Maggie was definitely not Jake's type. These were not attributes his flamboyant cousin desired in a woman. Maggie was earthy, real. Or maybe it was his imagination getting the best of him, for she felt so incredibly natural nestled in his arms.

Colin reached into a pocket and pulled out a handkerchief. When he handed it to Maggie, she came back to life, straightening and blowing her nose soundly. Definitely not Jake's type, he thought with a smile.

"What?" she asked defensively.

He rubbed her back, dreading relinquishing the feel of her. "Are you all right?"

"Just dandy." She blew her nose again, swaggering a little.

"Are you drunk?"

Maggie thrust his handkerchief into his lap, then stood, grabbing the porch railing for support. "Thanks to you."

Colin discreetly pocketed the handkerchief. "I suppose it was me sucking those ice cubes dry."

Maggie turned, an intense pain only Jake could inflict upon a woman shining in those adorable brown eyes. Colin rose to take her in his arms again, but she drew away. "And you're married!" she said, pointing an accusatory finger.

At this, Colin laughed. "What?"

"You lied to me. You said you weren't."

Who told her this? "Maggie, I'm not married."

She shook her head, in disagreement or to clear it, he wasn't sure. "Engaged then. Same difference."

"Engaged?" Now, this was a laugh. Years of playing the patriarch, managing the family business, the family estate, *the family*. He rarely had time for sex, let alone a full-blown relationship.

"I'm not engaged."

She didn't believe him, crossing her arms about her chest and narrowing her eyes. "My mother was right. You damn Yankees are all the same."

Colin couldn't help but laugh. "Are you for real?"

Maggie wasn't finding anything humorous, and her thoughts veered off as her shoulders slumped forward. "Why me?" she asked in a weak, pitiful voice. "He could have had any gorgeous woman he wanted at that convention and he picked me. Why?"

As was in anything dealing with Jake, Colin was clueless. "I don't know."

She softened a bit, still uneasy on her feet. Colin rose and reached for her, but Maggie backed away. "If he wanted to get out of the family business, why didn't he marry some blonde and have sex all week in Vegas?"

Again, the thought of Maggie being celibate with his cousin gave him hope, although he could hardly see why considering she was his cousin's widow. Still, Jake had always bested him when it came to women. Kathy was a prime example. It felt good to have an edge with Maggie, however remote.

"Shall I take you to bed?"

Maggie stared at him hard. "Excuse me?"

Dear God, Colin thought, he was finally losing his mind. "I meant you should go to bed. The funeral's in the morning and you need to get some sleep."

Maggie nodded, letting Colin take her elbow and lead her toward his car by the front of the house. They passed the bay window of the living room and spied Bonnie talking quietly with Maggie's father. Most of the guests had left and the couple sat deep in thought, silhouetted by the glow of one lone table lamp.

Odd, Colin thought. For a moment, he imagined his mother interested in men, being a woman as well as a mother, grand-mother and design manager of a major regional magazine. He hadn't seen that side of her since his father's death and doubted he was seeing it now.

Maggie paused, swaying into his shoulder. "I need to tell my dad where I'm going."

Colin led her forward again. "Bonnie has this all arranged. I'm sure he's informed."

"He worries..." She paused again at the passenger door of his Explorer, lost in thought. Then she frowned. "You call your mother Bonnie?"

Colin opened the door and helped her inside. "We work together. I can't tell my employees that 'Mom's coming with the proofs' now, can I?"

Sly Miss Georgia surfaced, if only briefly. "I don't see why not. I'll bet she calls you honey and baby, among other things."

Colin crossed over to the driver's door and dropped down behind the wheel. He roared the car into action. "At least she doesn't call me 'Magpie.'"

Her mouth dropped open. "How on earth did you know that?"

"And they say army men never reveal their secrets."

Maggie paused watching her father and Bonnie rise from their seats at the bay window and head toward the inner house, his hand lovingly placed at her back. "It's not half as bad as my real name."

She must be drunk, Colin thought, forgetting their earlier conversation. "The one you received in the Atlanta Airport? I heard."

Maggie twisted her face in a smile. "Most people think Maggie is short for Margaret. It's actually a nickname for Magnolia."

"Magnolia?"

She ran a hand through her hair and smiled grimly. "Yeah, I'll bet your Yankee sensibilities are having fun with that one."

Suddenly, they were back in Pittsburgh, trading barbs and enjoying each other's company. When Maggie's gaze flared back at him and her lips pulled up in a half-smile, half-pout, Colin wanted nothing more than to smother those lips with his own. He paused at the end of the driveway, watching the lone lamppost cast an orange glow about her face and considered doing just that. He reached over and brushed his knuckles against the smooth skin of her cheek and leaned forward, but Maggie's smile retreated and she began twirling her hair nervously.

"You were going to drop me off at the hotel, right?"

Colin straightened, cleared his throat, checked the deserted street before him and headed away from his mother's house. "Right."

What was this woman doing to him? Clearly he had left his rational mind in New York City.

"Now, what are you doing?"

Pulling into his own driveway, only a half mile from his mother's house, Colin realized he had forgotten to explain the housing arrangements. "There's no hotel."

Maggie appeared at him through the darkness skeptically. "Uh huh."

"Really. The closest hotel is in Freeport. We take care of our guests around here."

As he turned off the engine, she leaned away from him toward the passenger door. "And I take it this is your house."

Again, he wanted to laugh. Maggie was with the safest man in Maine, surrounded by family in all directions.

"Your father is staying at my mother's house along with some cousins and the Bradleys are at Edith's," he explained. "No one, but Mark's parents, wants to stay with Jude and Mark because Frederick is boundless energy."

"He's an angel."

"You're a new playmate, give it time. He's a handful."

Maggie sighed. "And I was relegated to your house, is that it?"

"You, plus my Aunt Sophie and Uncle George. They're sleeping upstairs next to my room so you have the first floor all to yourself."

She remained silent, staring up at his colonial money-sucker. "It's lovely," she whispered, her voice laced with liquor-induced emotions.

Colin worried that Maggie teetered on the brink of another crying spree, so he bolted out the door and retrieved her baggage from the trunk. He met her at the passenger side as she was climbing out of the Explorer, wiping her eyes with the heel of her hand.

"Hang in there," he said, and she sent him a half-hearted but appreciative smile through the tears.

"I don't want to put you out." She wiped her nose across her sleeve, then realized what she'd done. "Shit, I'm wearing a Ferrari."

Colin thought to pull out a clean handkerchief but his hands were full. "It's no problem. I live alone so company's welcome."

Maggie shot him a skeptical glance and Colin wondered if she still thought him engaged. He began to ask who the lucky woman was when fierce, deep barking ensued from the other side of the door. Damn, he'd forgotten about Frosty.

"Frederick's grandparents are allergic to dogs. I'm housing Frosty as well."

Maggie pulled her hair behind an ear, fingering the tips that fell about her cheeks. "Frosty?"

"Yeah, well, he's not the friendliest dog in the world." Colin dropped the suitcases and unlocked the door, which made the barking increase. "They got him at the pound, think he's been abused, so he's skittish around people. Don't be surprised if he barks forever, then goes and hides."

The door swung open and Frederick's pug stood facing the duo, feet planted firmly apart, popping up an inch or two off the ground as his miniscule mug howled away. Maggie took one look at the tiny pup, trying so hard to be ferocious despite his size, and started laughing. Personally, Colin was sick of the deranged dog no matter how amusing the situation, but it felt good to hear Miss Georgia happy again. "Definitely a bark worse than his bite kind of dog."

Maggie leaned down and offered her hand. "Hey boo boo. What's ya know good?"

Colin slipped over the threshold, bringing the suitcases into the hallway, and placing them next to the guestroom. Frosty barked at his intrusion but quickly turned to Maggie when he realized Colin was ignoring him. By the time Colin turned around, the dog had stopped howling and was allowing Maggie to scratch behind an ear.

"You're a sa-wee-tie-pie," she said, drawing out more syllables than Colin had ever heard. And damned if the dog didn't eat it up.

"Wow, he's never taken to anyone like that before."

Maggie looked up with a sleepy grin. "Maybe he's a Southern dog, doesn't understand your language."

Colin moved around the loving couple to shut and lock the front door. "Do me a favor then. Tell that pain in the ass to stop barking."

"We're not listening." Covering the dog's ears, Maggie picked up the non-objecting mutt, which shocked Colin further, and walked into the living room. "What a gorgeous house."

Colin followed his usual routine: turning off the outside lights, turning on the hallway lamp, pulling the mail out of the wall slot and dropping it on to the desk of the living room's secretary. "It was my great, great grandfather's, built in 1833."

"Was this the Civil War hero with the match?"

Colin leaned against the staircase railing, watching Maggie examine his home, pug cradled in her arms like a child and snorting with satisfaction. "No, that was William Sherman. Grandpa Theodore was the one holding the flint box."

Maggie shot him a caustic glance. "Cute."

"Can I get you something to drink?"

"Think you've done enough damage for one evening." She ran a lazy hand across the oak mantel, which housed Colin's collection of family portraits in assorted frames.

"That fireplace and mantel was part of the original cabin built on this spot before the Revolution."

Maggie shook her head in amazement. "It's fabulous. So…"

"Time-consuming? Expensive? A money pit?"

Maggie gave him that half-pout, half-smile again, a gesture that seemed to say she got the joke, but couldn't believe he was saying it. "So historic, so New England were my thoughts."

Colin removed his jacket and draped it over the back of a chair. "Same thing."

This time, he knew Maggie didn't approve. "You're living in an historical monument, one that's tied to your family for almost three hundred years. And you act like it's an anchor tied around your neck."

Her arrow hit a little too close to home. He felt it pierce his heart with a tangy mixture of truth and guilt. Was that how he really considered his family and business? Was it that obvious?

"You'll understand what I mean when you take a shower in the morning," Colin said to change the conversation, and his feelings, back to congenial terms. But the accusation seemed to hover in the air before him.

"Colin?" he heard an elderly woman call from the stop of the stairs. "Is that you?"

"Yes, Aunt Sophie. I'm locking up."

"Who's that with you?"

Colin glanced at Maggie, who appeared to have wilted in those few moments. "Just me and Miss Georgia."

"Who?"

"It's me, Mrs. Parnell," Maggie called out as if she had known his aunt all her life. "It's Maggie."

"Oh, okay." He heard the sound of slippers shuffling down the hallway. "Good-night then."

"Good-night," they both said in unison, then grinned at each other in response.

They stood staring at one another in the warmth of his ancient living room, unable to break what spell had befallen them. Colin knew he should turn away, but damned if he could stop gazing at the heavenly creature before him, one who was half drunk and carrying a mentally unstable pug. Her eyes twinkled too, as if she enjoyed the enchantment as much as he did. God, if only she hadn't been Jake's widow and caught up in this insane set of circumstances. If only they had met under different conditions, two travelers finding solace in each other's company in an airport lounge in Pittsburgh. He could be showing her his house on the way to his bed, where he would demonstrate some Yankee ingenuity.

"Colin?" she said, breaking the spell, her countenance wilting once more. "I really should get to bed."

Colin exhaled and smiled. "Right."

He showed her to the guestroom, made sure there were fresh towels — thank God for Joyce, his weekly maid, who had visited the day before — and explained the lay of the house, including kitchen and nearest bathroom.

"Are you sure I can't get you anything?"

Maggie shook her head. "You've been very kind."

Colin pulled the heaviest suitcase on to the trunk at the end of the bed, straightened and sighed. He hated leaving her company, hated not knowing the full details. God help him but he wanted to hear her say once more that nothing happened in Vegas.

"I'll see you in the morning, then."

Maggie nodded. "What time is the funeral?"

Hell, Colin thought grimacing, here he was having illicit

thoughts about Jake's widow when he was going to put his cousin in the ground in less than twelve hours. "Eleven."

He had to get out of there, had to get some rest and sear this woman from his brain. "Good-night," Colin said and headed toward the door.

"Colin?" came a soft, sultry voice from behind and he knew sleep would not come well that evening. He paused on the threshold while Maggie approached, standing only as high as his chin, but every inch adorable. She fiddled nervously with a button on her blouse and bit the inside of her cheek.

"I shouldn't bring this up, considering." She swallowed hard and Colin noticed red highlights reflected in her hair and a defiant cow lip gracing her forehead. Her eyelashes were too long for a face so small, which emphasized her expressive, friendly eyes. She really was so wicked cute.

"I know I acted poorly in Pittsburgh…"

Hell, not Pittsburgh. He hated thinking back to his embarrassing flirtations, especially knowing how hesitant she had been to even enter the damn lounge. "Maggie, if anyone's at fault, it's me."

This stopped her cold. She looked up at him with a soulful, almost hopeful gaze. She uttered the next sentence carefully, as if lightning might strike her on the spot. "Then you were attracted to me?"

Colin placed a hand high on the edge of the door and leaned against it, staring down into the eyes of a woman first used by his cousin, then cast aside. Why had he chosen Maggie in the first place? She was Colin's type of woman, not Jake's. Nothing made sense and now Miss Georgia suffered doubts of self-worth, no doubt comparing herself to the collection of ex-girlfriends gathered at the wake.

He leaned forward and placed a hand on her cheek, her face so near he could smell roses. She sucked in a breath as if wondering if he would kiss her. And he wanted to with all his soul.

"I don't know what occurred between you and Jake in Vegas, but I do know this. Jake was a fool if he didn't appreciate what he had."

She exhaled, started to speak and Colin silenced her lips with his thumb, which he let drift slowly back to her cheek. "We can talk in the morning. As for Pittsburgh, I wish I could say I was sorry for what happened, but the truth is I'm not."

The light in her eyes so evident in the airport's lounge returned, this time reflecting a semblance of hope.

"Yes, Maggie," Colin said softly, "I was very much attracted to you."

As he leaned forward, she did the same, and he knew he could steal a kiss that night. But, it wasn't the right thing to do, considering the circumstances, the alcohol and the memory of Jake lingering between them. Instead, Colin gently kissed her forehead, said goodnight and closed the door behind him.

As he headed up the stairs to his own bed, he was thankful for the ailing monstrosity of his home and its failing pipes, for a cold shower was just what he needed.

Chapter Six

TWENTY-NINE YEARS OF LIVING ON army bases had robbed Maggie of one of life's special pleasures — sleeping late. No matter how hard she tried, her eyes flew open before dawn, her body refusing to return to slumber.

This morning, sleep was particularly absent. She tossed and turned, her dreams a scattering of images from the night before, all ending with one particular man leaning against a door frame making her feel, for the first time that night, like a whole woman. When she finally gave up the fight and threw off the covers, tossing her socked feet over the edge of the early colonial bed, Colin was the first person to greet her.

"Dear God." Maggie gazed at the photo on the bedside bureau of a young Colin resting against the side of a Jaguar. He must have been high school age, maybe early college, for his hair was longer and the lines of worry about his eyes were absent.

The man sitting behind the driver's wheel looked as handsome and confident as the day Maggie had married him. Even though sunglasses masked those baby blues, Maggie could feel Jake's charm emanating from the photograph.

She didn't know which was more disturbing, the fire burning in her gut over Jake's deception or the blush creeping up her cheeks gazing at his cranberry professor cousin.

"This is all way too nuts." Maggie placed the photo facedown on the bureau and headed for the bathroom. Take a long shower, suffer through the funeral, avoid Colin and get the hell out of Dodge, she commanded herself. Find some explanation to give her father. Hell, to give Stacy and the Cajun Embassy! Then get back to Atlanta, find a job and get her life back in order.

The shower sputtered to life and steam quickly filled the room, but Maggie dunked her head beneath the stream and paused. Getting her life in order was one skill she had yet to master. Three layoffs since college, topped by a marriage to a man she barely knew who used her to rob his cousin of his own career, a man she was now attracted to. The absurdity of it all made her laugh, which quickly resulted in a pounding headache due to the lingering effects of the scotch. Holding on to her pounding temples Maggie wanted to cry instead, but she worried that might make the headache worse.

"Wow, could I be a bigger mess?" she asked the ceiling. "God, this is a very good time to strike this shower with a lightning bolt. I mean it, please put me out of my misery."

God ignored her, so she washed her hair, applied conditioner and removed herself from the sauna. She pulled out three outfits she had chosen for the occasion, and decided on the gray suit and black underlying sweater that she used for job interviews — conservative, neat but comfortable. Before she pulled it on, she checked the label in case Kathy was inquisitive.

It was five thirty when she left her bedroom in search of coffee, the sun not even a thought to the darkness outside. Even Frosty remained asleep at the end of the bed. Maggie tiptoed into the kitchen and groped the wall for the switch.

"Who were you talking to?"

Maggie jumped at the voice, turning quickly to find Aunt Sophie at the back door, a steaming cup of java in her hands.

"You scared me." Maggie exhaled, wondering between gasps where Aunt Sophie got her caffeine.

The elderly woman turned and smiled, a genuine gesture of affection as opposed to the endless superficial ones Maggie had received the night before from the stream of ex-girlfriends. "I'm sorry, dear. Didn't want to disturb the deer."

Maggie peered over Sophie's shoulder to view three deer munching on grass and clover in the back yard, their horns silhouettes in the fading moonlight.

"Sweet, aren't they?" Sophie said. "We get a lot of them this time of year."

"I haven't seen deer since I left LaGrange." A pain stabbed at Maggie's heart. She hadn't thought of those days in a very long time.

Sophie didn't answer, but sensed her discomfort and rubbed her arm. It was such a simple gesture, one that Maggie's family members did all the time, in addition to the endless hugs and kisses. Or maybe that was what undid her, remembering her family miles away in Georgia, for Maggie began to cry.

To her credit, Aunt Sophie didn't offer up condolences, just squeezed Maggie's shoulders. "You need a cup of coffee."

Maggie nodded through her emotions, wondering if a person could dehydrate from too much crying.

"I can't sleep anymore," Sophie started chattering, "especially in a strange place. And Colin, bless him, has the finest house of the lot, little good it does me."

Maggie heard coffee being poured somewhere in the darkness and the sound of a coffeepot returning to its cradle. "You want cream with that? Not sure if he has any. I may need to drive into town."

Suddenly, Maggie felt useful. She wiped her face. "I can make breakfast. I like cream but black is fine."

Sophie appeared at her side and placed a hot cup in her hands, the familiar scent drifting up to comfort her. "You drink this cup and by the time you're done, I'll be dressed and we'll go get some groceries."

Afraid the tears might return at Sophie's hospitality, Maggie merely nodded. Sophie headed out the door, but turned as if forgetting something. She grabbed both of Maggie's arms and squeezed. "Don't be talking to God that way, now. It's best if you ask for his assistance instead."

As the petite old woman with the friendly eyes disappeared down the darkened corridor, Maggie did speak gentler to God. Only this time she offered thanks.

It was a little after six when Sophie and Maggie had visited the closest mini-mart, bought up all the eggs, milk, bread and fresh maple syrup the store offered and began cooking what would become a several hours-long breakfast. Maggie's father and Bonnie were the first to arrive, no doubt on account of Stewart rising before the dawn like his daughter. He immediately planted himself between the refrigerator and stove hoping to speak to Maggie, but Bonnie always seemed to draw his attention away. Finally, when Edith arrived at quarter past seven, followed by Uncle Walter, Sophie's slow-moving husband, Maggie managed to get all the heaping plates of food on the table and her guests planted in chairs to eat.

And that was how Colin found her, serving up plates of scrambled eggs, bacon, flapjacks with syrup and biscuits and gravy, the latter her own family recipe. He stood in the doorway, his hair damp and disheveled but his dark suit pressed and neat.

Maggie tried to ignore him, but his gaze followed her movements back and forth from the stove as the menagerie inquired about butter, extra bacon, and more coffee.

"I hate to be rude," Edith said, holding up the gravy, "but what is this?"

"It's white gravy," Stewart answered, dipping a spoon into the bowl. "You pour it over your biscuits like this."

Edith grimaced while Stewart smothered his biscuits. "How on earth do Southerners eat like that and maintain a heartbeat?"

Stewart laughed. "One of the many wonders of the world."

He started to pass the bowl to Edith but she held up a hand. "Gluten intolerant."

They all began talking and comparing fattening foods between the regions, while Maggie added more butter to the skillet to cook up a fresh plate for Colin. She had managed to focus on her cooking and not on the way his shoulders filled out his jacket, was relishing the sound of her father laughing when he sneaked up behind her to pour himself a cup of coffee.

"Sleep well?"

His sepulchral voice, heavy from sleep, made her heart skip a beat. She cleared her throat. "Fine, thanks."

Maggie nervously pulled her hair behind an ear, still surprised to find so much of it gone. She didn't dare glance his way; his presence alone was nerve-racking. "Want some breakfast?"

When he didn't answer, she peeked sideways and found him staring, those dark brown eyes serious and examining. "Don't do that," she whispered.

Colin straightened as if waking from a trance. "Do what?" Then a sly glint appeared in his eyes and he leaned forward, his after-shave mingling with the scent of frying bacon and browning biscuits. "Am I making you nervous, Delta?"

There it was again, that familiar feeling like the one they had shared in Pittsburgh. Maggie didn't know whether to punch him in the arm like a brother or slide her hands up that starched white shirt. My stars, but the man looked good enough to eat.

"What smells so good?" Mark entered the kitchen carrying Frederick in his arms who quickly jumped to the ground and ran to Maggie's side. Jude followed, carrying a plate of sliced meats that she put on the bottom shelf of the refrigerator.

"Maggie, Maggie," the boy cried. "You're still here."

Grabbing the young tyke, Maggie hurled him into the air. "Didn't I promise to come see your tree house?"

"Can we go now?" Frederick asked excitedly.

"Not right now. I've got some bacon that needs to be cooked."

"After breakfast then?"

Colin reached over and effortlessly pulled Frederick on to his shoulders, heading off toward the back porch. "Maggie has to fin-ish breakfast and then we have to go to the cemetery. Remember what I told you last night?"

Maggie didn't hear the rest of the conversation for the screen door closed and Jude offered to help. While Jude tended to the bacon, Maggie poured herself a cup of coffee and piled biscuits on to a plate.

"We have to talk," she heard her father whisper beside her left ear as he returned his plate to the sink.

When she turned, Stewart was leaving the kitchen with Bonnie to pick up a relative Edith called Aunt Bochi. Their eyes met and Maggie swallowed hard. Sooner or later she had to explain to her father. Later seemed like such a better idea.

While Maggie served up the second round of breakfast, Colin and Frederick returned from the porch, grabbed a biscuit each and headed into the house to conduct some business before the funeral. Uncle Walter left for a shower, grumbling about the lack of hot water, which Maggie didn't understand since she had plenty earlier that morning, and a minister arrived carrying a large bowl of pasta salad.

Introductions were made, and thankfully the minister said nothing of Maggie's lack of yellow hair and voluptuous figure. Other cousins and different assortments of family and friends arrived, all willing to eat while Maggie was more than happy to keep busy at the stove.

Finally, the hour arrived when they had to leave for the cemetery. As Maggie finished up the batch of fried eggs, Kathy sauntered into the kitchen, the epitome of fashion perfection.

"Hungry Kathy?" Despite everything that had transpired the night before, Maggie was determined to be courteous.

"I don't eat breakfast," was her curt reply. "I would like some black coffee if you have some."

Maggie poured the last of the fourth pot and handed Kathy the cup, while the New Yorker examined her from her bare feet to her mussed hair.

"Karen Scott."

Kathy cocked an eyebrow. "I beg your pardon?"

"The name of the designer."

The woman offered nothing back but a blank stare and Maggie wondered in horror if this Scott woman topped the current what's out list. She seemed to be popular at Macy's.

"Where's Colin?"

"Living room I believe."

Kathy sighed and tossed back her hair. "I don't know how I will make it through this day," she said with a catch in her voice and then headed toward the front of the house.

Watching her perfect posture head down the hall, Maggie felt her blood boil. One, the woman was more distraught over her husband's death than she was, and anger felt better than the guilt lying under the surface, and two, Kathy was engaged to her cranberry professor. And there was something really wrong with that picture.

Her only consolation was Frosty following Kathy's every footstep, barking and nipping at her heels.

Maggie tore off her apron and began laying pieces of bacon inside the leftover biscuits. She was suddenly very hungry having been up since before dawn with only coffee to keep her going. Besides, she was angry, hurt, confused and Colin no doubt was in the living room offering comfort to his snotty fiancé. Food was her friend, always had been. Now that everyone was out of the kitchen, she would enjoy her comfort food in solitude without worrying who was watching and what he or she thought.

But, Kathy's voice interrupted her peace. "What do you want me to do with Aunt Bochi's food?" Maggie heard her ask Colin in the hallway.

"Bring it to the kitchen," she heard Colin answer. "And for heaven's sake, warn Maggie about the potato salad."

Kathy arrived, holding a bowl of potato salad about a foot in front of her as if she held the plague. "Here," she said, thrusting the dish into Maggie's hands. "It's funeral food."

Maggie gazed into the bowl and sure enough, it was potato salad with a sea of green olives floating on top. "Why do you have to warn me about this?"

Kathy paused and looked at Maggie as if she had no idea what she was talking about. The woman really was irritating; Maggie wanted so badly to fling the salad over her perfectly coiffed head. "I heard Colin saying to warn me about the potato salad."

This brought Kathy back to life, but she looked away. "It's nothing. Aunt Bochi makes the best potato salad in New England. Be sure and try some."

Something in Maggie's gut thought otherwise. "That's the warning?"

Kathy smiled, which made Maggie distrust her more. "It's a New England expression."

Maggie gazed into the bowl. It looked perfectly normal and she adored homemade potato salad.

"Really," Kathy said with a brighter smile. "He said to warn you about it because it's so good. That's how we talk up here."

"Okay." Maggie's stomach growled from the combination of lack of food and the aftereffects of too much scotch. "Think I will try some."

Kathy smiled nervously and hurried off.

"Great," Maggie said to herself. "Alone again."

She slipped off the plastic wrap and spooned out some on to a plate. After tasting a bite and finding it delicious, Maggie spooned out more and sat down to enjoy her meal. She had just finished when Bonnie appeared in the doorway, keys in hand. "It's time dear."

Maggie followed Bonnie to the front yard where everyone seemed to be arguing over who would ride with whom. She felt her father's hand on her arm. "You can ride with me. I have a rental." He leaned in close, his voice soft but stern. "It will give us a chance to talk."

Maggie cringed at the thought. But like an angel swooping down from above, Bonnie lightly touched her other arm. "She's riding with Colin and Frederick, the boy insisted."

To Maggie's greater surprise, Bonnie slipped her arm in the crook of her father's elbow. "You'll ride with me, Stewart, if you don't mind. I could use some help with Sophie and Walter."

As if Bonnie's attention to her father wasn't eye-opening enough, her father's reaction sure was. He smiled down at her and placed a hand over hers. "I'd be happy to, ma'am."

"Stop calling me that," she said with a teasing grin. "You make me feel old."

"My dear," Stewart said with a charming bow, "you are ageless."

Dear God, Maggie realized watching the interaction, but the two of them were flirting. When they caught her staring, they both cleared their throats and straightened, Bonnie removing her hand and heading towards her Oldsmobile. "We need to get going," she said over her shoulder. Stewart appeared to blush — although Maggie was certain she was seeing things — and followed.

She felt a tug on her pants leg and found Frederick gazing up at her with a huge grin. "You're riding with us."

Maggie pulled the young tiger into her arms. "Wouldn't dream of riding with anyone else."

They headed toward the familiar Explorer, Colin leaning against its hood like in the photo. Anxiety gripped Maggie's chest, cutting off her air, as she braced herself for the myriad emotions the day would bring. Kathy had nothing on her today.

All three entered the car silently and remained so as they followed the long line of cars to the cemetery. When Colin paused to let his mother's car pull in front, he glanced over at Maggie.

"Have you told your father yet?"

Maggie shook her head.

Another silence ensued, until she remembered what she had been dying to know since her arrival. "Colin, how did Jake die?"

Colin glared at her until Edith honked her horn behind him and he resumed driving. "I thought you would tell me."

"Me?" Maggie straightened her jacket nervously. "How would I know? I haven't seen him since Vegas."

Frederick leaned forward in his car seat, his restraint near the breaking point. "Haven't seen who, Maggie? Cousin Jake?"

Fearing the boy might hear too much, she tried to mask the conversation. "Colin, doesn't your mother know? She made all the arrangements, didn't she?"

"Yes, but she has yet to tell me."

Colin pulled on to the main highway running through Madison

and they passed the magazine building, its white paint shining in the morning sun with four American flags blowing in the breeze. Maggie sucked in her breath, thinking of the possibilities. If only Jake would have hired her instead of marrying her she could be working there right now.

But then, Colin was publisher. It was the wrong thing to do, considering the circumstances, but Maggie couldn't help herself. "Are you still looking for staff?"

At this, Colin smirked good-naturedly. "You're not exactly Yankee material."

This time, ten skunks did a dance on her grave and an intense shiver ran up her spine.

"What?" Colin asked, noticing her discomfort.

Maggie sighed and looked away, her heart splintered in so many places. "That's what your father used to tell me."

A silence ensued and remained until they reached the cemetery, then they all entered the funeral home for a brief, but poignant service in which all of the blondes from the day before wept in the back of the sanctuary. Maggie sat up front with family, feeling every bit the impostor, while her father sat next to Bonnie offering solace.

Kathy remained one pew behind and not liking it one bit, her eyes sending needles into the back of Maggie's head, which seemed to be working since Maggie's head pounded. Every time Jake's name was mentioned, her chest constricted and her neck muscles coiled. She longed for the actual funeral, anything to get outside and breathe fresh air.

Finally, the pallbearers were called forth, Colin being one of them. As he carried the coffin to the waiting hearse, Maggie witnessed the anguish on his face, as if he carried his cousin's weight all his life.

Thankfully, the gravesite was nearby and they were able to walk through the cemetery's lovely gardens, which did Maggie's headache some good. But, by the time they reached the spot, the pounding returned, coupled with sweats and a queasy stomach.

"Are you feeling all right?" Stewart asked her.

"Just nerves," she whispered back, although she wondered if it was something she ate.

To his credit, he didn't pressure her further, merely draped an arm about her shoulders and held her tight. Maggie surrendered, savoring the feel of her father's rough wool uniform against her cheek and for once not minding the cold brass buttons and medals. She closed her eyes like she had as a girl, letting her father hold her against the pains of the world. And while the minister said prayers over the grave, she took comfort in knowing her father ached as much as she, that he, too, wasn't thinking of Jake at that moment, but of a cold Georgia morning years before when the light in their life has been unfairly extinguished.

Neither father nor daughter said a word, even when the service concluded and the crowd began to disperse. Instead, Stewart turned toward the waiting procession, still holding his daughter tight.

"We still need to talk," he finally whispered to the top of her head.

"I know," she whispered back. "It's not what you think."

To her surprise, Stewart laughed, the second time that day. She couldn't remember the last time he'd appeared so jovial. Truly happy. And they had made it through a funeral, the first time in ages. For years, they had politely given excuses to family members and friends because they couldn't bear going miles near a cemetery. For years, the pain had remained sharp and biting like a blade refusing to rust.

"Well, that's not very comforting, Magpie," Stewart said. "Because I have no idea what to think."

It really was funny, considering, and Maggie was thankful her father could see humor in it all. But a sonic jet had pulled up alongside her and was blasting its engines in her ears.

"Are you sure you're all right?" she heard her father ask.

"Just need to lay down a little." And put a gun to my head.

This time, Maggie rode with Bonnie, Stewart, Edith and Sophie, while Colin visited the local grocery for reinforcements and Frederick headed home for a nap. When they arrived back at Colin's house, Maggie slipped away before her father could corner her, found a quiet spot on the back porch and rested her head against her purse while downing a glass of ice cold Pepsi and petting her favorite pug. She decided to made a quick call to Stacy.

"It's about time you called me."

"I've been a little busy." Maggie gulped down two Advil, followed by giant gulps of soda. Her stomach was glad for the refreshment but did a little dance.

"What happened? I've been worried sick."

"I'll explain later when I get home tonight. You're going to pick me up right?"

Stacy snorted. "Good thing I love you. Otherwise there would be no way I'd go to the Atlanta Airport in the middle of the night." Maggie's stomach flip-flopped, so she sipped more Pepsi. "I'm sorry Stacy, but the red eye was the cheapest flight."

An ugly burp escaped her lips before Maggie could catch it. "Are you drinking again?" Stacy asked.

"My stomach is upset and I have the worst headache." Maggie couldn't help but laugh, which made another burp emerge. "Not to mention I just buried a husband who used me to get out of a family obligation."

Faint as it was, Maggie heard Stacy harrumph. "I knew that boy was trouble."

Somewhere inside the house, Maggie heard Bonnie call her name. "I have to go, Stacy. Bonnie's calling me."

"Bonnie? His mother?"

Now it was Maggie's turn to sigh. "Drink a lot of coffee. We'll be up all night talking. It's quite a story."

Bonnie called her name again, this time from the top of the porch. "What about that Colin guy?"

The pounding in Maggie's head increased along with the pain in her heart. Leaving Madison meant leaving Colin. She probably would never see him again.

On the other end, Stacy harrumphed again. "That pause tells volumes."

Bonnie was now at Maggie's side, tapping her on the shoulder.

Maggie didn't have time to inquire what Stacy inferred. "Gotta go," she said and ended the call.

"We're getting ready to read the will," Bonnie said.

Maggie struggled to get on her feet, amazed at how even her bones were aching. "I doubt that has anything to do with me."

"Well, regardless, you need to be there." Bonnie took her hand and headed toward the back door, Frosty following behind.

"Really, Bonnie, Jake wouldn't have left me anything." They headed down the hallway toward the living room where she and Colin had talked the night before. "We were only married a month."

Bonnie said nothing, dropping her hand as they reached the living room.

"Great, the wife is here." A balding man dressed conservatively and carrying a briefcase motioned for Maggie to join the other family members sitting around the fireplace. Since everyone had places on the couch and easy chairs, Maggie chose a hardback on the periphery of the room. Edith gave her a hard stare, Bonnie smiled and Colin eyed her curiously.

"This is the last will and testament of Jake Adam Webster," the man began, and proceeded to list items in Jake's possession and who they would be endowed upon. Mark, trying hard to repress a grin, received Jake's prized Jaguar. Bonnie inherited some land and a cabin that was willed to Jake by a grandfather. A set of leather books and his furniture went to Edith, some stocks to Frederick for college. And to Colin, Jake willed him an historic trunk filled with memorabilia, an item that appeared to make Colin uncomfortable.

The man continued with smaller items but uneasiness filled the room, as if something unspoken was circling among them like vapors of a ghost.

"And to my wife, Maggie Delta Webster…"

Maggie knew she heard wrong or that her head had finally split open and she was hallucinating. Jake couldn't have included her in his will. When had he found time to make a new one? Or even thought to do so?

"…I leave my life insurance benefits, my liquid cash assets…"
It couldn't be. It didn't make sense.
"…and my stake in *Yankee Living* magazine."
Maggie knew for sure she was hearing things until Colin rose abruptly and turned toward her, his eyes blazing. "What?"
"Just as I said, Mr. Parnell, your cousin…"
"This is madness," Colin yelled, still staring at Maggie as if she were the devil sitting in on the proceedings. He pointed a finger in her direction. "What have you done?"
Everything seemed to burst apart at once, all family members on their feet and talking, some trying to calm Colin while his furious gaze remained fixed on Maggie. Her father came to her side, urging her to talk sense to him, to make things right, but all she comprehended was the roar of the voices talking in unison and the bile rising in her throat.
"Now, Colin," Bonnie pleaded, "Jake had the right to leave his stake to whom he pleased."
"To a stranger?" Colin's rage refused to abate. "He was only married a month!"
Stewart raised his hands to calm the emotions. The uniform seemed to make a difference, for everyone gave him their attention except for Colin, who paced the floor furiously.
"There must be some mistake," her father said. "I'm sure Maggie didn't mean to take a portion of your magazine. It's probably all a misunderstanding."
This, Maggie heard and registered. Despite the little men playing drums in her temple and the room spinning, Maggie saw the contrition in her father's eyes. He wanted her to deny it, say it wasn't so, give it back! And through her haze, Colin's glare demanded she do just that.
She probably shouldn't accept anything, she thought for a moment. She had no right to this family's possessions. But she wanted desperately to work for *Yankee Living*, had wanted to all her life. And through all the heartache of the past few weeks, suddenly something felt right.
She tried to speak, tried to reassure Colin she was fully capable

of working for the magazine, that she would be an asset to his or any publication. She really didn't care about the stake or the money, she wanted a job! But while all eyes glared, waiting for her to speak, something more sinister seemed to take control of her throat.

"Tell them what they want to hear," her father whispered.

And with that thought reverberating in her head, Maggie revisited the morning's potato salad all over the antique Persian rug.

Chapter Seven

"FOOD POISONING?"

Colin stared at the potato salad pushed to the rear of the refrigerator, a bowl of Aunt Bochi's latest find with three spoonfuls off the side. It could be the only answer.

"I don't understand," Stewart said behind him. "Why would Maggie get food poisoning?"

Colin straightened, but the weight of his family felt heavy upon his shoulders. Kathy was to blame for this, he was sure.

"Aunt Bochi, uh my Aunt Martha is a bit cheap. She likes to buy food past its expiration date to save money, claims it's perfectly fine. Only her ham sandwiches got us all wicked sick one Fourth of July and we've been cautious ever since."

Stewart sighed, looking equally tired, and took a seat at the kitchen table. "Maggie loves potato salad."

"I'm sorry." Despite the rage still roaring through his veins, Colin *was* sorry. The poor girl had been retching repeatedly in the other room and a doctor had been called. No doubt her father had changed his plans to be with her.

"Can I get you anything, sir?"

"She missed her plane."

Colin sat across from him, watched him roll the antique saltshaker between his fingers. "I don't think she had a job to go back to."

This seemed news to Stewart, and Colin sensed it pained him to hear it from someone else's mouth besides his daughter's.

"We haven't spoken in a while." He took the opposite pepper shaker, a replica of a windmill, and turned it round and around. "We had a falling out over her career choices."

"You don't approve of journalism?"

A raw pain filled Stewart's eyes. "I don't care what she does, I want her closer to home. She's the only family I have anymore." His voice caught and he paused to regain his composure. "But she keeps getting laid off from jobs and moving farther away."

Remembering that Maggie was now part owner of *Yankee Living* — *his* magazine — brought back the fury. Colin rose and began pacing the kitchen floor.

"I don't know what's going on here," Stewart said, "but you can't possibly think Maggie had anything to do with this."

Colin paused at the kitchen window, noticing the rain clouds moving in. Jude would be calling soon about that leak over her back bathroom. "I don't know what to believe anymore."

Stewart stood, straightening his uniform as if trying to straighten out his life. "Got any alcohol in this house? I think we could both use a drink."

The man was reading his mind. "What's your pleasure, sir?"

Stewart grinned, if only slightly. "For you to stop calling me sir."

Colin couldn't help himself; he liked this man, despite the fact that he and his daughter could be conspiring to rob him blind. "What's your pleasure, Stewart?"

The colonel seemed to relax. "Scotch if you've got it."

Colin reached into a cabinet and produced two glasses and a bottle of his best Isle of Skye. "Like father, like daughter."

The familiar pain resurfaced. "Maggie doesn't drink scotch, does she?"

Colin had no idea how to respond to that, since it was difficult to explain Pittsburgh on top of everything else. "I gave her some at the wake last night and she appeared to enjoy it."

The explanation worked, but Colin sensed Stewart still grieved from knowing so little about his child. He poured them both a glass and they drank, Colin savoring its warm aftertaste.

After a few seconds, Stewart broke the silence. "What do you know about Maggie and Jake?"

Colin sighed into his glass. "Besides wanting to kill my cousin all over again?"

"Your mother said you two weren't very close."

They were about as far away from each other as Bill O'Reilly and Bill Maher. The lawyer's words came back all too clear: "... and my stake in *Yankee Living* magazine." What on earth was Jake thinking giving away their family legacy? Or was this one last attempt by Jake to drive Colin insane.

"It was his lifelong goal in life to compete with me," Colin said softly, leaning back in his chair. "He was reckless and wild, had any girl he wanted, took off whenever he felt like it, never cared about the magazine. And yet, whatever I had, he had to have it too."

Stewart downed his glass. "I don't understand what Maggie saw in him, even if it wasn't a real marriage."

Colin poured them another drink, but he eyed Stewart curiously. "You know about the marriage?"

To his credit, Stewart was equally cautious, gazing at him as if perusing a chess move. "Do you?"

"Only that they pulled a Britney Spears and Jake took off soon afterwards."

"And told you all that he was working for me in my failed oil company in Mexico." Stewart laughed as he drank his scotch. "Only company I keep these days is Uncle Sam."

"How do you know, then? Maggie said she hadn't told you about the marriage."

"She hadn't." The old pain returned to his eyes. "I dragged it out of her roommate. Plus, your mother called me."

This news stopped Colin cold. "My mother?"

"She felt Maggie needed family here."

Colin rose and began pacing again. When his father and Jake's parents had been killed in the car accident, the family business and the family had passed on to the two of them but had, in truth, landed square on Colin's shoulders. And Jake had been the one with the journalism degree. Still, he and Jake had been partners. He should have known everything about him.

"If he wanted to back out of the agreement we had, all he had to do was tell me." He was talking to the kitchen walls, but Colin didn't care. He needed to vent. "Whatever happened, he could have told me."

The rain began to fall outside, first lightly, and then stronger followed by a burst of thunder. Colin gritted his teeth, waiting for Jude to call complaining about the leak. And Edith's car was acting up again. Not to mention that everything at the magazine had been put on hold during his trip to New York and no doubt a pile had been growing on his desk. In two weeks, the autumn foliage issue would be published, their biggest to date.

Colin's shoulders fell. He was so incredibly tired, hadn't slept at all the night before, tossing and turning trying to make sense of the madness.

Then there was Miss Georgia with those precious brown eyes and that adorable smile, a Southern belle who could be stealing his family business.

"May I make a suggestion?"

Colin turned and found Stewart studying him again. "Drink heavily?"

Stewart rose and removed his wallet, pulling several cards from its holds. "This is Maggie's personal card," he said, handing him the first one. "It's got her Yahoo email and website on it. I was always misplacing her address, since she was always moving around."

Colin glanced down at the card with an old-fashioned pen and inkstand on it. "Magnolia "Maggie" Delta Mallory, professional writer and editor" it read. If he weren't so pissed, he would have laughed at her so typically Southern name.

"These are her collection." Stewart handed him several other cards, all from different publications. "I kept them as a joke, although she never saw it that way."

Deep South Trails, *A Taste of the South* magazine, *Georgia Road-*

ways. "What do you want me to do with these?"

Stewart downed the last of his scotch. "Start with her website or LinkedIn. She has her resumé there. Then check out the others and make sure you read the piece on the South and a sense of place in *Georgia Roadways*, it reminds me a lot of you all."

Colin shuffled the cards, finding five publishers in all, two where she was listed as intern. "I don't understand."

"I may not know a lot about my daughter right now and she may not be deserving of what she just inherited," Stewart continued. "But, I do know she thought the world of your father and would give her right arm to work for you."

"That may be true, but I still have to contest the will."

Stewart nodded. "Of course you do."

Best to get it all upfront, Colin thought. "I've also hired a private investigator."

Again, the colonel nodded. "Have him call me and I'll make sure he accesses my army records. It's got every place we ever lived in there." Stewart grinned. "Otherwise, he'll have a helluva time."

Colin really shouldn't be friendly with the guy. Who knew what was the truth here? But, he held out his hand and Stewart shook it firmly.

"Gonna go look in on my baby now." And with those words, he headed off to the guest bedroom.

Colin stared at the menagerie in his hands — web editor, features editor, copy editor, staff writer. Maggie sure had made the rounds. Pocketing the pile, he grabbed his raincoat and car keys and headed toward Madison. Jude would have to nurse the leak for now. Colin had questions needing answers.

He pulled into the magazine's empty parking lot and waved to Teddy MacIntosh, the night watchman.

"My deep condolences on your loss, Mr. Parnell."

"Thanks Ted, just tying up some loose ends here." Colin paused, remembering that he only carried his keys. "Ted, can you let me into Jake's office?"

"Be happy to." The watchman sauntered over to the back door.

"But your mother is already in there."

Everything about Jake's death confused Colin, but his mother's involvement was baffling. He headed into the darkened building, stopping to check his messages and made sure Casco, the magazine's pet cat, had enough food and water.

"What are you doing here?"

Colin dumped a healthy scoop of cat food into Casco's bowl and stood up to find Bonnie examining several color swatches in her hands. "I could ask the same of you."

"I'm way behind on the Christmas home shoot and Marianne's doctor wants her home early so she's going to start her maternity leave after next week."

Colin rubbed his forehead. "Great."

"It's going to be a rough fall."

Good thing he came in. Best to get through that pile on his desk before the start of the week and the endless problems awaiting him. "I'll get right on it."

"When is the new copy editor starting?"

Colin entered his office, throwing his stack of messages on the desk. Sure enough, mail, memos and page proofs were piled high on top. "Not for another three weeks. She's having problems finding an apartment."

Bonnie settled into the chair before Colin's desk, fanning her swatches before her as if studying a hand of cards. "Of course she's having trouble. There's no place to rent around here. She'll have to commute from Portland."

"She doesn't want to do that, mom. Puts her too far away from her kids."

The olive green swatch won; Bonnie placed it on the edge of his desk. "Then that's a big problem." Colin looked up to decipher her thoughts. "If she doesn't take the job, sweetheart," she said, leaning in close to whisper, "we're in deep shit."

Colin dropped the mail and fell into his own chair. If the copy editor didn't show, they would be down three people by the end of the month, including a web editor whose college internship was ending before the holidays. Deep was an understatement.

"I hate to bring this up now, sweetheart, but we do have an in-law who's a journalist."

Colin couldn't believe his ears. "Whose side are you on, mom?"

Bonnie took offense to the remark and stood up, ready to return to her office. "I'm not on anyone's side, Colin. Maybe you need to stop being so defensive when it comes to Jake."

This beat all — his cousin had betrayed him, lied about a marriage, disappeared for a month and left his share of their family magazine to a perfect stranger, a woman, he added to himself, that was driving him crazy with lust. Had everyone around him gone mad? He knew he had. "Do you realize, mom, that you haven't even told me how Jake died."

Bonnie paused on the threshold, but she didn't look back. "You know Jake. He never wanted anyone to know."

"Know what?"

Bonnie sighed and met his gaze. "He made me promise that I wouldn't tell anyone how he died."

The night felt like a *Twilight Zone* episode, every moment turning more and more bizarre. "You sound like this was planned."

She turned again and waved him off with her collection of swatches. "I can't speak of it."

Colin bolted out of his chair and reached his mother's side. "Where were you all last week?"

She stared blankly into the darkened newsroom, then met his gaze and smiled like she had when she broke the news of his father's death, like a mother offering comfort to a young child in the midst of despair. "I loved him, you know."

Colin leaned against the doorway, the pain of grief pressing on his heart. "I did too, little good it did."

A tear trickled down Bonnie's check, but she appeared at peace. "I think he figured that out at the end. But it still wasn't enough, was it?"

"What wasn't enough?"

Bonnie awakened from her trance and sobered. "The trunk will be here in a couple of days. I think you'll find answers there." She pointed to the desk. "Definitely use that color for the page border."

Colin grabbed the green swatch off the edge of the desk and fell back into his chair. "I don't want his trunk. Do you know what's in there? All his conquests. All the times he followed me into some sport I enjoyed for the sole purpose of being better than me."

"Perhaps." Bonnie placed her hands on the desk and leaned forward. "You won't know until you look."

And with those final words, she straightened and exited his office. "Wait," Colin yelled after her. "I deserve a better explanation than that."

She popped her head in the doorway. "I'm sure your private investigator will help. In the meantime, hire Maggie."

For a moment, Colin wondered if his mother was in on the Georgian conspiracy. "Why don't I make her publisher then?" he yelled. But, the only answer he received was the back door closing.

Frustrated that he was more confused than when he arrived, Colin ran his hands through his hair and leaned his elbows on to the mound of mail. Everything would have to wait until morning. He couldn't bear to deal with the endless work before him that night.

Then a thought occurred to him. He flipped on his computer and opened the database of subscribers. He typed in "Maggie Mallory" and waited while the rainbow wheel turned around and around. Finally, her file emerged, all two pages of information, including several changes of addresses and two interruptions in delivery due to failure to forward. Maggie had told the truth about being a long-time subscriber; her records dated back fourteen years. She would have gotten a ten-year subscriber prize of *Yankee Living's Prized Country Recipes* if her mail hadn't been interrupted that year. Funny, Colin thought, that was the year his father died.

Which made him think of something else. He headed to Jake's office, wondering if Bonnie had left it opened. The door was shut, but unlocked, so Colin gingerly entered the office that had remained mostly a mystery in the years the two had worked together.

Everything remained in place as it had when Jake departed for Vegas. His *Blue Dog* painting and the Hockney still graced the walls next to an assortment of photos of Jake with famous people who had come through Madison. The designer furniture sat untouched and polished — the Mission desk, the Arts and Craft pottery collection Jake passed on to Jude and the Tiffany lamps given to Jake by Kathy.

But, it was his files that interested Colin most. Since Jake had served as editor, he had been in charge of hiring the editorial staff. At least, when he was around. The personnel files of most of the editors were stored in his cabinets.

Colin opened the middle drawer and searched through the names, wondering if Maggie existed among the many *Yankee Living* wannabes. There, stuffed in the back, was a thick file with her name on it.

He couldn't believe how enormous it was, filled with letters, resumés, articles, Christmas cards and carbon copies of letters his father had mailed to her. Colin sat on Jake's black leather couch and spread the file before him on to the coffee table. Then, he began to read.

He started at the beginning, finding resumés Maggie had mailed to his father, a few dated in the past couple years after his father's death. He turned, instead, to the back and the phone message dated 1996. The note simply read, "Ms. Mallory, University of Georgia, wants you to help with dissertation."

What followed was a series of letters between Maggie and his father, stating purpose and the general idea of her thesis. Then a formal letter with a series of questions. Next, came the actual dissertation titled "Regional Journalism" and his father's comments to her work, which were, as always, critical but compassionate.

Maggie had then mailed him articles from her various places of employment, an occasional resumé and, every year, a Christmas card. His father had always replied with extensive criticism, although praising her efforts, and reiterated how Maggie "wasn't exactly Yankee material."

"Holy shit," Colin said, remembering their conversation earlier that morning. Or was it yesterday, he thought, looking at the clock that read twelve fifteen.

Regardless of the time, Colin made himself comfortable, and started reading the myriad of articles before him, beginning with the one titled "South and A Sense of Place."

Maggie dreamed of being ten years old, running through the piney woods of her uncle's house in Marietta in the apex of summer when the air was still and hot and perspiration rolled down her back in droplets. Her father grilled hamburgers, holding an iced drink in one hand and laughing at her Aunt Cecily's jokes. Somewhere in the background kids played and dogs barked and all was right with the world.

Suddenly, Maggie's mother appeared, the epitome of Southern womanhood, her lipstick the perfect match to her outfit. Maggie wondered how she managed such a feat and was about to ask when her mother's brow creased and she placed a loving hand on Maggie's forehead.

"Are you sick, sweetpea?"

"Momma?" Maggie asked aloud, wondering how it was possible.

When Maggie opened her eyes she realized the large, brawny fingers belonged to a masculine hand. And even in the intense darkness of the room, Maggie could make out those haunting brown eyes.

"Are you feeling better?" Colin asked.

The headache abated and her stomach quiet at present, Maggie nodded. "No thanks to your Kathy. Why are you here? To finish me off?"

Colin rubbed his eyes and grimaced; he actually appeared contrite. "I brought you some ginger ale."

She rose on her elbows until the pounding began again, then

settled her head into the pillow to quiet the noise. Colin handed her the glass and she sipped the liquid gingerly to quench her intense thirst, the result of an endless night of potato salad reruns.

"I'm sorry about the rug."

At this, Colin managed a smile. "It's been barfed on before, not to worry."

"I'll take care of the cleaning."

Colin leaned back and rubbed his eyes again. Maggie wondered what time it was. "Don't worry about the damn rug," he muttered.

He was still angry, she was sure of it. She couldn't blame him, especially after everything Jake had done. Still, he was going to marry a woman who had poisoned his guest and that put a major twist in her panties. "She's wrong for you."

He stopped messing with his eyes. "Excuse me?"

"Tell me you're not seriously going to marry that witch."

He was difficult to discern in the darkness, but she thought she spotted a good-natured smile. "What witch is that?"

The ale tasted heavenly, but one sip was enough for now. She placed the glass on the night table and was about to object to his relationship with Kathy, but within seconds Maggie's eyes drifted shut. Just before sleep overtook her, she felt two large hands pull her blanket tight about her chin.

"Get some rest, Miss Georgia. We'll talk in the morning about you working at the magazine," was the last thing she comprehended.

Chapter Eight

THE ANTIQUE CLOCK ABOVE THE mantle chimed five, causing Stewart to jump awake. He was still in uniform but someone had graciously draped a quilt over him sometime in the night. How long had he been asleep there? He honestly didn't know. Obviously, he was more tired than he thought for the last thing he remembered was checking in on Maggie.

He bolted upright, ready to head to her room, but he noticed the shadows near her doorway move.

"She's fine," a voice whispered, coming closer. "But you have a plane to catch."

Stewart pulled his feet over the couch as Bonnie sat in the opposite chair, her hands in her lap clenched together. For a moment, they stared at one another in the darkness, neither one speaking.

"Stewart…" Bonnie began.

He reached over and touched her joined hands. "Please don't."

She jumped at his touch but she didn't move away. "Heaven knows what you must think of me."

Stewart slipped his fingers inside hers and squeezed. "You're an amazing woman, Bonnie. That's what I think of you."

He moved closer, so that he was practically kneeling in front of her chair. "We have lost people dear to us and the funeral brought back those horrific memories. We took comfort in each other.

There's nothing to be ashamed of."

"But I haven't been with a man since…"

Stewart smiled grimly, thinking back on those long, lonely years since his wife's death. "That makes two of us."

Bonnie sighed and met his gaze. "Shall we chalk it up to melancholy then?"

Stewart reached up and touched her cheek, letting his thumb caress the soft reaches of her skin. He could imagine a million reasons for his behavior the night before, but melancholy wasn't one of them. "Will I see you again?"

Her eyes sparkled in the gloom. "You'll have to if your daughter stays here."

He considered the possibilities. Funny, but all those years he wanted Maggie close to him in Washington, D.C., always trying to convince her to work for the Army's *Stars and Stripes* publication, and now he couldn't imagine a better scenario than Madison, Maine.

Stewart stood and straightened his uniform. Two days ago the familiar cloud hovered over his heart, furthered hindered by the news that his daughter had married a stranger without his knowledge or consent. Today, in the darkness before dawn, he felt as if the room was filled with light.

"Tell Maggie to call me when she wakes up."

Bonnie stood and met him eye to eye. "Of course."

"I'll be on base by thirteen hundred." He smiled, thinking how silly that must sound to a civilian. "That's one o'clock."

Bonnie unraveled his collar and brushed out the wrinkles of his jacket. How long had it been since a woman cared for him? And did she?

"Do be careful," she whispered.

He wasn't sure how to interpret that, but he told himself it was a good sign. He slid both palms about her face and kissed her passionately, savoring her lips as if searing the moment into his memory.

Then without saying goodbye, Stewart grabbed his hat and coat and left for Washington.

Maggie wasn't sure what woke her up, if it was Frosty needing to go out or the incredible rumbling in her stomach. She pulled on her sweats and let the pug out into the backyard. Standing in the kitchen, surrounded by dishes of every kind brought to the house by family and friends, she found herself incredibly hungry. Only she didn't know what to do about it considering her fragile constitution.

She gingerly opened the refrigerator door and gazed at the mounds of aluminum-covered bowls and platters. She wanted to delve into one of them, but feared she'd make the mistake of eating Aunt Bochi's food again.

"Watch out for the potato salad."

Colin's voice startled her, causing her to hit her head on the freezer door handle.

"Hey, be careful." He rushed over and gazed down with a concerned but hesitant look, like the attitude he had exhibited the night before. Maggie knew he wanted to like her but was conflicted over the events of the funeral and will. She needed his approval, wanted his trust.

"I'm fine," she said, offering up a smile although her head began pounding all over again.

Colin took her arm and led her to a chair. "Sit. I'll make you breakfast."

That was out of the question. She owed this man on many levels. She shook her head. "I'll do it."

But before she could rise from her chair, Colin pointed a stern finger at her like a big brother. "Sit."

And sit she did. "Can't I…?"

"No."

Colin opened the refrigerator and leaned on the door. "Holy crap."

"People always bring food to a funeral," Maggie offered, trying to make small talk, but all it did was rehash memories of her mother's death. She closed her eyes briefly, wishing away the images that still tormented her.

"Yeah, well, I never have more than milk in the house. How the hell am I going to eat all this?" Colin looked up when she didn't respond. "Are you all right?"

Frosty whimpered on the screened porch, which gave Maggie a chance to regain normalcy. "I'm fine," she said, opening the screen door and letting the pug make himself comfortable on her lap. "A cup of coffee and a piece of plain toast will do me just fine."

"Are you sure? I can make you some cream of wheat."

Maggie shuddered. She had oatmeal once at the army base in Germany and couldn't get it past her lips. Her mother had called it "Yankee slop," offering up yet another of her dissertations on how only Southerners knew how to cook. "Uh, no thanks. The only hot breakfast cereal I eat is made of corn."

Colin gazed at her puzzled. "Corn?"

She should have politely said no; she didn't feel up to explaining grits to a Mainer who was rather pissed that a Southerner inherited part of his Yankee magazine. "Thanks, but toast is fine."

Now, that she thought of it, her situation was ludicrous. What the hell was she doing there? And was Colin giving her a job to be kind while he investigated her intentions? "Are you sure you want me to work for you?"

Colin threw a scoop of Starbuck's into what looked like a fancy coffeemaker. "No," he said rather too quickly, then sighed. "But, what else am I going to do with you?"

Maggie could think of plenty things, namely getting on a southbound plane. But, she didn't want to lose whatever flimsy momentum she had going. Still, she didn't want a job this way. "Look, Colin, you don't have to…"

"Do you not want to work for us?"

She leaned an elbow on the table and rested her head in her hand. "Hardly. You know what this magazine means to me. Or do you?"

Colin paused at his task, but he didn't look at her. "Yes."

"But I don't want to cause any problems for you."

He finished pouring the water into the machine and then faced her. "I've seen your work. It's impressive."

Maggie's mind reeled. Where had he obtained samples in a twenty-four hour period? Was her work still on the Internet?

"I'm short three people," he continued. "A news editor, soon a web editor and a home and garden assistant to my mother. And if my new hire can't find a place to stay, possibly a copy editor."

Maggie disseminated that information immediately. "I can help in all those areas."

Colin nodded soberly. "I know."

"You know?"

"I've seen your resumé."

Now things made sense. "My father gave you one." Maggie smirked, thinking how her father would do anything to get her to D.C. "He keeps a copy on him and every time he sees an editor from the *Stars and Stripes*, he talks me up."

Colin didn't answer, which unnerved her more than his constant cold gaze, so she kept on talking. "Ever since my mother's death, he's been possessive, always trying to get me close to him. He keeps setting up interviews for me with the *Stripes* but I've been there, done that, you know? I've had enough of army life. Although he does have a point about job security and heaven knows I've never had that."

Colin pushed a button and the coffee machine sprung to life. "Am I talking too much?" she finally asked, knowing damn well she was.

"Your father didn't give me your resumé."

Well, at least the man was answering, even if it confused Maggie more. "How then…?"

"Look." He leaned back against the countertop, another starched Polo stretching across those wide shoulders. "Let's make it a trial period, say three weeks? You can fill in for a while and we'll go from there. Okay?"

Maggie had a million questions, but she simply nodded. Three weeks was better than the Atlanta unemployment line. "I need a place to stay."

Two slices of pumpernickel popped out of the toaster, startling them both. Colin placed both on a plate and handed it to her with the butter dish, then resumed getting the coffee ready. "The closest rentals are Freeport and Portland. Freeport is closer but you'd still have to have a car and commute."

"I can rent one." Hell, she could walk.

He poured a cup before the carafe was filled, adding cream. How'd he know how she liked it? "You can stay here," he said softly.

She said nothing as he handed her the cup announcing the anniversary of some tall ship named the Majestic. He met her gaze then, no doubt wondering what stilled her tongue.

"I can't put you out," she finally said, although deep down she wanted to do nothing but. "It's a lovely invitation but three weeks..."

"Don't worry," he said with a wave of his hand. "I'm never here. As long as we coordinate showers, we'll be fine."

Maggie savored the hot coffee after a bite of bread, amazed at how good something so simple tasted. "I don't understand about the water. It was perfectly hot for me yesterday."

Colin poured himself a cup and almost smiled. Almost. "That's because you were the first one up."

The knowledge hit her like a wall of Georgia humidity on the first ninety-degree day of summer. "Oh shit."

Her language surprised him somehow and he again gave her that look that stretched between wanting to be hospitable and wanting to kick her butt. "I'm afraid I took one this morning," he offered. "I thought you'd sleep all day."

Maggie shook her head. "I'm ready to go to work."

He looked at her hard, big brother returning. "You need to go back to bed."

For a second, Maggie wished his instruction to be an invitation and a delicious shiver ran through her. Maybe a cold shower was in order. "I can't go back to bed. Sun rises and so do I. The government brainwashed me that way." She placed the dog on the floor and grabbed her coffee. "If you give me a few minutes, I'll be ready." And hopefully I'll have washed away that image of you in my bed.

Colin reached over and took her arm. "Maggie, the water's cold. Give it a couple of hours. I can come back for you around lunch."

She couldn't wait until lunch. She was dying to see the inside of her beloved magazine. "A little cold water won't bother me."

Colin leaned in closer, reintroducing her to his fresh aftershave. He smelled divine, a heady mixture of good old-fashioned masculine scent, soap and Old Spice. His still damp hair curled about his ears, while his eyebrows burrowed in a frown above an intense gaze. The only thing Colin lacked was a smile, something that had disappeared since the reading of the will. And as God was her witness, she aimed to see that smile again.

"Cold water?" she said in her most coquettish, Southern accent. "Fiddle-lee-dee-dee."

Finally, a smile emerged, his eyes sparkling, mirroring in the merriment. Before he could regain his composure, return to the angry publisher and the admonishing big brother, Maggie hurried off. "I won't be long," she yelled back, closing the guest door behind her.

⚜

Colin watched as her rumpled petite figure disappeared around the corner, the door closing shut to the dismay of Frosty, who stood whimpering at the threshold. He heard the water starting, then a feminine yelp, which made him smile again.

"Crazy woman," he said to Frosty, who immediately began growling at him. And that was all it took to wake him from the spell.

What was he doing, giving the girl a job? She could be robbing him senseless and he was practically holding the door open. And all that cute Southern charm, was it nothing more than a put-on to warm her way into their homes and hearts?

Somehow, Colin doubted it. So many things didn't add up. He

ran into her in Pittsburgh, not the other way around, and convinced her to join him for a drink and he was hard-pressed to believe that Maggie's hesitation to leave the plane was an act. There was the phone call to Stacy, the tears, that helpless look viewing the parade of Jake's ex-girlfriends at the wake. Not to mention that she really, really wasn't Jake's type.

Still, anything was possible. Bottom line, they knew nothing about her.

Expect that she owned the cutest set of brown eyes in North America. And the sweetest smile.

Frosty's nails clicked on the wooden floor as he sought refuge in the kitchen, barking at some entity coming down the hallway. "Are you planning on standing there all day in a trance?" his mother asked.

Colin rubbed his eyes. One of these days he was going to get a good night's sleep. "I'm waiting for Maggie to finish showering. Remember, it was your idea to give her a job."

Bonnie kissed him hello and headed toward the coffee maker. "And I'm sure she'll do fine."

Sweet smile or no, Colin wasn't about to take chances. "It's temporary, mother. I told her three weeks."

Having made her coffee to her liking, she turned and leaned against the countertop in deep thought. "Three weeks will be a big help. Three months would be even better."

Colin studied the woman who had brought him into the world, the one person he trusted above all others.

"What?" she asked.

"What aren't you telling me?"

Bonnie sipped her coffee. "That if we don't get to town soon, we're going to miss the editorial meeting."

Just then, Maggie came rushing into the room, her shoes in one hand and her hair freshly blown dry. She pulled on her loafers one by one as she spied Bonnie. "Oh hi, Mrs. Parnell."

"Hi Maggie. Feeling up to helping me out today?"

"Absolutely." Maggie pulled a pair of earrings out of a pocket and attached them to her ears, then smoothed her hair in place behind each ear. Within seconds, she stood before them dressed, made up and ready to go. Colin never saw a woman pull it together so quickly.

He must have been starring for she sent him a side-glance, then started straightening her clothes self-consciously. "Am I dressed okay?"

"You like fine, sweetheart," Bonnie answered.

And she did. A navy pinpoint Oxford shirt matched a pair of blue twill pants topped with a red and blue plaid cardigan sweater, a casual change from the fashionable attire she had worn at the wake and funeral. She appeared perfunctory but sophisticated — downright preppy — as if she walked out of New England instead of Georgia. Teach Maggie how to lose her r's and drop the y'alls and no one would be the wiser.

"I wasn't sure what to wear." Maggie twisted a lock of her hair nervously. "I brought three suitcases of clothes just in case."

That piece of information stopped Colin cold. "How convenient."

Maggie comprehended his tone instantly and her eyes narrowed. "Right. I planned all this." She slid her hands into her pants pockets and lifted her chin. "I seduced your cousin in Vegas, which wasn't hard since I'm tall and blonde, then made him change his will so I could inherit your magazine. Only I had no idea he had a will or that he was close to death or that I'd even see him again."

Electricity charged the air between them, Maggie bristling with anger. After all his fury over the will, Colin never expected this from her. Obviously, he touched a nerve. Or maybe Maggie was finally unraveling after such a trying weekend. Whatever the reason, he faced her soberly. He had every right to doubt her intentions, especially since now she owned one-fourth of his livelihood.

Bonnie immediately stepped between them. "Okay then. Why don't we head on out."

Colin needed no further encouragement. He placed his coffee in the sink and headed for the front door, Frosty yapping at his heels. He grabbed his car keys and jacket, slamming the door behind him.

"Don't let him bother you," Bonnie said when she noticed Maggie flinch. "He's naturally upset."

"I don't blame him." All her fury spent, Maggie smoothed out her hair, rubbing her neck where her fingers fell free.

When had she cut that beautiful hair? Bonnie wondered. Jake had given her a photo of Maggie and her hair had fallen halfway down her back. This new look suited her, perhaps offered her a second lease on life. No doubt Maggie had spent the last month agonizing over what she had done and why Jake had disappeared. Bonnie prayed Maggie would put Jake behind her and move on.

Working at the magazine would help; Bonnie knew that was what Jake had in mind. She had to admit, having Maggie in Madison could attract her father back to Maine.

Bonnie's cheek flushed. "Your father left early this morning. He said to call him after one o'clock."

Maggie nodded, turned pale and grabbed the back of the kitchen chair.

"Are you sure you're up for this?" Bonnie asked her.

"I'm up for anything." Maggie straightened and offered up a smile, but Bonnie knew she was hurting inside. She touched her arm. She didn't know why, but something about this child tore at her heart. Was it Jake and his desertion? She doubted someone as strong and intelligent as Maggie would carry a torch for a man she barely knew.

Or was it something more? Maggie had lost a mother at sixteen, her father a wife. And both father and daughter had yet to move past that pain. Bonnie understood that quiet, lonely sense of grief, when no one but the darkness inside you could offer solace. She recognized it in her own children's eyes, the way Edith built an angry wall around her heart and Jude holed away in her house, using Mark and Frederick as an excuse.

Then there was Colin. Strong, reliable Colin. She worried about him most of all. They had all come to rely upon him, the new patriarch of the family, hanging their heartaches upon his shoulders without realizing what they had done. Not only had he helmed the magazine these past years with little of Jake's help, but he had patched up their lives, unclogged their toilets, changed their flat tires. And pulled Jake out of trouble on more than one occasion.

Now he had to hire Jake's widow, a woman who had literally become his partner in business overnight.

Bonnie doubted Maggie wanted anything more from *Yankee Living* than a job. She had seen the file, heard her husband gush about the ambitious journalism student from Georgia. Every year Gavin had shown her Maggie's Christmas card and read her stories with pride. In a way, Maggie had been part of their family, the writer Gavin had always wanted.

Jake had shown promise, penning such amazing prose, tales that brought tears to one's eyes or incited one to change. But, he had failed them all, then failed himself.

Maggie touched Bonnie's sleeve. "Are *you* all right?"

Bonnie sighed, looking into the sweet eyes of her new assistant. Jake had been right. She really was an angel. And perhaps Jake had managed one decent thing before he died. He sent Maggie to Madison.

Bonnie squeezed Maggie's arm lovingly. "Let's go to work then."

Chapter Nine

A HEAVY PAUSE SETTLED OVER THE dinner table like the morning fog sneaking into town, swallowing everything in its wake. After two weeks in Madison, it was something Maggie was getting used to.

Well, maybe the fog.

Jude and Mark had invited her over — again — for a meal and visiting, but after the usual small talk and "how are you getting on" adult conversation ceased and rarely came back to life. If it weren't for Frederick's endless chatter, Maggie would have gone stark raving mad.

The Willoughbys were motormouths compared to Edith. The tight-lipped sibling would invite Maggie over — at Bonnie's instance, no doubt — offer her take-out, and then plop down on the couch for hours silently watching the Discovery Channel. Somewhere around nine p.m. and the elephant sea lion mating rituals, Maggie would yawn, claim fatigue and practically run for the door.

Bonnie was a better conversationalist at the several lunches she and Maggie had shared. But if Maggie were honest with herself — and she couldn't be, considering that Bonnie was her elder and there were rules in that regard — Maggie would admit that although she found Bonnie friendly and certainly more talkative than her children, she, too, seemed to lack a spark. Her voice and demeanor were devoid of passion, although her work glowed with it. Her home designer spreads burst off the pages, teeming with color and flair. Yet, one-on-one Bonnie would rarely laugh, often staring off into the distance, pondering some thought.

But it was the Willoughbys who invited Maggie over for dinner all the time. Unlike Edith, they actually seemed to want her company and asked repeatedly, although Maggie had a hard time wondering why, unless they longed for someone to warm the empty fourth seat at their table.

Or maybe New Englanders weren't the talkative type. Maggie had heard as much, but this endless silence seemed beyond even the most stoic of people.

"Everyone at the magazine treating you well?" Mark asked, startling Maggie.

"Everyone has been very helpful, thanks."

Well, almost everyone. If the Parnell family were the silent type, Colin was invisible. Ever since that morning in the kitchen he avoided her, would refuse to meet her gaze in editorial and staff meetings. The first day at the magazine, Bonnie introduced her around, showed her the ropes and gave her instructions, but Colin remained holed up in his office. Since Colin was publisher and manager of the business side of the magazine, Maggie hardly expected to deal with him on a daily basis. But she did live in his house, work with his mother and dine with his siblings, not to mention inheriting part of his family business that once belonged to his cousin. Surely, they had something to discuss.

Plus, Colin was never home. Maggie knew he worked late, but most nights he arrived home long after she had gone to bed. He would awake early to shower — Colin left a note indicating this would allow her hot water at a normal waking time, even though her usual waking time was closer to his — then hurry out the door.

Maggie started sleeping in more, waking to a leisurely breakfast and hot shower, then head to the office for nine, Bonnie's starting time. She loved her work, adored the magazine and cherished the lovely home she resided in, but a constant loneliness gripped her heart that was hard to shake. She tried to reason with herself that a new job always felt this way, but the truth was Maggie felt as low as a toad in a dry well. She had yet to make friends with coworkers and she had no family or Cajun Embassy members nearby. Frederick and Jude came the day after the Aunt Bochi incident to retrieve Frosty so she didn't even have the dog to keep her company.

The person she really missed continually refused to make eye contact, the only reminder of him the sounds of his footsteps on the stairway late at night.

Feeling the emptiness creep back over her, Maggie made a mental note to call her college buds first thing in the morning. She needed a Cajun Embassy fix, even though her best friends were hard to reach these days. Maggie's morning hours, although one hour ahead, were still too early for the slow waking roommate who worked nights at a newspaper and her California comrades were three hours behind. Nighttime was best, but Dewey covered Hollywood happenings and Lizzy was busy planning a wedding.

Maggie sighed thinking of it all, adjusting her roast beef on the plate with her fork.

"Are you bored?" Frederick asked. "Nobody talks at dinner, do they?"

Jude choked on her water and practically spit out her ice cube. "Frederick, what a thing to say?"

"Well, you always say I talk too much but nobody talks at all!"

His parents exchanged looks as if they hadn't a clue what the boy was talking about.

"It's an after-work thing," Maggie whispered. "When you work all day, you get really tired and don't feel much like talking."

Frederick looked at his parents for approval, and then turned back to Maggie. "You don't have that problem."

Again, Jude gasped, but Maggie raised her hand and laughed. "I talk way too much, Frederick. Everyone will tell you that."

Mark rose and picked up his plate. "I am a bit tired." He headed toward the kitchen and the adjoining sunroom that Mark had transformed into a home office. "Think I will try to get some work in and then call it a night."

Jude watched her husband disappear into the back of the house, sadness creeping across her features. Then she, too, rose and began clearing the table.

Maggie jumped up. "Let me do that."

Jude smiled grimly, then took the dishes from Maggie's hands and methodically headed toward the kitchen. "It's fine. I've got it."

Something was off here, Maggie knew it. She first suspected problems between the couple, but there wasn't marital tension between them. She wondered if it was work-related but Jude seemed content at the office, although her stoicism continued there as well. Maybe it was Mark. Every time she visited, some time during the evening he would excuse himself to the back room.

"What does your dad do in his office?" she asked Frederick.

Frederick shrugged. "He's writing the great American owl."

Maybe it was the endless torture of the silent dinners, the loneliness of the past two weeks or the fact that all of these people still wondered if she had hoodwinked their cousin into cutting her a piece of the *Yankee Living* pie, but Maggie began to laugh. It began as a reaction to Frederick's innocent remark, then quickly gained speed until she had a hard time controlling it.

"Are you okay?" Frederick asked, which made Maggie laugh harder. She felt her eyes tear and her ribs hurt from the excursion.

"I think she's hysterical."

Suddenly that voice — the one she dreamed of despite her best logic, the one with the adorable accent that sent goosebumps skittering over her body — sounded from behind and robbed her of all merriment. She sobered up faster than a longtailed cat in a room full of rocking chairs.

Frederick ran into Colin's arms while his uncle lifted him high in the air. Colin was still dressed in work clothes, a tweed vest underneath a corduroy jacket and his usual starched button-down. Maggie wasn't sure if it was the fact that she rarely knew men who dressed this well in the media — at least not on the editorial side — or that Colin wore the vest like a romantic lead out of *Masterpiece Theatre*, but suddenly laughter became the farthest thing from her mind. She stared at him, enjoying the view, while he exchanged preschool talk with Frederick.

"Colin, great, you're here." Jude entered the dining room wiping her hands on a dishrag. "That roof is going to be the death of me."

Colin frowned and placed his nephew on the floor. "You can always call that roofer in Portland."

Jude opened the door underneath the staircase and withdrew a toolbox. "You're the one who said he was too far away and cost too much."

"He is," Colin answered, a hint of fatigue in his voice.

Jude handed him the tools and placed her hands on her hips. "I thought you liked working with your hands."

Colin stared at her with a stone face. "I live for it." Then he headed up the stairs.

Maggie caught the sarcasm in that statement but Jude failed to. She seemed pleased to have big brother coming to the rescue. "I'll be right up," she yelled at his back and was answered with a grunt. "Just have to give Frederick a bath."

"I can do that," Maggie offered.

Frederick started jumping up and down. "Yes, please, let Maggie do it."

Jude ran her fingers through Frederick's hair in an effort to calm him, but he failed to notice anything. He bolted up the stairs to be with his uncle. "I appreciate the thought," she said to Maggie, "but I have to give him his asthma treatment tonight."

Maggie nodded, glancing at the pug at her feet, wishing she could snatch Frosty home with her — anything to break the monotony of returning to that empty house.

"You can do me a favor, though."

Jump off the nearest bridge? Maggie thought. That would solve some people's problems, particularly the man upstairs.

"I always bring Mark a cup of coffee at night, when he's working. I have the pot on. Would you…?"

"Sure," Maggie quickly said. "I'd be happy to."

Jude grinned her typical don't-give-the-world-too-much-teeth smile and hurried up the stairs. Maggie entered the kitchen, happy to be doing something useful, and was greeted by the fresh aroma of percolating coffee. Mark's door stood open by a crack, the light from his office spilling on to the kitchen floor, but no sound emerged from the secret chamber. Maggie was glad to finally see what was behind the mysterious door.

"What do you want with your java, Mark?" she yelled to him.

"Cream and sugar," he answered, making her giggle at the sound of "sug-ah."

She poured two cups of the same and tiptoed inside his office. The site before her was amazing.

"Cool place."

When Mark looked up at her exclamation with a wide smile, she nearly spilled the coffee. "You really think so? Let me show you around."

He stood beaming and started showing off his collection of books, trophies and photos that lined the walls and bookshelves within the tiny sunroom, now an author's sacred space. It reminded Maggie of Uncle Frank in LaGrange who loved to brag of his latest Craftsmen tools and cousin T-Paul in Louisiana who had a collection of fishing equipment used in catching blue crabs and catfish. But this was something Maggie could relate to: writing and books.

"This was my creative writing award I received in college." Mark pulled the framed certificate off the wall and displayed it proudly. "It's nothing big, but I got five hundred dollars with it and my short story was published in the school literary magazine. Not the student one either."

She had never seen him verbally construct so many sentences within a five-minute period. "That's great, Mark. I had no idea you were a writer."

Mark's features darkened slightly. "I'm not published."

Maggie pointed to the frame in his hands. "Sure you are."

Mark sighed and placed the certificate back on the wall next to a row of leather-bound books. "I'm sure you heard by now by someone in the family that I had a book contract and lost it."

He plopped back into his chair and Maggie took the leather Queen Anne to his right. "I didn't even know you were a writer."

Mark huffed beneath the rim of his coffee cup. "Not like anyone speaks of it around here."

Now Maggie was confused. Did he expect his in-laws to speak of his writing or just the failure part? But it wasn't the first sarcastic comment he had made about the Parnells.

Maggie touched his arm. "Why don't *you* tell me about it."

Mark smiled but the pain shown through. "Nothing to tell really. I wanted to be a novelist, thought I had what it took. I sold my first novel to a publisher with only a few chapters written. Bad idea."

He paused, staring at the screen before him. "So let me guess," Maggie inserted. "You never finished it."

"Had to give the advance back."

Maggie never wrote fiction, but she knew plenty who had and an advance was not something easily gained. "If you sold one, you're bound to sell another."

"They did say they would look at it if I ever finished it."

That was encouraging. "So?"

Mark offered that painful grin again and waved toward the screen, which held one line of type upon the page.

"Let me guess," Maggie said. " 'It was a dark and stormy night…?' "

Mark laughed, which shocked Maggie further. "How about, 'And then the rains came…'?"

Maggie leaned over to see if that were true, only to learn that the actual sentence was more like a note to himself of what he wanted to write, something dreadful about love lost and the darkness of the soul. She leaned back in her chair and grinned. "Why Mark, you have a sense of humor."

He ran a nervous hand through his hair. "Yeah, well, little good it does me."

"What are you writing about?"

He waved at the screen again. "Nothing."

"Oh come on." Maggie looked around hoping to find a pile of finished papers. "You've written something, haven't you? You've been in here every night I've been over."

"Sure." Mark shifted the keyboard in front of him. "I wrote three chapters once."

Maggie didn't know much about fiction but she knew deadlines well. "You need an editor."

"I need the muses to shine on me."

"Apparently they already have and you've pushed them away."

Something in his gaze made Maggie think she hit a nerve.

"She was close to him, you know? Really close."

Maggie searched her brain in an attempt to follow his thoughts, coming up with the only logical choice. "Jude's father?"

Mark nodded. "They could talk about everything. She told me she loved me because I reminded her of him, that she could talk to me the same way. But when her father died, the light in her went out."

"But she still has you…"

Mark picked up his coffee and gazed into the black liquid. "She has a failure. How can I help her when I've failed myself? I mean, look at me. I'm a preschool teacher."

This was defeatist talk and Maggie would have none of it. She shook herself to brush off the sadness that had descended upon the room. Then she leaned forward and looked into Mark's eyes. "Totally unacceptable."

Mark moved back in his chair, surprised at the change in conversation. "Excuse me?"

"First of all, what's wrong with being a preschool teacher? When I picked Frederick up the other day, the principal was raving about you. Maybe it's not what you want to do with your life, but it's one of the most noblest professions around."

Mark huffed again. "Tell that to the Parnells."

She wondered what he meant by that, but bottom line, the Parnells had nothing to do with what he did for a living. She learned that first hand defending her career to her father. "It should only matter to you, Mark. You're the one doing it every day.

"Second," she continued, leaning in closer, "I can't deal with a writer who says he can't deliver. My dad is coming in tomorrow so I'm going to be busy all weekend but I'm coming over here Monday night and I better see more than notes on a page."

She shouldn't have spoken to him like that — she barely knew him — but sometimes people needed a good kick in the pants. Anyway, that was how Maggie saw it. Now, as she waited for a rebuttal, she prayed it had been the right thing to say.

To her grateful amazement, Mark smiled. "Yes, ma'am," he said in the most awful Southern accent she'd ever heard.

Renewed by his approval, Maggie crossed her arms and gazed at him sternly but smiling all the while. "I mean it. Pages by Monday."

"Are you going to be my editor now?"

Maggie picked up the coffee cups and rose. "Yes sir. Everybody needs a deadline, you especially."

He grunted, but his attention returned to the screen. "I'll do my best."

Maggie paused on the threshold. It was none of her business what he wrote, but something told her it was the right thing to say. She had a feeling that having someone interested in his work made all the difference to Mark. "How about writing about what you just told me? Sometimes writing down the experience of life is therapeutic. It's better than that darkness of the soul stuff. That was downright depressing."

He stared at her for a long moment, than nodded. "Maybe you're right. It's just so…"

"Personal? Aren't writers supposed to write about what they know?" She shrugged. "What's the worst that could happen? You have words on pages and you get your feelings out?"

He nodded again, still contemplating a course of action. Then he looked at her as if coming out of a fog. "Are you headed home?"

She really didn't want to; she was hoping to run back into Colin. Maybe Jude would invite them all into the living room for conversation and scotch and she could enjoy the way he looked in that suit. But who was she kidding? He probably had no desire to speak with her.

"It's getting late," she told Mark, then shook an authoritative finger at him. "Monday. Pages."

He saluted her, and then returned to his computer. At the corner of her eye, Maggie swore she saw a smile.

She placed the cups in the dishwater, then moved to the foyer. If Jude were still upstairs, she would yell her goodbyes and head on home. She grabbed her sweater on the back of the dining room chair and began looking around for her purse.

"It's on the umbrella tree."

Colin leaned against the back of the couch, his vest and jacket long discarded and his shirt sleeves rolled up exposing dirty hands. He was writing down something on a pad and didn't look up.

"You should have changed. You probably got that nice shirt all dirty."

He gazed up briefly at the comment but didn't respond, which only made Maggie nervous. She headed to the umbrella stand to retrieve her fancy Mitzi Baker handbag, the one Dewey had loaned her for the funeral and the one Kathy had found so intriguing right before the barfing episode. Personally, Maggie hated it. She needed to purchase a new one, a purse big enough to hold a reporter's notebook. Now that the nights were getting cooler, she had to purchase some warm clothes as well. Only she didn't know how long she would be there. That last thought twisted in her gut.

"Did you fix the roof?" she asked Colin, trying, like so many other times, to initiate conversation among the Parnells.

"For the time being."

Maggie stared at him, still ignoring her by writing on the pad. Funny, but his silence bothered her more than the others. In fact, it made her downright mad and she wasn't sure why.

"Well, you're busier than a moth in a mitten." She didn't mean it to sound so flippant, but it came out that way.

And it got his attention. Colin looked up, as if he finally wanted to give her the time of day. Or decipher what she said. "And you're a smart one, aren't you?"

His comment stopped her cold. She planted her hands on her hips and cocked her head. "What do you mean by that?"

He straightened, sticking the pad inside his breast pocket. "Valedictorian of your high school, full scholarship to Columbia, journalism fellowship to the University of Georgia and graduation with honors at both. Have I missed anything?"

Some of this was on her resumé, but somehow she doubted that was where he had obtained the details of her scholastic career. Then it dawned on her. "Oh, I get it. The private detective."

"I especially loved the Georgia State Fair award. The local newspaper even wrote a story about it. What was it? The LaGrange Democrat? Funny name for a newspaper in a state that always votes Republican."

Maggie crossed her arms. As stupid as it sounded, she was proud of that award, not to mention that she made the Democrat's front page in color. "I won that award for a quilt in the home-ec division."

Something about that little piece of information made Colin shift nervously. And something about the whole conversation made Maggie want to laugh, even though she was fuming inside for being part of some invasion investigation.

"That's it?" she asked. "That's all you could dig up? Don't you know you're supposed to get the dirt on someone, not the accolades."

He stared at her hard. "I'm working on it."

Just then Jude appeared, handing Colin a piece of metal piping that looked as if it belonged to an old heating unit. "Working on what?"

Colin frowned at the corroded piece of hardware. "Working on getting your furnace going before the first frost."

Jude rose on her toes and kissed her brother on the cheek. "What would I do without you?"

For a moment, Maggie swore she saw Colin cringe. Colin, the bedrock of the family, the leader of the clan. Maggie wondered about that job in New York, the one Colin lost because of Jake.

How much did he want that position? Was it because of a personal career choice or a chance to get away from aging houses and a demanding business? On more than one occasion, Bonnie had mentioned Colin taking the brunt since the death of his father, only she never explained. Was his family too used to him coming to their aid?

"You're going to pick Frederick up tomorrow, too, right?"

Colin rubbed the bridge of his nose. "That's tomorrow?"

Jude's shoulders fell. "You promised. Mark and I have to be at the country club by five at the latest."

This time he definitely cringed. "I have a meeting at four. Can't Edith do it this time?"

"She has her accounting class then."

Tension filled the air as one person grasped at straws and the other feared the worst.

"I can do it," Maggie offered.

The two looked at her as if they had forgotten she was standing there.

"I'm working a half day tomorrow, to pick up my dad from the airport."

Jude waved her off. "I don't want to intrude on your time with your father."

"It's no trouble at all," Maggie insisted. "My dad would love to see Frederick again. He's always saying he wants grandchildren."

Holy crap, where did that come from? Not only was her thirtieth birthday approaching, making that biological alarm sound, but it was starting to come out of her mouth.

"Are you sure?" Jude asked.

"Consider it done. I'll bring him to my house." When Colin sent her a sideways glance, she quickly stammered, "I mean, Colin's house."

"Great. I'll get him around ten."

"I'll bring him home," Colin said, still gazing at Maggie.

Jude thanked them all again and a silence ensued. Maggie couldn't bear yet another awkward moment, so she slipped on her sweater and said her goodbyes.

Before she headed out the door, she stole one last look at her illusive roommate. "See you back at the ranch?"

She shouldn't have asked. It was none of her business. She kicked herself for doing it, even though she was dying to know.

"No, I'm going to be awhile," Colin answered.

Maggie tried to hide her disappointment, offering instead a cheery smile. "Well, I'll see you at work then."

Jude, on the other hand, asked the question she longed to. "Where on earth are you going this time of night?"

Maggie felt her heart constrict waiting for the answer. Until it came and then she wished she had never brought the subject up.

"I need to go over to Kathy's tonight."

For once, Maggie didn't care about pleasantries and conversations. Maybe Mark had it right all along, for as clichéd as it sounded a darkness was invading her soul.

Yet, she had to have the last word.

"For the record," she said to Colin, one hand on the doorknob, "I'm a voting Democrat."

Maggie grabbed her overly expensive purse and tripped over the threshold, retreating to her company car and heading back to Colin's home. She fought back tears as she struggled with the cell phone.

Of the three, Lizzy was the one who picked up.

"Where have you been?"

"I called you twice this week."

"Not at a decent hour."

"Are you busy? Do you want me to call you back?"

"Hell no." Lizzy paused. "What's wrong?"

"Nothing." Maggie bit her lip to keep from crying. The Cajun Embassy could read her better than anyone.

"You sound like you're close to tears."

"I am." Might as well as be honest, they were going to come forth sooner or later. The road suddenly blurred. "And I'm a little pissed."

"Damn Yankees. Maggie, get on the next plane and get your ass back South. What are you doing up there?"

She honestly didn't know, considering she didn't belong in Madison, Maine, where people ate meals in silence. But then she passed her beloved magazine, the row of American flags floating in front, and she remembered her dream. "I love it here."

Lizzy snickered. "Yeah, sure sounds like it. Who are you mad at?"

One particular Damn Yankee. But she wasn't up to explaining Colin, Pittsburgh, scotch and all. "My dad's coming in tomorrow and I still haven't explained everything to him."

"That's why you're pissed?"

She couldn't put anything past her friends. The last time they spoke, Stacy even asked about Colin, although how she sensed there was anything between them Maggie didn't know. But then, there really *wasn't* anything between them, which made the tears come again, this time harder. "I'm just feeling blue tonight, that's all. And mad at getting in this mess to begin with. Wish you all were here."

A pause followed and Maggie could hear a nail file in action. "I can be there first thing tomorrow, *chér*. Want me to help break the news to daddy?"

Maggie really did, but she owed it to her father to do it alone. She got herself in this mess, she needed to get herself out of it. "I'm okay. Just glad for the talk."

Voices were heard in the background and a door closing. "Maggie, darlin', I hate to break this off now, but…"

"I know." Maggie hated saying goodbye; it felt like casting off a lifeline. "You go and have fun."

"We're planning the reception meal. I'll call you in the morning, sweetheart."

"Okay."

Lizzy hesitated. "Are you sure you're all right?"

Maggie pulled into the driveway, Colin's house looming above her dark and empty. What was she doing here?

"I'm all right," she assured Lizzy and ended the call.

But she doubted every word.

Chapter Ten

WHAT WAS HE DOING HERE at this hour of the night, Colin wondered driving up the long driveway to Kathy's palatial estate. The massive house loomed down on him beneath a moonless, stormy night.

Early morning showers, late nights at the office investigating Jake and his whereabouts the past few months — not to mention juggling magazine business during the toughest time of the time. The foliage season was upon them with the peak arriving in a couple of weeks. The copy editor bowed out, as his mother had predicted, which left him short-handed once again.

Colin was exhausted, needed a week to catch up on sleep, but here he was babysitting Kathy only minutes after saving his sister from a leaking roof, story of his life.

New York called again, another contract assignment for the architecture firm that had initially offered him a job. Colin told them it was next to impossible to get away this time of year, but he hadn't said no. Deep down inside, despite all the work and family obligations, Colin hoped he could take off for the city and escape all these insane problems. Have a social life. Work for someone else for a change.

Through the haze of fatigue and frustration Colin kept seeing Maggie's face, and the hurt expression she exhibited knowing that he was both digging through her personal life and seeing the woman who tried to poison her.

"I'm not seeing anyone," he yelled aloud, jamming the shift into park and turning off the engine.

The fact that he cared that Maggie thought he did, made him madder. "Damn it, Jake, why did you have to marry *her*?"

He was going crazy, pure and simple. It wasn't the first time he had spoken to his dead cousin. But he needed answers — and no one living seemed to have any except his faithful private detective who continually found nothing on Maggie. At least no dirt, as Miss Georgia so eloquently put it.

One thing that might offer answers was Jake's chest, which was arriving over the weekend, his mother informed him, although she refused to say from where. Bonnie encouraged him to riffle through Jake's many accolades, trophies and conquests, but Colin didn't want to rehash the past. He wanted his mother to explain Jake's death, explain who his wife really was and assure him that this Southern siren was not here to steal his family business, not to mention his sanity.

Or his heart.

Despite his attempt to remain levelheaded and objective while the private investigator looked into her background, Colin longed to be back on casual terms with Maggie. Hell, he longed for a lot more than that.

"I'm a voting Democrat!"

Colin grinned, thinking of how such a mouse of a woman could pose such a proud stance when provoked. And her twang emerged full force when she got incensed, making him smile wider at the memory of it.

He prayed there was no dirt on the woman, that she was only a pawn used by Jake to get out of his obligations to the family and magazine. Still, Maggie now owned twenty-five percent of his business. What was he to make of that?

Colin glanced up at the house, dark and silent among the sugar maples. The sky flickered with streaks of lightning while drizzle decorated his windshield like a Jackson Pollard painting.

Kathy must have gone to bed, a good sign. During the past week, she had followed her doctor's orders and taken her meds. For the past two days Kathy had called but insisted she only wanted to talk, needed some company — in a rational mind, no less.

Definitely a good sign.

He slid down in his car seat, making himself comfortable while debating whether to knock or go home. He thought of calling on his cell, but he'd wake her parents, two other people not accustomed to sleeping these days. The rain fell harder and the wind blew leaves against his windshield, making it harder to see the house. Colin let his eyes drift shut, relishing the feel of a rare moment of silence and solitude. Within seconds, Colin fell fast asleep.

He would have slept past noon had Kathy not tapped on his window. Colin jerked awake at the sound of knuckles hitting glass.

"What are you doing?" Kathy asked, gazing inside the car beneath a brightly colored golf umbrella.

Colin rolled down the window to find the rain still falling, but that morning had arrived. "What time is it?"

"Almost eight." Kathy looked inside the car suspiciously. "Did you sleep out here?"

"Eight?" Crap, he had to get home and shower. He should be at his desk by now. He had a meeting at ten.

"Want to come in for breakfast?"

Colin gazed in the rear-view mirror to find a man staring back who had just slept in his car. "I'm losing my mind."

"No kidding, is that a yes?"

He gazed up at Kathy while the rain spit on his face, which actually felt refreshing. "No, that's a rain check," he said with a sleepy grin.

She didn't get it, but he wasn't surprised. Kathy had absolutely no sense of humor. "Okay, fine."

"Last night the lights were off. I thought of knocking but I didn't want to wake you and I guess I fell…"

"Yeah, whatever." Kathy turned to go which made the water

gathered on top of the umbrella slap him in the face. "I'll see you around."

Colin watched her walk toward the house, dodging puddles in her pink house slippers, while he mopped his brow with his handkerchief. Even though the conversation had been abrupt, she looked good, sounded calm.

He roared the car into action and headed home, checking the clock to make sure he saw right. For once he was thankful the town was as tiny as it was, for he hit the driveway within minutes. He soon realized, however, that Maggie was still at home, the company car parked in its usual spot.

"Crap." How to explain this one? He really didn't have to justify his actions, but he felt guilty as a schoolboy. And the fact that she knew he was at Kathy's house all night only made it worse.

He entered the house quietly but it was no use. He had to speak to her. He followed the scent of toast and coffee into the kitchen and found her seated at the table, her head buried in the Portland Press Herald. Maggie gazed over the headlines and examined him, but said nothing.

"Did you take a shower this morning?"

Maggie lowered the paper and Colin made out the dampness in her hair. Crap.

"I thought that was the agreement. Shouldn't I have?"

Colin paused on the threshold, debating whether to hurry upstairs to the cold water or beg a cup of coffee. "No, it's fine. I'm just running late."

"I see that."

He expected some smug look, but instead Maggie turned back to her newspaper, adding, "You look like hell."

Colin ran a hand through his hair, trying to tame the wild beast. "Thanks. Did my mother call?"

Maggie dropped the paper. "Yeah, sorry. She said the meeting has been moved up to nine."

"Crap."

Her expression changed from one of condemnation to concern. "I wrote it down on a note and put it by the front door. I thought you'd see it this morning on your way out."

He wanted to say something in his defense, but he was so damned tired he hadn't a clue what that would be.

"Can I help in some way?"

Colin forced his brain to clear. What was she asking him?

In a flash, Maggie's countenance changed again. "Never mind. Like you're going to trust me to go to some meeting for you." She stood, grabbing her jacket off the back of the chair. Before she could pass him on the way to the door, Colin grabbed her elbow.

"It's an advertising meeting. All I need are the figures for August and the projections for Christmas."

She met his gaze, anger and frustration still brewing behind the finest pair of eyes he'd ever seen, only inches from his face. He wanted to explain he had slept in his car. Hell, he longed to express how he wanted to believe she was an innocent party to his crazy cousin and that her excellent work at the magazine had been a lifesaver. But, he still wasn't sure she should be going to this meeting.

Instead, Colin released her elbow and backed away. "Just get the information, pass it on to my mother and tell her I'll be in around noon."

She softened a bit, although he knew she still steamed inside. "Anything else?"

Besides wanting to drag her upstairs to his bed?

Colin shook his head, trying his best to remain apathetic until the P.I. cleared her name. "Thanks."

Maggie nodded and headed off to work. He watched her walk to her car, get in the hybrid and drive away. Then without a beat Colin gave up all thought, Maggie and otherwise, landed on the couch, and, still in his work clothes, fell instantly back to sleep.

"I'm an airplane!"

Maggie searched the oncoming line of departing passengers while Frederick flew circles around her knees. The kid had talked nonstop all the way to the airport and was now literally bouncing off the terminal walls.

"Frederick." She grabbed him before he crashed landed into an elderly woman after jump-kicking the ticket podium. "Watch out for the people coming off the plane."

Frederick paused for a moment, then started up again, arms outstretched. Maggie prepared to chase him again, but she caught sight of the familiar uniform and waved. Stewart saw Maggie instantly and bolted to her side, wrapping his arms around his daughter and swinging her in the air.

Maggie laughed at her father's ritual and hugged him close, so glad for those strong arms around her. When he finally returned her feet to earth, he smiled and rubbed his nose against hers. "How's my Magpie?"

Maggie returned the smile but her dad offered a loaded question, one not easily explained. When she sighed, he gave her a knowing look. "We have a lot to talk about."

"Yes." Maggie felt a rush of tears starting. "Yes, we do."

To his credit, Stewart said nothing while pulling her close, letting her expend her tears into his shoulder. With his free hand, he grabbed Frederick by the collar before he collided with a stewardess.

"Who are you trying to be, young man?"

Frederick looked up, recognizing Stewart but his gaping mouth proved he wasn't sure how. "I'm a plane."

"A plane?" Stewart let go of the collar and patted him on the back. "What kind of plane?"

He shrugged. "Why is Maggie crying?"

Stewart squeezed his hug about her. "Because she's so glad to see her dad."

Frederick relaxed, knowing the man was related. "You talk funny, like Maggie."

At this, Maggie chuckled and the tears abated. "We already had this discussion, Frederick. Who talks funny?"

"Yankees," the child said proudly.

Stewart shook his head and gave her a look, although she spotted a grin underneath that unspoken paternal reprimand. "What are you teaching him?"

Maggie pulled away from his embrace, grabbing the plane ticket out of his coat pocket. "He's got to learn someday."

Before he had a chance to retort, Maggie took Frederick's hand and began moving them all toward the baggage claim. She was so happy to see her dad, so glad to have family who enjoyed talking and laughing.

Then Frederick reminded her of the conversation before her. "You cried the last time we were here."

Stewart placed an arm about her shoulders again. "Was this when you arrived for the funeral?"

Maggie nodded, but she wasn't recalling grief. Walking down this very corridor, Colin had stared at her as the fraud she was. "We really have to talk," she whispered.

"We have plenty of time," Stewart said, kissing the top of her forehead. "I'm here all weekend."

They collected Stewart's bags, stopped at a food cart to supply Frederick with an ice cream cone, then walked — Frederick hopping — to Maggie's company car. As Stewart placed the duffel bag in the trunk, Maggie grabbed Frederick before climbing on to the car's roof.

"Maybe sugar wasn't such a good idea," Stewart said.

Maggie finally managed to get the tyke into the back and locked into his car seat. She fell into the driver's side, hair mussed and falling about her face. "Believe me, he's like this on celery."

Frederick chattered until they made it to the highway and Stewart nearly jumped out of the car, exclaiming, "Heavens to Betsy. Will you look at that!"

Maggie was slowly getting used to the brilliant foliage of New England, but it still took her breath away. Every day was a new adventure, as if every time she uttered the phrase, "This is the most beautiful site I've ever seen," God proved her wrong the next morning.

"It's not the peak," she informed her father. "We're still building up to the big moment."

Stewart stared at the rolling hills of gold, crimson and burnt orange, rolling down to the edge of a cerulean sea. "It's gorgeous," he whispered in awe. "And it looks fine right now."

Maggie reached over and grabbed her father's hand. It was so wonderful having someone with which to share this experience, someone equally enthralled with the country's undisputed finest display of fall color. The Parnells and members of the *Yankee Living* staff seem genuinely enchanted with the annual event, but they weren't exactly running through the leaves with glee, which was what Maggie wished to do, given the chance.

"So, where do we start?"

Give it to her father to get down to the nitty gritty. Maggie peered in her rear view window but couldn't make out if Frederick was asleep. The boy had fallen silent, a good sign.

"I got laid off again."

Stewart's gaze left the foliage and he abruptly straightened in his seat. "The Parnells laid you off?"

"No." She waved her hand in the air as to brush off the silly thought, but she wondered if that scenario was coming.

"Then what are you talking about?"

"*Georgia Roadway* magazine."

Stewart gave her that look, the one she used to receive coming home from concerts smelling of pot and alcohol. The one a parent gives after spending time not knowing where his child has been. Only this time, it carried something more. "When?"

Maggie cringed. "Several months ago."

Now, she knew what lingered behind her father's gaze. Hurt. Not only had she failed to tell him about Jake, but she kept her unemployment a secret as well. "I'm sorry, Daddy," she whispered, but he looked away. "I didn't want to tell you. I didn't want you to worry."

When he looked back, his gaze flared with anger. "I worry about you every day, whether you want me to or not. It makes it worse not knowing. How could you think not to tell me?"

He was right. She should have told him. He would have given her the same lectures, how journalism wasn't a stable profession, that working for the government offered job security and great benefits. All true things. She could have suffered through his ministrations, politely turn down his offers of money and referrals to *Stars and Stripes* and moved on to a new publication, all the while glad there was someone in the world who cared.

But there was one other element to the story.

"I thought if I went to Las Vegas for this journalism convention, I could schmooze, make some contacts, get a new job and then I could call you with good news, instead of the usual."

Stewart remained quiet, waiting for the Jake explanation. Now that Frederick was asleep in the back seat, the world took on that uncomfortable silence again, like visiting with the Parnells.

Maggie relaxed her iron grip on the steering wheel and exhaled. "That's where I met Jake."

She explained the whole story, including the conference cocktail party, the alcohol-infused dinner, the passionate kisses on the balcony overlooking the Strip and the drunken quickie wedding with Elvis presiding. Then she recounted every detail after Jake said goodbye at her hotel door that night and she never saw him again.

"Never?"

"His lawyer called me with the news of his death the day before I got on a plane to come here."

Stewart grappled with this information as she had done for one long month. "It doesn't make sense," Stewart said, adding, to make sure Jake hadn't violated his daughter in other ways, "And you never slept with the man?"

"No."

"Never?"

"Sheesh, Dad, do I have to say it again?"

Stewart seemed pleased by the news. "That's a good thing."

Maybe fifty years ago. To Maggie, it appeared like the insult it was. "Not really. I'm the only woman on the face of the earth who apparently didn't and ironically I was his wife."

Stewart patted Maggie's knee sympathetically but she knew he was still pleased they hadn't become intimate, as he would have put it. "Well, you did say he was marrying you to get out of that obligation to Colin."

Speaking of, Maggie pulled off the highway into Madison and drove pass the magazine, spotting Colin's Explorer out front. "There's more."

Stewart passed her a look that was thankfully more lighthearted. "I can't wait."

"On the way up to the funeral, my plane was delayed in Pittsburgh. I had drinks with this good-looking guy and we, ah, kinda flirted with each other."

At this, Stewart smiled warmly, which decreased the tension tenfold. "Under the circumstances, Maggie, who would doubt you? It's not like you were really married or anything."

Maggie turned on to the street leading to Colin's house, following the rolling lane of colonial houses, rock fences and towering maples in a variety of colors. She inhaled deeply, hoping it would bring her courage to face all the craziness before her. "I didn't know who he was, Dad. He didn't tell me his name."

"So?" He gazed at her, trying to decipher where she was heading. "Is he contacting you now? If I were you, I'd give it a little while, then go see him." He paused briefly, then added, "In a public place, though. You don't know what kind of man he is."

She knew exactly what kind of man he was, that was her problem. The kind that made her heart race.

Maggie parked the car in front of the colonial. She paused to gather her thoughts, then turned toward her father. "It's a little more complicated than that. I think I really like this guy."

"Does he live in Maine?"

"Yes."

"Does he live close by?"

Maggie glanced up at the house that was as attractive as the man who lived in it. In two weeks, she had fallen in love with the place, foliage and all. "Oh yeah."

"Well I'd be respectful of the Parnells and their feelings toward Jake, then give it some time and contact him. He has to understand your situation."

Another silence ensued, Maggie's mind reeling with confusion. How to explain this one? She could barely explain it to herself.

"Dad," she finally said, "it was Colin."

There was a moment of solitude while Stewart comprehended it all, a moment of peace when the birds sang outside and a soft wind blew a painter's palette of fall leaves around the windshield.

Then everything clicked in her father's head and he burst out laughing.

She was relieved he wasn't angry by all the news, but his reaction startled her. "You think it's funny?"

Stewart calmed himself, a wide grin still playing his lips. "Maggie, you married a man you barely knew who disappeared on your wedding night, then flirted with his cousin in a Pittsburgh airport, a man you now work for who is furious that you're stealing his magazine." He paused, fighting back laughter. "Am I missing anything?"

Maggie grabbed her purse and jacket. "Yeah, like what am I going to do about it all?"

Her father started to say something, then paused. A frown creased his forehead. "I haven't a clue."

Then the laughter began again.

Maggie shook her head, leaving the car and her guffawing father. "You have to admit it's pretty funny," he yelled at her.

She really did, but she still wanted answers. Plus, Colin could be home any minute, and facing him and his usual grouchy mood and suspicious stares wasn't funny at all.

Maggie opened the back door to find Frederick wide-eyed and bushy tailed. "I'm hungry," he demanded.

"I thought you were asleep." She unbuckled the car seat and pulled the tyke to the ground, where he immediately took off running toward the house. For a moment, she worried he had heard the entire conversation, although she doubted he understood any of it. Still...

"So, what needs fixing?" Steward retrieved his duffel and came to Maggie's side, staring up at the historic home.

My heart, Maggie thought. I keep falling for a gorgeous pair of

Yankee eyes. When it all came down to it, though, Jake, with that earth-stopping charm and leading man looks had nothing on his cousin.

"It's the hot water heater," she told her dad. "It needs replacing. I bought a new one and it's in the basement, but I haven't a clue how to install it."

"And your airport Casanova doesn't either?" He sent her a sly smile.

"He's too busy. Besides, he never had to worry about it when he was living alone."

"Come on," Frederick shouted from the porch. "I want some pop."

Maggie headed for the house. "He wants some *pop*. And they say we talk funny."

Stewart carried his duffel over a shoulder, lost in thought. "Did you ever consider Jake might have known he was going to die?"

Her father's words brought her to a standstill. "Why would you say that?"

He glanced up, squinting into the sunshine. "Why else would a man his age change his will? And include a wife he barely knew and hastily married in Vegas? I can understand why he'd have a will, considering all that he owned, but to alter it like that to include you? Doesn't make sense."

"No it doesn't." Maggie opened the front door and Frederick bounded inside, heading toward the kitchen. "I know the marriage was all arranged to get out of his obligation to Colin, but it's odd that Jake would just hand over his stake in the magazine to me."

The refrigerator door opened and Maggie heard something fall to the floor. "Get one coke, Frederick, and share it with us. I don't want you drinking all that sugar."

Frederick raced back toward the front of the house, a Mountain Dew in his hands. "It's not a Coke, Maggie."

"Same thing," Stewart added, opening the can for the boy.

Frederick didn't understand, but he didn't care. He darted off again.

Maggie thought to remind him not to drink the entire can, but she gave up. She had other thoughts running through her mind. "If Jake was dying, surely the family would have known. I don't know where he spent that last month. Or where he was the day he died, for that matter."

Stewart chewed that for a bit, then shook his head. "Bonnie knows something, but she's not telling."

This was news. "Bonnie? But why?"

Her father appeared to blush slightly, or perhaps Maggie was seeing things. "I don't know. I couldn't get her to tell me anything about the boy."

Maggie thought to ask when they had such an intense conversation, but Stewart glanced up as if coming out of a trance. "Did I ever tell you that you look like your mother in that new haircut?"

Suddenly, the air disappeared inside her lungs and the room began to spin. How long had it been since he discussed her mother? She honestly couldn't remember. The words refused to come, so Maggie shook her head.

"She was a lot taller, of course, but her hair used to fall across her shoulders like that."

Something forceful rose in her chest and Maggie bite her bottom lip to keep it from shaking. Stewart noticed and grabbed her shoulders. "What's wrong?"

Maggie shut her eyes briefly to fight back the tears. "You haven't talked about mom since the day you came into my room to tell me about the accident."

Her father appeared ready to dispute that fact, incredulity passing across his face. Then, something stopped his tongue and pain replaced confusion. The cloud Maggie had seen so many times hanging over her father — hanging over their lives — threatened again, pulling him deep inside himself.

"No," Maggie commanded, touching his cheek. "Please don't go back there."

The darkness passed as quickly as it arrived and the sun shone again. Another first. Usually, her father would beg for solitude and retreat to some far room, closing the door behind him. This time, Stewart smiled, leaning his forehead against his daughter's. "Maybe it's time we stopped being silent with one another. Maybe it's time we truly talked."

"I want to know everything," Maggie whispered. "I want to know all about her."

Stewart straightened and swallowed hard, but the cloud didn't return. "Why don't we find that rascal child, save him from a deadly sugar rush and then get to work on this water heater? We can talk while we work."

"Okay." Maggie couldn't help being excited at the prospect. Plus, she could pay Colin back, if only a little, for his two weeks of hospitality. "And Colin will be so pleased we did this."

"Colin." Stewart eyed her curiously. "I'll tell you about your mother if you tell me about him."

Maggie really didn't want to, but fair was fair. There was still so much to explain. "He's not like Jake."

For some reason, she didn't have to explain that one; Stewart seemed to know. But then her father knew everything.

"I like him," was all he said before they sauntered down to the basement with Frederick at their heels.

And that meant all the world to Maggie.

Chapter Eleven

THE FLOORS SAGGED IN THE middle, their original pine twisted from years of use and abuse. Holes gaped down from the ceiling and tiny feet scattered above. The original molding was cracked and peeling, while wallpaper in various shapes and colors tilted back in corners, as if begging to be removed.

In short, the house was a mess.

"It's got potential," the owner said brightly.

"When did you say this was built?" Bonnie studied the brick fireplace and hand-carved woodwork, estimating the date around the turn of the nineteenth century.

"Eighteen twelve, like the war."

Eighteen twelve — would make great fodder for a story lead, Bonnie noted. "And you said it's already been approved by the society?"

The owner handed Bonnie a series of documents relating to the New England chapter of interior designers that sponsored, along with the magazine, an annual showcase house. Each year, an owner provided a house like a raw canvas, and a group of carefully picked designers created the painting, decorating each room in their own unique style, while landscape experts completed the exterior. Then the house was presented to the public who pay for the privilege to see both an historic home and a collection of expertly designed interiors.

"We have all the designers lined up and I begin the major renovations this week," the owner said.

"You have your work cut out for you," Bonnie answered, stepping over a hole in the floor.

"Historical homes as wonderful as this one should be preserved." The owner looked around, seeing the majesty of the old American home, not her flaws. "She's a true classic."

Bonnie paused at the back bay window, looking out on to what must have been an elaborate English garden. Now, overgrown vines swallowed the trellises and weeds littered the yard. Hadn't Gavin called her that once? A classic New Hampshire beauty?

They had met at college in Boston, both studying publishing. Gavin, with jet-black hair and aquamarine eyes, was the handsome son of an old publishing family with no problem wooing girls. He tried his charm on Bonnie, but she would have none of it. "I want a career," she told him firmly. "And no bewitching pair of Parnell eyes is going to keep me from it."

Of course, Gavin won her over, convincing her to marry him and dragging her back to Maine. She got a position at the magazine in the process, and she had loved both dearly ever since.

Maybe that's why Bonnie understood Maggie so well, understood how charming the Parnell men could be. Only Maggie didn't know the whole story. Time would answer all the questions, Bonnie knew, and maybe her presence at the magazine would help heal some still smarting wounds.

"As long as she's at *Yankee Living*, everything will turn out fine." The owner reached Bonnie's side. "Pardon?"

Had she said that aloud? She straightened, adjusting her thinking with her posture. "When do you think we'll be able to photograph?"

The owner literally lit up at the news. Her home was going to grace the cover of *Yankee Living* come next spring. "I have to get the approval of the inspectors. They don't want anyone coming in without the shoring and other protective measures first."

"I understand."

"I'll be doing that this week. I can get back to you within the month."

The two women shook hands.

"I see you don't have the gardeners chosen yet," Bonnie said as they walked down the foyer. "I can give you a list of some amazing designers, if you like. A couple have already done showcase houses, so they know the routine."

She didn't think the woman could shine any brighter, but she did. Or maybe Bonnie underestimated the power of her magazine.

"I'd love that," the woman said. "I was thinking of creating a tool shed in the back, like the one you guys wrote about in June, the one with the blueberries on the cover." The woman laughed. "The magazine had blueberries on it, not the shed."

Bonnie smiled. She knew exactly what the woman was referring to — every month *Yankee Living* provided plans and instructions on how to create outbuildings and other projects, plans mostly created by her son, the frustrated architect. "Good idea. That was one of our best. I'll have Colin give you a call. He was the designer of that project."

The two exchanged parting pleasantries and Bonnie headed for her car. She paused in the front yard, admiring the expansive view. The front yard rolled down unhindered to the property line and a typical New England rock fence, one, no doubt, created when the house was built and the fertile land first tilled. In the distance the foothills of the White Mountains hid under a mist, her childhood home. And in between stood acres of gorgeous fall foliage, an endless sea of auburn, crimson, gold.

Bonnie had spent her life in New England but its beauty reaching up to the sky never failed to amaze her. She mentally made a note to contact Maggie when she returned home, to make a date for a foliage tour of the area surrounding Madison, to show off how much New England shined once a year.

Then she remembered Stewart was visiting.

The thought of Maggie's father created a lump in her throat and tightness in her chest. In one sense, she didn't regret what happened with Stewart, didn't lament the intimacy they had shared both in and out of bed. But somehow she felt guilty of adultery, that she had cheated on the only man she had ever loved.

Which was ridiculous. Women became widows and learned to live and love again, why shouldn't she?

Because it felt strange, she thought. It felt uneven, like an earthquake cracking open a surface and tilting the land sideways. Her life existed on an even keel, no disruptions, no emotional outbursts. This take-charge Southerner had entered her life and all rational thought had disappeared. How could one man create such a disturbance?

Bonnie had to admit her feelings for Stewart felt like a schoolgirl crush. Maggie would mention her father's name and she would tingle inside like the minutes before Christmas. She even caught herself twirling a strand of hair, remembering how amazing he looked in his army uniform. As much as she loved Gavin, had adored her husband and the great father that he was, she couldn't remember feeling quite so giddy about a man.

"I'm losing my mind," she whispered to the wind.

Bonnie glanced up at the massive home one last time. On the outside, one couldn't detect its faults and fissures, how inside its floors sagged and its walls crumbled. The house stood like the majestic queen she was, New Hampshire architecture at its finest.

"Oh Gavin," Bonnie uttered, "give me a sign. Tell me it's okay."

Just then, her cell phone buzzed. "Bonnie Parnell," she answered.

"Bonnie, I found you. I was hoping I would."

"Maggie?" The coincidence rattled Bonnie and she felt her lungs constrict.

"We're on the coast, although we're not sure where." There was a bout of Southern laughter, joined by what sounded like Stewart in the background. "There's a lighthouse here, like the one you see in all the commercials."

"Sounds like the Portland Head Light. You're outside of Portland in Cape Elizabeth."

"That makes sense, we passed through Portland on the way down." Bonnie heard Maggie pass on this information to another party. "I'm sure we'll find our way back but I thought if you were nearby, you could meet us and help two wayward Southerners be proper tourists for a day. We haven't a clue what to see."

Bonnie's pulse quickened as she considered seeing Stewart again. "I'm in New Hampshire, checking out the new showcase house."

"Oh." Disappointment came through the airwaves. "Okay, just thought I'd ask. Wow, New Hampshire. Will you be out of the office for a while?"

Bonnie laughed and the feeling felt good. "Our states are rather small, Maggie. You could put all of New England inside Georgia."

There was a short pause. "Yeah, I guess you're right."

"I'm only two hours away, maybe three."

"Wow, you're kidding?"

Bonnie heard Maggie relay this to her father. Suddenly a throaty male voice boomed over her phone, one sounding a lot like Rhett Butler, God help her. "If you're that close, how about meeting us for dinner?"

Bonnie's mind whirled. She needed to get back to the office and make plans. She had a photo shoot to arrange, needed to read through garden book proposals that were beginning to create a stack on her desk as high as the Washington Monument, start working on next year's budget.

"I'd love to."

She swore she could hear Stewart smiling and that image caused her insides to do a little dance. "Great." He was genuinely enthused. "Tell us what to do."

After a few minutes of sightseeing instructions, the Southern pair was on its way to foliage hot spots and Portland's finest attractions. They agreed to meet at Hugo's, an elegant dining establishment that offered haute New England cuisine, at six o'clock.

As Bonnie hit the end button, she stole one last look at the cover of April. "You're still a New Hampshire beauty," she told the house, silently thanking Gavin for the sign.

Dusk settled over the hills as Colin made his way home, a pile of work sitting next to him on the seat, topped by Jude's corroded piece of hardware. Thankfully, Maggie had called him at the office Friday afternoon, saying Frederick could spend the night and to not worry about rushing home. He had taken the opportunity to finalize his budget plans and write up the advertising report for the Board of Directors. Then, he had fallen asleep on his office couch, waking up the following morning to start all over again.

Saturday he visited Boston to make a presentation to a prospective advertising client, an old college friend who invited him to stay the night, which he gratefully accepted. He wasn't in any shape – particularly after the two had visited a round of Irish pubs – to make the long drive home. And these days, it felt good to get away.

Sunday evening and he was exhausted, but if he finished the work gracing his passenger seat, he could steal away to New York in the morning for that contract assignment and get away from the problems plaguing him.

But, that left Jude's ailing furnace. He had promised her he would take care of it before the end of the month and the prospect of the coming frost. In New England in autumn, that could be any moment.

He loved his family – he truly did – but this constant reliance on him was going to bury him alive. Jude had never been a needy one, always the family drum major leading the band on to the field, but after their father's death she seemed to long for Colin's company as well as his handyman assistance. Her marriage appeared healthy, at least to the outside, but Mark had retreated into a blue funk ever since the publisher rejected his book and Colin doubted he was of much help as a sounding board.

Edith remained holed up in her house, eating too much and watching hours of television alone. In the past few years she had both gained weight and disappeared. For all her outward bravado and abrasiveness, Edith was putty on the inside, scared to venture out and brave a social life. Visiting her ancient house to fix its many ills, Colin let his sister boss him around knowing that it boosted what little self-esteem she owned.

And there was his mother, the proud matriarch who never let her husband's death keep her from leading the magazine on to more awards and a larger circulation. But, Colin knew the pain she carried quietly inside. He knew it well.

Colin grabbed the pile of papers, including the hardware, and stumbled into the darkened house. He was glad for the solitude, glad not to have to explain another night away to his latest family member and roommate — as if he had to explain anything.

Amazingly enough, Maggie had turned out to be self-reliant and unassuming. According to his mother and other editors, she learned quickly, worked efficiently and took initiatives that were fruitful to the magazine. Even at home, her presence was inconspicuous and beneficial. In between the maid's visit once a week, Maggie kept the house clean and neat and, on several occasions, left him dinner in the microwave.

For once, someone was actually assisting *him*.

Colin grunted, throwing everything on to a chair by the side of the foyer, then tossed the keys on top of the secretary. Maggie was the wrong person to be helpful. She should have been a horrid worker with a sordid past. Then he could have easily removed her from his life, absorbed the quarter interest in his magazine and returned his life to normal.

Yet, what was normal? Was his life of three weeks ago something he wanted to maintain? Did he really want to lose the most interesting woman to waltz through his door, even if she was From Away? Like way down South.

He needed a scotch, then a hot bath. In that order.

Yet, before he could take a step in that direction, Colin spotted mail placed upright on the foyer table. The top envelope offered only his name, written in his mother's handwriting. Colin grabbed the stack and headed for the living room, where he poured himself a Chevas. In the process he nearly stumbled over a massive chest lying before the fireplace.

He knew immediately it was Jake's trunk. He recognized the

cheesy bumper stickers: "I'm with stupid," "My drop-out beat up your honor student," "Your body may be a temple, but mine is an amusement park." It was moments like these, gazing at Jake's prized possession, that Colin wondered if his aunt had had an affair.

Colin fell into his favorite chair and downed the scotch. He was in no mood to deal with Jake's chest – why the hell did his cousin leave the damn thing to him anyway? One last laugh at Colin's expense? One last chance to rub Colin's nose in Jake's successes, the ones he acquired all those years while Colin ran the family business and gave up his own dreams? He would open the damn thing another day.

Instead, Colin tore off the back of the envelope on top of his stack, pulling out *Yankee Living* stationary.

> *Colin,*
> *Jake's chest arrived today so I had it delivered to the house.*
> *Maggie let them in and put it in the living room. Do go*
> *through it, sweetheart. Let me know if you want to talk.*
> *Mom*

Talk? How many times had he asked his mother about Jake and now she wanted to talk? As soon as the private detective was done with Miss Georgia, he would set him on Jake's trail. Try to make sense of it all, sans his inheritance of Jake's obnoxious trunk.

Grunting, Colin threw the letter on top of the chest, gazing at the Hallmark card he now held in his hands, one adorned with feminine handwriting. Could it be that one of his sisters thought to thank him for the many times he had come to her assistance. Maybe, it was a card from Jude, thanking him for the numerous times he had patched her roof.

Renewed with the prospect of being appreciated, Colin opened the card that began with "For all you've done…." But what he found inside surprised him.

Colin,
I can't thank you enough for letting me stay in your house and for letting my father stay here as well this weekend. As a token of our thanks, we have left you a present in the basement, just beneath the stairs. It was a bit large, considering what we were trying to do, so my father made some adjustments. I hope you don't mind — he's an engineer and can be trusted. Anyway, thanks for the hospitality. Enjoy your next shower.
— Maggie and Stewart

Curiosity got the better of him and he dropped the rest of the mail on the chest, heading for the basement. As he turned the corner on the last step, he was greeted by the pungent smell of freshly cut pine. He spotted a shiny new water heater, one twice the size of the old one, built inside a revised space underneath the stairs. New wood and lack of some old two-by-fours indicated Stewart had removed some obstacles, then reinforced the area to make way for the modern appliance. Stewart had added a little door to hide the monstrosity, and covered the water heater with an energy-saving blanket.

"Well I'll be damned."

Colin paused, admiring the Mallory handiwork. The duo had even painted the new wood to match the surrounding walls — and this in the middle of an ancient, damp basement that didn't deserve such treatment.

A hot shower, Colin thought. A long, hot shower.

For the first time in days, Colin smiled. Maybe it was the colonial style latches on the makeshift door or the large red bow draped around the water heater's middle, but the thought of Maggie and her father installing the massive appliance made him happy. And forgetful, if only briefly, that Maggie now owned a significant segment of his family's business.

Colin ran a grateful hand down the side of his metal savior, and then headed back upstairs. A half hour later, after a long deluge in heat and steam, Colin called Jude to try to find the Southerners who had delivered such an awesome gift.

Jude answered on the fifth ring, a party in progress in the background. "Where are you?"

"At home. Just got back. Have you seen Maggie?"

"Sure." Jude laughed at something being said. "They're here. We're all here. Come on over."

"What's going on?" Colin began, but Jude had hung up the phone.

He really had way too much to do; all he had wanted was to find Stewart and Maggie and offer his thanks and not get involved in a large family gathering. But now they expected him. And if memory served him right, Stewart had a plane to catch in the morning.

Colin threw on some casual clothes and a thick cardigan sweater, for the night had turned chilly and damp. They were laughing at Jude's house, he thought as he closed all the windows to escape the bite that suddenly appeared in the air. What was that all about?

When he arrived at his sister's house, several cars littered the driveway, including his mother's, Jake's old Jaguar — his trademark bumper stick, "If it's tourist season, why can't we shoot them?" on the back — and Maggie's company car. The house was abuzz with lights and activity, oblivious to the sudden storm that had descended outside. Colin pulled his sweater's lapels together and entered the house, grateful for the roaring fireplace and the warmth it offered.

But Bonnie's presence next to the comforting blaze startled him to his core.

His mother was laughing. Not a polite smile or chuckle as Colin was used to hearing these days, but an honest-to-God, deep-throated, from-the-heart laugh. The source of the merriment was a tall, muscular man with an accent as thick as Georgia honey.

"I swear to you that's how it went down." Stewart paused as if finishing the story, enjoying the laugher around him. "Ask Maggie if you don't believe me."

Everyone turned toward Maggie, but her gaze was fixed at the door. "Hey."

"Hey," Colin answered back, finding some obscene joy that

Miss Georgia spotted him first.

"Colin." Bonnie cleared her throat and sobered, a slight blush gracing her cheeks. "You're back."

"Jack agreed to three months of inserts. I think he'll opt for more once he sees the numbers."

Why was he talking business? Clearly everyone was enjoying the leisurely Sunday evening and that didn't include magazine advertising. He could have kicked himself for the energy in the room dropped ten degrees.

"That's great Colin," Bonnie said. "Anyone want dessert?"

Frederick jumped off the couch and grabbed Bonnie's hand. "I do, I do."

"I'll help," Edith said, but Stewart patted her shoulder.

"Sit back down and relax. I'll go help your mother."

Whatever hint of rouge dotted his mother's cheeks before, it flushed bright pink at Stewart's declaration. Colin could hardly believe it; how long had it been since his mother blushed? He might have imagined it all, had Maggie not stared at the couple, equally surprised. She turned her gaze to his, perhaps searching for confirmation that their parents may be flirting with one another, but Colin hadn't a clue what was going on. Besides, looking at her reminded him why he came.

"Thanks for the present." He grinned thinking of the heavenly shower he took. "You really shouldn't have, but I'm glad you did."

Maggie pulled a wisp of hair behind an ear. "My dad did most of it." She appeared as if she wanted to smile, but something held her back. She shrugged. "I painted the door."

"You shouldn't have done that either. It's only a basement."

"Do you like it?" She looked at him hopeful, as if that question covered more than a new water heater.

"Are you kidding? I love it. It's fabulous." And somewhere deep inside, beyond wills and private detectives, he meant every word.

"I held the tools." Frederick came bounding into the room with a plate of apple pie a la mode in his hands. Stewart grabbed the child's tilted plate before the ice cream fell to the floor. He straightened it with a smile, but cookies and cream splattered across the front of his shirt.

Oblivious to his state, he offered his hand and Colin accepted the handshake, thanking him for the incredible gift, which Stewart dismissed with a wave. "It was nothing. I don't own a house —never have — so you did me a favor. It felt good to work with my hands and feel useful for a change."

"He fixed the furnace," Jude said proudly from behind.

Again, Stewart frowned, uncomfortable with the attention. "All it needed was a good cleaning – the thing was full of junk. I simply took apart the burner and cleaned out the attached pipes and we had it up and running."

A new water heater. Jude off his back. The man was a saint.

"I suppose you're going to tell me the roof is fixed too."

Bonnie arrived with two plates of pie and handed one to Stewart, along with a napkin that he used to clean his shirt. He barely looked down, as if a five-year-old smearing ice cream on his button-downed shirt happened every day.

"You need to call a roofer," Stewart told him. "I think all your patch-ups are going to be just that. It needs work on the outside and in." He paused, gauging Colin's reaction. "Unless you enjoy doing all that work."

For the second time that night, Colin smiled broadly, but tried to contain himself for Jude's sake. "I think I can live without it."

Stewart patted Colin on the shoulder, as he had Edith. One thing about these Southerners, they were always touching people. He had noticed Maggie doing it to just about everyone at the magazine over the past two weeks: smiling and touching, laughing and touching, talking and touching. It was kinda nice, actually, but it took some getting used to.

"Thanks again," Colin said to the colonel. "You really made my night."

"Well, now you and Maggie can take a shower together."

It was innocently said — after all, he was her father — but Colin felt his own cheeks begin to burn imagining that scenario. When he felt a warm, familiar hand on his forearm, the sensation increased.

"Are you hungry?"

Understatement. "Excuse me?"

She removed her hand as if she sensed his discomfort. "Do you wish to put food in your mouth?" she asked, folding her arms across her chest.

For all his reservations about Miss Georgia and his anger over the marriage and the will, Colin suddenly felt awkward as a teenager. "Sure."

"I made chicken, mashed potatoes and salad."

"Don't forget pie," Frederick called out.

"And pie."

She gazed up at him, caution guarding her smile. She looked so wicked cute in her polo shirt, jeans and Mary Janes. He wanted so badly to kiss her, to tease a smile back on those lips now curled up in a crease. He wanted to get back to Pittsburgh and their dueling accents. But he couldn't go there now, not until he knew for sure.

Instead, Colin offered sarcasm. "Wow, is there anything you can't do?"

To her credit, she didn't miss a beat. Maggie leaned in close and said for his ears only, "I can't seem to think before I say the words 'I do.'"

With a mixed look of hurt and irritation, Maggie disappeared into the kitchen, leaving Colin to wonder if she regretted staying in Madison and working for the family. When she returned, she brusquely handed him a plate piled high with food, but not before he got another chance to absorb the bushy eyebrows, the upturned nose and those adorable brown eyes that stretched wide when she got excited.

Only now, they appeared as slits, eyeing him suspiciously.

Colin decided it was best to avoid Scarlet for a while, to join Edith on the couch and enjoy the hot meal.

"It packs a punch," Edith said, nodding to the chicken.

Colin bit into a leg and found a symphony of spices, so unlike the bland food his family traditional served. "It's wonderful," he managed between bites. Another understatement.

"If you like it hot."

He wanted to explain to Edith that adding spice to food didn't make it hot, but she was the last person to venture out of her safe bland harbor. Once in New York he convinced her to try Thai food and she never forgave him.

Instead, Colin peered over Edith's head, caught Maggie's eye and mouthed another "thank you." She managed a slight smile, but was immediately interrupted by Mark, who handed her a pile of papers.

"Didn't want to wait until tomorrow," he said eagerly.

Colin noticed him glance in Jude's direction and his sister broke out in a wide blush. Now, what was going on with them?

"We have plans for this evening," Mark said to Maggie and winked.

Maggie smiled knowingly and accepted his papers. "I understand. I'll read them tonight."

"It's rough," Mark hastily added. "It came out in a rush. Don't be too hard on me."

She touched him, as usual, but this time also kissed him on the cheek. Colin felt a rush of jealousy, although he knew he had no reason feeling that way. Did Southerners kiss a lot, too?

Just then, Frederick pulled on Colin's sleeve. "I have to go to bed now. Will you tell me a story, Uncle Teddy?"

Colin wolfed down the last of the potatoes, then pulled his nephew up and over his shoulders and headed upstairs, the tyke giggling all the way. When they reached the landing, Colin turned back to view his family from above.

Stewart was telling Bonnie a new story while his mother laughed at the telling, Edith actually piping in at one point. Mark joined his wife by the fireside, placing an arm about her shoulders and hugging her close. They kissed softly, their gaze holding as if some secret passed between them.

When had Colin seen his family so happy, so joyous in one room? Not since his father died, for sure. The air in the house seemed charged with affection and comfort.

"Uncle Teddy." Frederick kicked his heels as if Colin was a pony.

"We're going," Colin said, but he paused to absorb the rare sight one more time.

Who took credit for this?

Maggie sat on the periphery of the action, seeming to both enjoy the revelry and feel apart. She laughed at her father's story, but wrapped her arms about legs, like a turtle curling up inside a shell. Something was missing here.

"Uncle Teddy," Frederick cried louder, which made Maggie turn and look up. In that instant when their gazes met, Colin knew exactly what that was.

Tomorrow he would head to New York City, but not before talking to the detective. He needed to get to the bottom of things, needed to know what her story was and why this all happened.

More importantly, he wanted Maggie back in his life.

Chapter Twelve

IT WAS FRIDAY AFTERNOON, THE weather spectacular during the finest time of the year and all her work was completed. Yet, Maggie felt like she'd been chewed up and spit out. For the life of her, she couldn't explain why.

Careful not to bother Malick, the magazine's new Webmaster who was busy working out the kinks of the upcoming Christmas pages, Maggie leaned over his shoulder to glance at the calendar. Nope. Too early to be PMS.

"Something wrong?" Malick asked.

"I don't know," she said, falling into her chair. "I'm out of sorts today, feeling grumpy. I'd probably complain if Jesus came down and handed me a five dollar bill."

The slender twenty-something with long hair and a goatee sent her that confused look Maggie was getting used to, the one Yankees bestowed on her when she offered up colorful speech. "You're doing it again," he said.

"Sorry." Sheesh, what did she have to do, spell it out in plain English?

"I take it you're angry about something."

"Yeah, and I don't know what or why."

Like a typical male, Malick left it at that, careful not to enter that realm of unstable feminine emotions. Meanwhile, Maggie wondered what bug had flown up her butt.

The day had started stressful — now that she thought about it — when she broke one of Colin's picture frames gracing the living room bookcases. She was sipping her coffee, waiting for her pants to dry downstairs in the dryer, and got bored. Digging through his belongings like the snoop that she was, she knocked a family portrait on to the floor, shattering the glass into a thousand pieces.

The frame shop assured her it would be finished that evening, but the incident made her late for work and without a breakfast. God must have decided to punish her for being so nosy for Maggie stumbled into the magazine's kitchen, hoping to snag a muffin from the vending machines, and ran smack dab into Kathy. She didn't know what irritated her more, the fact that she was eating again in front of the witch or that the woman continually lured Colin into her lair while Maggie barely saw the man — and he lived in the same house!

Not to mention Kathy had yet to apologize for poisoning her with potato salad.

"How are you?" Leave it to Maggie to always be hospitable. She should have yelled at the bitch, not offer pleasantries.

Kathy gave an impression of the Mona Lisa and scurried away, leaving Maggie furious that she had been kind at all.

Then there was Edith, who invited Maggie to lunch only to sit for one full hour saying practically nothing. Maggie tried to start a conversation several times with the woman, but Edith responded with an endless stream of one-word answers.

"I've got Frederick tonight." Amazingly, Edith had finally managed a sentence.

"That should be fun. What are y'all going to do?"

Edith shrugged. "There's a wonderful National Geographic special on penguins."

Maggie tried to imagine her wild five-year-old sitting quietly on Edith's couch watching a nature documentary. She shook off the disturbing image. "You know what you should do?" she said brightly. "Go bowling."

At least Maggie had finally made Edith laugh. That was a first. For all her clever jokes and expressions, Edith never cracked a smile in her presence. But this blunder had cheered her up for sure.

"Are you kidding?" she had asked, then sobering added, "You are kidding, aren't you?"

Maggie frantically searched her brain for some Mason-Dixon rule on bowling, but didn't Norm belong to a bowling league on *Cheers?* Surely, Yankees bowled.

She still fumed recalling the conversation. What was so dang funny about her suggestion?

"Malick, do you bowl?"

The Webmaster paused in his programming. "Sometimes."

"It's not a crazy suggestion then? I mean, people in Maine bowl, right?"

Malick grinned, causing a deep indentation in his right cheek. The guy was cute, if one preferred the quirky, silent type who liked foreign films and science fiction. "Yeah, people in Maine bowl. Why?"

Maggie shrugged, wondering if she was making more of it than she should. She really had a bee in her bonnet today. "Something Edith said."

Malick turned in his chair, appearing as if he wanted to ask Maggie a question, but the words got stuck on the end of his tongue. He scratched his head and frowned, then rubbed his hands together.

"Something on your mind?" Maggie asked.

He slid a nervous hand through his hair, which pulled strands out of the tie in back, making him seem more frazzled than usual. "Does she have a boyfriend?"

Well, shut my mouth, Maggie thought, Edith has a beau. "Not that I know of."

Malick digested this information, nodded his head with a grin and returned to his work. This could be good, Maggie thought. This definitely could be good.

Just then the phone rang, but the voice on the other end did nothing to relieve her blue funk. More than likely, he was the cause of it all.

"Hey," Colin said, imitating her.

"Hey," she said back. What, Yankees didn't greet people that way either?

"Are you busy?"

"I'm helping with your website."

She really wasn't, had finished the feature pages a half hour ago, but she didn't want Colin thinking she was wasting time at his magazine. Which only made her madder considering she worked at least fifty hours that week.

"I'm getting ready to board the plane at LaGuardia, was wondering if you'd pick me up at the airport."

Maggie needed a second to swallow this. They lived together and her retrieving her roommate made sense — sort of. It would, that is, if he could stand the sight of her. "Sure."

"If it's no trouble."

"What else do I have to do?"

A pause ensued and Maggie mentally kicked herself for sounding so snide. The man had given her a job under the craziest of circumstances, why was she being so rude? Still, it had been three weeks and the combination of Colin's suspicions and her lack of job security was getting under her skin.

"What time are you getting in?" she asked.

"Seven fifteen. American Airlines." His accented voice sounded throaty and amiable, like it had when they had shared scotch in Pittsburgh and she imagined him owning cranberry farms. Thinking of how they bantered flirtations that afternoon made Maggie shiver. It seemed a million years ago.

"I'll be there with bells on."

Maggie swore she could hear him smile. "Great," he said, more than likely laughing at her choice of words like everyone else.

"It's an expression my mother used to say," she said in defense.

"Uh, huh."

"You Mainers sure talk a lot, did you know that?"

"Ah-yah," he answered in typical Maine fashion, although Maggie knew he was imitating a stereotype.

"Funny. Do you want me to use my car or yours?"

"Mine. And bring your appetite."

Before she had time to inquire, Colin made a quick farewell as the boarding announcement was heard in the background. She hung up the phone wondering what he meant. And just why he sounded so happy for a change.

Two hours later, still confused, she watched a jovial Colin walk off the plane.

"Hey," he said again with a teasing smile.

Maggie was tired of being the brunt of jokes regarding her accent. She decided to imitate a Mainer.

She said nothing.

Colin looked like a hound dog finding a bear instead of a rabbit. She could almost see his ears turn back.

"Are you hungry?" he asked, as they headed toward the parking lot, his week's clothes conveniently in one large carry-on bag.

Was she hearing right? The man who had spoken less than two words to her in the past three weeks wanted to have dinner with her? Or maybe this was the moment he would let her down easy and tell her to pack her own bags.

"Why?"

Colin laughed. "Because then you could put food in your mouth?"

Smart ass. "I know what it means. Why do you want to know?"

When they reached the lobby doors, Colin paused, staring at her as if she had lost her mind. Which she probably had, considering her mood. "Has something happened?"

Yeah, she thought, noticing how cute his mussed hair looked and how his tweed jacket sported leather circles over the elbows, her typical cranberry professor. Three weeks, exasperating circumstances involving suspicions and doubt and she still dreamed about him at night.

"Kathy came by looking for you today."

He didn't bat an eye. "Great."

Was that sarcasm she heard? Dear God, she prayed, let it be sarcasm. "She wants you to call her."

He ignored the remark. "I repeat, are you hungry?"

"Yes."

"Good. Can we go now?"

"Fine."

They marched to the car, a sharp coastal wind cutting through her flannel-lined raincoat. Maggie pulled her collar up around her ears, but it did little to relieve the dampness permeating her bones.

"Where's your coat?" Colin asked, comfortable in his tweed jacket and underlining vest. From everything Maggie had seen so far, maple syrup ran through the veins of Yankees. They were rarely cold, although they constantly assured others that preparation was the key.

"This is it."

"No, I mean a real coat."

Maggie sent him a side-glance, careful not to move too much and expose any skin. "I live in Atlanta. It doesn't get that cold there."

When they arrived at the car, Colin threw down his bag, and then leaned in so close Maggie could smell that dang wonderful aftershave. "I'll let you in on a secret, Maggie." He leaned in closer, making her pulse quicken before whispering, "It gets really cold here."

He was trying to be funny with his usual deadpan face. She had noticed him do this a dozen times with his family and Kathy, all who failed to grasp his wry humor. But there was nothing funny about winter in Maine. Not if she wasn't going to be here to see it.

"What's the point?" she asked him. "I may not be here when it gets cold, remember?"

Colin straightened, a frown playing his forehead. He started to speak, but the familiar frustration rose in her chest and she thought it best to retreat to a safe position. She handed him the keys and headed to the passenger side.

After he threw the bags in the back, he unlocked her door. Then they rode in silence toward the waterfront, the heater full blast.

"Has anyone fed you a lobster dinner yet?"

"No, no one has fed me a lob-stah."

Colin grasped his chest and gaped at her. "Was that a joke?"

She sent him a don't-mess-with-me glance, but she felt a hint of a smile curl up in her lips.

"I know just the place. Great chow-dah too."

She folded her arms. "Are you putting me on?"

Colin laughed, his face lighting up for the first time in weeks. "No, 'fraid I really speak this way."

"How come Jake didn't?"

All semblance of happiness vanished in a flash. She shouldn't have brought him up. "He spent a lot of time away. Besides, he wasn't proud of being from Madison."

"Why not? It's slice of heaven."

Colin studied her hard, waiting for a light to turn green. "You really think so?"

Slowly thawing out, Maggie forced her muscles to relax and her jaw to unlock. "Are you kidding? It's postcard perfect. Every day is a new adventure. I love the way the mist hugs the valley in the morning and all you can see are the rooftops and the church steeple. Last night, when this cold weather came through, the fireplaces were fired up and it smelled like the eighteenth century. Not to mention the magazine office. I mean, it *is* the eighteenth century."

And something she would eventually have to give up.

Maggie stared out the window as they approached downtown Portland and the waterfront with its many cafes, quaint shops and cobblestone streets. Maine really was the most charming state, an endless display of calendar photos. But perhaps it wasn't meant to be.

Colin parked near a secluded restaurant close enough to the harbor she could hear the halyards rattling against the masts. Colin tapped her arm when she grasped the passenger side door handle. "Wait here," he commanded.

Maggie searched through the frosted windshield to find him,

only to have her door open and Colin offer her his hand. "Mademoiselle."

"Madame," she reminded him.

That pinched look appeared again on his forehead, but Colin didn't falter, taking her hand and leading her to the front door of an establishment named "Charlie's." The maitre'd instantly recognized Colin and began a conversation as he led them to a table overlooking the water on one side while a roaring fireplace warmed the other. Colin offered Maggie the chair next to the fire, a seat that also faced the windows and the breathtaking view of Casco Bay.

"My dad used to take me here," he whispered as he pushed her chair into the table.

Being reminded of Gavin Parnell only soured her temper, even though she sat at the most romantic spot she had ever seen. As much as Gavin had encouraged her in her early journalism career, she wondered if he'd approve of her sitting there at the family table now. As usual, she felt she was trespassing on Parnell property.

"Would you care for something to drink?" the maitre'd asked.

"Two scotches," Colin answered.

Maggie's eyes shot up. So they were back to scotch?

"What happened?" she repeated, wondering what turned him back into an agreeable human being.

The answer came so sudden she swore she could hear the bricks landing on her skull. "Of course." She shook her head, wondering why she hadn't figured it out before. "The private detective told you I was clean. That I didn't brainwash your cousin into marriage."

Looking as guilty as he knew he was, Colin said nothing as two glasses of scotch were placed before them. Maggie rubbed her eyes, weary of so many things she didn't know which one to choose.

"Pretty boring, isn't it?" She took a gulp of the alcohol, enjoying its burn. "My pathetic, innocent life."

Colin, the stern publisher of the past three weeks, met her gaze then, which caused her to shiver. "What did you expect me to do? We barely know each other and you said it yourself that you were married less than an hour before Jake disappeared and you never saw him again. Am I'm supposed to hand over my magazine to you, no questions asked?"

He had a point, one Maggie agreed with from the beginning. She didn't know why she was being so difficult. "Of course not. I don't blame you."

He picked up his glass and tilted it in her direction. "Yes, you do."

He had a point there as well. "Yes, I do," she admitted.

Colin took a long drink of his scotch, stared at the harbor and exhaled. In that brief moment, with the firelight casting shadows about his features, Maggie saw a man with the world on his shoulders.

"I'm sorry," she said. "I haven't had much job security in my life. Hell, outside of college I haven't lived anywhere longer than two years. It's wearing on me. Especially after all that's happened with Jake."

He ran a lazy finger around the rim of his glass. "Are you happy here?"

Maggie felt a lump rise in her throat. She was too happy at the magazine, that was her problem.

"My mother says you're the best assistant she's ever had and Malick said production is ahead of schedule."

"Your mother is too kind and we're only a few days…"

"The copy desk was thrilled with your help last week on the almanac. We were close to missing deadline, which would have cost a small fortune."

Maggie sucked in one side of her cheek. "I doubt I'm the reason for that."

Was it the firelight casting a glow in his eyes or was Colin softening up again? He appeared genuinely concerned about her staying.

"Are you happy here?" he asked again.

Now, it was Maggie's turn to exhale. "Yes."

"Then stop worrying about job security."

With that announcement, Colin signaled the waiter and ordered two cups of clam chowder, a scallop appetizer and steamed lobsters to follow. Maggie had always loved lobster, but had only tried the Florida kind — the ones with antennas where the claws should be — and all the locals seemed to think calling those creatures lobsters was akin to blasphemy.

Warmed by the fire and the scotch entering her veins, Maggie relaxed and slipped deeper into her chair. Outside the fishing boats bobbed in the harbor as the ferry announced its trip for Peaks Island and silently left the dock.

It was all so tempting. Could it be she had finally found a home?

Doubt gripped her like a lobster claw. Maggie straightened in her chair. "I can't do this."

"Do what?" He motioned toward her glass, nonverbally asking if she wanted another scotch.

Maggie shook her head. "I don't belong here." She slid up even more. "Colin, have your lawyers draw up the papers and I'll sign my stake in the magazine back to you."

He stared at her dumbstruck and she could only imagine the thoughts swirling around in his head. "Why?"

"Because I'm tired of moving around and I want to get on with my life. And I don't deserve any of this. Your father was right, I'm not Yankee material."

Now it was Colin's turn to relax. He dropped back in his chair and motioned to the waiter to bring a bottle of wine. She started to object, but he ignored her, gazing at her the way he did in Pittsburgh, with a sly twinkle in his eye. "Just what is Yankee material, Maggie?"

"Well, for one thing, y'all talk funny."

Colin scratched his head, trying to suppress a smile. "Granted."

Maggie groaned. Talk about the fire calling the kettle black. "I know. I talk funny too. But yesterday this guy calls up wanting to place an ad and for some reason he got me. And I didn't understand a word he said. It wasn't a few 'ahs' here and there, it sounded like he had a mouth full of cotton."

Colin nodded his head, a full-fledge smile still hiding under his polite grin. "Understandable."

"I'm serious, Colin. He got mad and hung up. I may have lost you a client."

"Doubtful. More than likely he was calling about the piece we did on wooden boats. You write about the best way to build something and everyone in New England calls claiming their way is best."

He leaned forward studying her, resting his elbows on the table and rubbing fingers against his lips. The image nearly undid her, which reignited her resolve.

"I'll stay until you hire someone," she said firmly.

"Because of one call?"

"Because of lots of things."

"Name three."

"Bowling for one."

Colin's eyes widened. "Bowling?"

Maggie grimaced, thinking how stupid that sounded. But she didn't know where to begin.

"You all talk different, you eat different, you have different words for things that I haven't a clue what they mean. How am I going to work for a magazine that brands itself as the 'heart of New England' when I don't even know the lingo? When I have a Southern accent, for heaven sakes."

Colin shook his head as if trying to follow her logic. "And I can't teach you any of this?"

Maggie imagined him teaching her lots of things and shivered. He started to remove his jacket. "You're always cold."

"I'm fine." She spoke too harshly, but it was all so aggravating.

"It's something else, isn't it?" His voice was calm and soft, like maple syrup pouring off a tree.

She gazed out the window, watching the ferry disappear into the darkness of the bay. "I live with you," she whispered. "Even if you're not there, I still live with you."

It took a few seconds for him to digest this statement and she waited for the questions. Hell, she wasn't sure what she meant by that. Instead, he reached over and took her hand, slowly rolling his thumb along the inside of her palm.

"Maggie." He stared at their hands, deep in thought. "I have never enjoyed time with a woman as much as I did in that airport lounge with you."

She gulped, forcing herself to exhale. If only he would stop plying her palm that way, his thumb massaging her lifeline like a lover, she could object to the turn in conversation. Instead, she agreed, whispering, "I did too."

Now, it was his turn to exhale. He glanced up, a sad smile telling volumes. "I'd say it's not meant to be, considering everything, but I don't want to lose you."

When she started to object, thinking of a million reasons why he should, he held up a hand. "I shouldn't be telling you this — my mother will be furious; she meant it as a surprise — but she has a friend with a guest house on her property and they are fixing it up for you to live in."

Maggie opened her mouth, but she truly was speechless. How his mother could arrange such a thing, despite not knowing if she was a fraud out to steal their family business, floored her.

"If you like it, of course."

She forced her mouth shut. Could this work? Could she really stay? And what about Kathy?

"It won't be ready for a while. A few weeks perhaps."

Reality came crashing back. A few weeks meant living with Colin all that time. Living with him, not being able to have him, watching him steal away to Kathy's in the middle of the night.

"I should go back to Atlanta, let you have your life back."

"I don't want my life back."

It was said with such force, Maggie wasn't sure it was Colin talking. There was a determination in his eyes, something raw and longing.

"We agreed you would stay three weeks," he said, more calmly. "And those three weeks are up today," she reminded him.

"Are they really?" He honestly seemed surprised. "Okay, then how about staying until Christmas? The job is yours, there's no question there. But at least give it to December to decide if you want to go back to Atlanta. Everything will be in probate for a while, so we can't talk legalities until then anyway."

Two waiters arrived, one carrying soup and another a bottle of wine. As they approached the table, Maggie pulled her hand free.

"What about Kathy?"

Colin didn't bat an eye. "What about her?"

She created a pattern in the tablecloth with her knife. "I don't want to cramp your style." Sure, she did, but she couldn't be that honest.

"Cramp my style?" At this, Colin almost laughed. "I have no style, Maggie. Just work and family."

"Right, and you staying out all night at Kathy's was about work and family." Damn, she really didn't want to go there. She sounded like a jealous fool.

He leaned in close, a smile teasing those inviting lips. "Believe it or not, I went over there to check on her and she had gone to bed. The house was all dark, so I closed my eyes for a second and fell asleep in my car, didn't wake up to the next morning."

Maggie didn't know how to respond to that. He appeared sincere, but it was the craziest explanation she had ever heard. But if she denounced it for the lie it appeared to be, she would look the jealous lover.

"Stay until Christmas," Colin repeated, adding with a grin, "You won't be sick of the cold weather by then. Otherwise, I would have suggested March."

Something milky white and smelling of clams was placed before her, along with a platter of scallops wrapped in bacon and smothered in butter. It all looked so delicious. But could she keep her hands off the dessert, mainly the cranberry professor sitting across the table?

"Christmas then."

Colin brightened, but she knew he doubted the working arrangement as much as she did. Still, a twinkle of hope glittered in his eyes, a sparkle that lit her own fire of optimism.

Would it be possible for everything to work out? It was all so

complicated. She wanted the job, she wanted to stay. She especially wanted the man sitting across from her. But she had the
Parnells' feelings to consider. Not to mention that she never, ever
wanted to do anything foolish and impulsive with a man again,
and that included flirting in airport lounges and Portland harbor
restaurants.

The second waiter poured them each a glass of wine after Colin
approved and the two men bowed away. Colin lifted his glass in a
toast and she tentatively touched her glass to his.

"Let's start over, shall we?"

She wasn't sure what he meant by that, but she sipped her mer-
lot as he did his. When he placed his glass back on the table, Colin
rose and came to her side, stretching out a hand.

"I'd like to introduce myself. Colin Theodore Parnell, publisher
of *Yankee Living* magazine."

Maggie couldn't help but smile and meet his handshake. "Maggie Delta Mallory… uh, Webster."

They shook, arriving at a truce.

"Welcome to the family, Maggie."

Chapter Thirteen

COLIN WOKE TO THE SMELL of coffee brewing and bacon cooking, knowing that Maggie had risen early, as usual. Coffee would be nice, just the way she made it, too — strong, hot and with "pet milk."

He smiled thinking of her quirks, including adding that thick, sweet canned milk to coffee. Surprisingly, most of them actually tasted good. Yet, God only knew what he was in for this morning. Before they made their goodnights and traipsed off to their separate bedrooms the night before, she had warned she was going to make something special — something "Southern" — for breakfast.

Arriving home after a week's absence meant an endless pile of work sitting on his desk at the magazine but at that moment, Colin refused to think about work. It was Saturday morning, breakfast was cooking, and he was going to join the rest of the world and take the day off. Or at least die trying.

Besides, if his instincts told him right…

Colin threw open the curtains. Gazing out on the scene before him like Scrooge on Christmas Day after his visits with the spirits, Colin absorbed the brilliant spectacle with a smile. He hadn't missed it, after all. There was still time.

He threw on his jeans and college sweatshirt and headed for the kitchen, following the smells that grew more intense and more delicious the closer he came. He found Maggie in her bathrobe, pouring a cup of something white into boiling water. When she sensed his presence, she turned quickly, hiding the box.

"Hey." A blush spread up her neck into her cheeks and it was everything Colin could do not to grab her terrycloth lapels and kiss her soundly.

"You're so wicked cute."

He hadn't meant to say it out loud, but he couldn't help himself. Those enormous brown eyes entreating him from beneath overgrown bangs were driving him crazy. And that sweet smile. How was it possible he had ever doubted her?

"What?" she asked, her smile fading, as her gaze turned serious. They had made an agreement, after all, one that didn't include attraction.

Colin quickly recovered. "I said, 'What are you hiding?' "

The smile and the blush returned. "Nothing. Go sit down."

He did as he was told, finding a placemat, cup of hot coffee and crispy bacon waiting. He delved into the bacon, realizing he was enormously hungry.

"Hey," Maggie called out from the stove. "Save some for the…"

"For the what?" Colin waited until she turned back to her cooking and stole another piece.

"You'll see."

"What are you doing today?" he mumbled between bites.

Maggie grabbed her coffee and inched close to the table, careful not to veer too far away from the pot that was making unusual gurgling noises. "I thought I might go work on the Design House."

"You're going to install the water heater?" He looked up at her askance, wondering if he had bacon traces on his face.

"Funny." She reached over and wiped his chin with her thumb and he resisted the urge to grab that hand and pull her into his lap. How on earth was he going to last until Christmas? Even if his mom finalized the guesthouse and Maggie moved out, they would still be working in the same office, attending magazine and family functions together. Whatever resolve he had felt the night before was now fading in the bright sunlight.

"Have you looked outside yet?"

Maggie peered out the back porch window. "Gorgeous day."

"That, my dear Rebel, is an understatement."

She squinted, her gaze roving across his enormous backyard and its acres of maples, sumac, birch and tupelos in various shades of autumnal color. She peered back, looking like a schoolgirl hoping her answer is correct. "It's the peak?"

Colin laughed. "Ayuh," making the stereotypical New England expression sound between the real thing and a "Duh!"

Maggie looked again, then rushed off to the pot that now sounded possessed. "How can you tell it's the peak?"

How can you not? Colin thought. "Isn't it obvious?"

Maggie stirred her cauldron, then poured something white and semi-liquid on to plates, adding a giant slab of butter.

"I thought it was impressive when it all began." She shook salt and pepper on to the creation. "It did get better every week, amazingly. But every day someone said it wasn't the peak, I couldn't see how all this amazing beauty could improve."

"Well, now is the peak and it's all downhill from here. After this, it doesn't get warm again until June."

Maggie turned around with a start, two steaming plates in her hands. "June?"

Colin shrugged. "Easter. June. Something like that."

"You're putting me on." She placed a plate in front of him, standing back proud with a mischievous grin.

He recognized the white glob immediately. "It's grits."

Her attitude shifted and he mentally kicked himself. "I, ah, had it before." She looked like a balloon caught on electrical wire, its hot air slowing leaking out. "But, I doubt it was good as this," he quickly added.

Maggie recovered, placing her hands on her hips. "When did you have grits?"

"My best friend went to Georgia Tech, remember? I visited him a couple of times."

Colin picked up a fork and stirred the butter around the plate, making the white gritty substance turn yellow with specks of black pepper. He took one bite and rolled his eyes. "Definitely the best I've ever had."

She punched him lightly on the arm. "Liar."

"It is. The kind I had was lumpy."

She sat down, stirring her own. "You should add bacon. My mother used to serve it that way and we'd crumble it up and mix it in."

"Great idea." Colin took a slice and did just that. Grits wasn't what he'd call tasty, but the mixture of starch, butter and salt was a nice wake-me-up, especially on an autumn day that carried a bite in the breeze.

"What did you think of Georgia?"

She asked the question expectantly, as if his opinion of her home state mattered. If she were as proud of her homeland as he was of his, he understood that feeling well. "I only saw Atlanta and I was quite impressed, beautiful city. The people were friendly too. I was amazed at how friendly they were."

"Best people on the face of the earth," she said between bites.

"Well, I know a few Mainers who would disagree."

"They don't talk much, do they? Mainers I mean."

Colin shook his head, wanting to laugh thinking how strange that must be to someone who did. "No, they aren't touchy-feely either."

This stopped her cold. She gazed up at him like a deer in head-lights. "What are you saying?"

Damn, he didn't mean it that way. "Nothing. I noticed that you like to touch people more than New Englanders tend to do. That's all."

She considered this, looking off in the distance lost in thought. "I did notice how y'all don't hug and kiss each other much. Not even family."

"We see each other every day."

"So?"

Now that Colin thought about it, when was the last time he hugged and kissed his mother, his sisters? "You hug and kiss your family every day?"

Maggie had a mouthful of grits, so she nodded, then said after swallowing, "My mom and I used to do the hugging sway every morning."

Colin smiled. This he had to hear. "Okay, I'm game."

Maggie stood, wiping her mouth and placing her napkin on the table. Then she motioned for him to do the same.

"Give me a hug," she ordered him.

This was dangerous territory, but Colin complied, standing up, wrapping his arms about her waist and pulling her close. Maggie snaked her arms around his neck. "Now, sway."

She giggled as they swayed back and forth, Colin completely ignorant of what this all meant.

"People used to think we were crazy, but I think my mom was in the habit of doing this with me when I was a baby and never stopped."

He had to admit, the swaying hug felt nice. But then being this close, feeling the way her body melded into his charged him like a bolt of lightning.

"Mom always said that hugs make you healthy. You should have them as often as possible."

"I'm all for that," he said softly, slowly pulling her close enough to catch the fragrant scent of her hair.

She rose on her toes to move her head above his shoulder, so Colin let his hands drift across her back. Maggie slipped both arms about his neck then, while Colin closed his eyes and nestled his face in her hair, pulling her tighter against his chest. Suddenly, the swaying stopped and they stood in the middle of the kitchen embracing.

He knew he should move away, but damned if he had the power to do anything but hold her close. It all felt so natural, so right — like breathing.

Just then Maggie exhaled and released her hold. She pulled back, resting her feet back on the floor and subconsciously pulling her hair behind an ear. "Well, that's how it's done."

She started to move away, but Colin grabbed her hand, pulling her back into his chest and kissing her soundly. She tasted of condensed milk and coffee, tangy and sweet. A little slice of heaven.

It all unfolded so fast, Colin hadn't allowed himself to fully take advantage of the situation, which, if his logical mind had been at work, shouldn't have happened to begin with. Maggie had fallen upon him with one hand braced against his chest and she used that advantage to gently push away. He had only a few seconds to savor her sweet Southern lips before they were gone.

She glanced up at him expectantly, as if he had a perfectly good explanation for what he just did. Outside of pure lust, he had none.

"You said Yankees should hug and kiss their families more," he said with a grin.

Before she had time to react, he placed both hands on her shoulders and turned her around. "Go take a shower and get ready. I'll clean up in here."

With a little push, he had her heading down the hall but not before she turned back and sent him a scrutinizing look while sucking in her lower lip. Colin nearly audibly groaned. If she didn't get out of his sight soon, he would lose any semblance of control he had managed to gather.

"Away with you," he called. "New England's peak is calling."

She disappeared inside her bedroom, closing the door behind her. He half expected to hear the lock clicking shut.

Colin braced his hands on the back of the chair and hung his head. Suddenly, Christmas loomed a million years away. If she decided to stay — which he was going to damn sure talk her into doing — how would he manage to keep his hands off her all that time? How long would be enough before his family accepted a union between he and Jake's widow, if Maggie accepted him? Something else he had to talk her into.

Thinking back on the kiss, he knew that wouldn't be difficult. Even though their lips had met for only a brief time, in that second Colin felt the longing that was kissing him back.

He had to be patient. He had to go slow. He had to convince her he wasn't Jake, that a commitment with him meant just that.

One day at a time, he commanded himself. He had to take it one day at a time.

"So, where are we again?" Maggie glanced at the map spread out haphazardly in her lap. Once they had left the ocean side of Maine, she hadn't a clue where they were heading.

Without taking his gaze from the road, Colin pointed to a small speck in a tangle of roads. "We're coming into town right now."

Sure enough, a sign appeared. Norway, population 4,611.

"Boy, we have been traveling far to get all the way to Norway."

He sent her one of those looks, the kind her dad used to bestow when she told a corny joke. It almost made her laugh, but another sign appeared that garnered her attention.

"How the hell do you...?"

Without a beat, Colin announced the name of the lake like honey slipping off a tongue. "Lake Pennessewassee."

She was speechless. She couldn't have pronounced that if her life depended on it. Colin gave her a smug look, almost daring her to try.

"That's better than that funny county name."

"Androscoggin?"

Maggie had to laugh. The only thing funnier than naming towns with oscots and quoddys and English names where only half of the syllables were pronounced was hearing natives speak them aloud.

"Do you think we could stop in IthinkIhavetofindapoddy?"

Now it was Colin's turn to laugh. "Good one."

"Thanks." She had to admit, it was better than the stupid Norway joke.

He pulled into a mom-and-pop store off the side of the road, the kind with screen doors on the front and chairs out front for sitting and spinning. Maggie had to blink, noticing the signs for RC Cola and Pabst Blue Ribbon. She could have been driving in Mississippi if she didn't know better.

"I'll only be a minute."

Before she could exit the car, Colin grabbed her elbow. "Don't let them know where you're from," he said sternly. "They don't take to foreigners around here."

"Cute." She slid the sunglasses up her nose and headed for the nearest restroom, realizing cute described everything about that man. She rubbed the place where he had touched her elbow, feeling as if she'd been singed. The man sent her skin — and various internal places — burning with a seductive fire. She thought to recall that kiss, that ever so brief but ever so magnificent kiss, but she didn't dare attempt to travel down that enticing road. It had taken her a ten-minute cold shower to shift her heart rate back to neutral.

"That man is going to be the death of me."

An elderly gentleman sitting on the porch looked up. "Pardon?"

"Just rattling on to myself again. Sorry if I disturbed you, sir."

The man stared as if she had grown horns. Maybe they really weren't partial to outsiders. They were out in the country, after all. Isn't that what people did in the middle of nowhere, kidnap visitors stopping by? Or maybe she had seen way too many horror movies.

Just then Colin passed her on the way to the store. Ever so slightly, he hummed a stanza from *Dueling Banjos* in her ear. The seated man gave her a harsh stare so Maggie followed Colin inside, trying hard not to laugh.

"That wasn't very nice," she said over his shoulder.

"Yeah, wrong state."

It took her a minute before she got it; the film *Deliverance*, about several men on a river outing attacked by local residents, was set in a remote spot in northern Georgia. She slapped him good-naturedly on the arm.

He grabbed two sodas from the cooler. "Touchy-feely woman."

"So y'all don't play-hit each other either?"

She nearly tripped over him as he paused in the aisle. "Don't say y'all in here," he whispered. "They might catch on."

He placed the cans on the counter and handed the woman a

five. Then he turned and punched Maggie in the arm.

She opened her mouth to object, but he had that look again, that sly, mischievous smile like he wanted to kiss her. You're treading in dangerous waters, her little voice warned.

"I'm going to find the potty," she said, inching back.

"You need a key," the woman behind the counter said, handing Maggie a piece of wood carved into a maple leaf with a key dangling off the end. "'Round the cor-nah."

"Thank you kindly, ma'am," Maggie said in her best Southern accent, sending Colin a daring look and hurrying out the door.

As the screen door slammed behind her, she mentally berated herself. "Stop flirting with him," she commanded herself, which made the porch man look up, no doubt wondering if those horror films about crazy people rolling into country towns had any truth to them.

After she took care of business — and bought a few moose postcards while returning the key — they were back on the road, heading to the White Mountain National Forest and upwards towards the Lake Country. Colin insisted on showing her prime fall foliage, but it all looked spectacular to her. Every corner of the road, every top of a ridge provided new extravagant displays of stunning color. It was the world's oldest cliché, but the views truly took her breath away.

"Look at that," Maggie shouted as they turned another bend and spotted a collection of trees looking as if they had burst into flame. "You have to let me take a picture of that."

"It won't do it justice, trust me."

"But…" She knew she wasn't capable of truly capturing this experience and that the magazine had stacks of professional photographs she was welcome to take home, frame and hang on her wall. Still, Maggie wanted to seal the moment, capture the day that belonged only to the two of them and keep it safe. "Just one?"

Colin slowed down and pulled off the road next to several SUVs with Massachusetts tags. "You're going to see this again next year, you know."

She hesitated, thinking of how wonderful enjoying seasons year after year in one place would be. Still, she wasn't ready to commit to anything, including Colin, so she left the car and joined the group taking pictures at the stone fence.

As she snapped photos of the brilliant crimson tree Colin had called a pin cherry, she heard him turn off the ignition and exit the car. "Here," he said, taking the camera from her hands. "Go stand over by the fence."

He took a photo while Maggie smiled beneath the most gorgeous tree she had ever seen – until she saw the next one, of course – and then one of the Massachusetts tourists approached them. "Want me to take one of you both?"

She swore she saw Colin smirk, but he handed him the camera, then joined Maggie at the fence.

"Not used to being a tourist in your home state?" she asked, trying hard not to giggle.

"Shut up and smile," he said before placing an arm about her shoulders and grinning for the camera.

An older woman who was traveling with the tourists watched the interaction, seeming to enjoy their playful report. When they thanked the man for taking their picture, the older woman approached them, grinning like she held some great secret. "You make a nice couple," she said.

Maggie didn't know how to answer that except to offer a nervous thanks.

"Are you off on a romantic weekend?" the woman asked with a sly glint in her eyes. "Foliage time is the perfect getaway, isn't it?"

"Yes, ma'am." Maggie hadn't a clue what the perfect getaway weekend was, considering her limited experience with men, not to mention vacations that weren't the result of being laid off. Right now, her idea of a hot romantic weekend was anywhere with the man driving the car. But she couldn't think about that.

"Are you coming?"

Obviously, Colin had found the conversation equally uncomfortable, for he was back at the car ready to go.

"Have a great time," Maggie said to the woman, climbing into the Explorer.

"You, too." Her eyes twinkled as she added, "Fall foliage makes for June weddings."

Maggie took her seat as Colin roared the car into action, no doubt alarmed at hearing *that* particular comment. They drove for several miles without speaking, the woman's remarks hanging in the air between them. Heavens, did she have to mention weddings?

Maggie stared out the window as they passed acres of brilliant foliage, an occasional grouping of pine trees breaking up God's magnificent palette with its mediocre forest green. She took pity on the modest pine, with its straight trunk and awkward branches reaching out into the world like a clumsy teenager. She knew how those pines felt. How could a tree, so common and welcome in her home state of Georgia, possibly fit in among the majestic russets, coppers, scarlets and peach?

Still, a perfect stranger said they looked good together. After that scrumptious hug earlier that morning, she knew they certainly fit together as well. And it wasn't the same as Jake — Maggie knew that for sure — even though Jake's kisses certainly curled her toes. With Jake, Maggie was definitely a common pine among maples, happy to live in his shade. With Colin, she imagined them more like two oaks growing side by side, their roots intertwining.

She shook off the thought. What difference did it make what tree she resembled? She and Colin were worlds apart and his family believed her to be the grieving widow of their nephew and cousin. 'Nuf said.

That didn't stop her from slowly turning her gaze sideways, studying Colin's profile as he drove. His hair needed a cut, but she liked the way it curled up at his collar, as if daring its owner to step outside the line of propriety. His nose seemed to offer a similar juxtaposition – classic yet slightly turned as if his Irish heritage insisted he remember his roots. But those lips... Maggie sucked in a breath thinking how they had kissed her that morning, how one simple gesture had sent shockwaves traveling down her spine.

Colin must have heard her gasp, for he turned. "Have you seen enough? Want to turn back?"

Did she? Her head said yes, but her heart wasn't listening.

"I don't think one could ever see enough, but yes, I guess we should turn back."

They rode in silence as dusk settled over the land, Maggie wondering if she would ever see the New England fall again. Then Colin reached behind his seat and retrieved a small, rectangular box. "I meant to give this to you last night."

She accepted the box, held together with a bright pink bow. "What is it?"

"It's a picture of my Civil War ancestor." He sent her an impatient look. "Open it."

Maggie untied the bow, then pulled the top off to find dozens of business cards inside. When she raised one up, a lump the size of a pumpkin lodged in her throat.

"If you don't approve of the title, we can change that. And remind me first thing Monday to get you covered under our health insurance."

Associate editor. *Yankee Living.* Not only had he asked her to stay, but he had taken the time to produce business cards. With her name on it. Maggie Delta Parnell, Associate Editor.

She started to speak but the pumpkin wasn't budging. And somehow, the words on the cards and the surrounding foliage all started to blur.

"Why are you doing this?" she finally asked. "You of all people."

Colin reached over and tucked her hair behind an ear, then let a finger briefly caress her cheek before taking the wheel again. "Maybe because I know you better than anyone else."

Maggie cringed thinking of what he must have unearthed during the past three weeks. Lots and lots of nothing and endless layoffs.

Colin must have read her mind for he tapped her chin. "You're a talented journalist, Miss Georgia. I'm hiring you because of that and nothing else."

Again, the moment rendered her speechless, the pumpkin reappearing, but Colin didn't skip a beat.

"Okay, lesson time. What do you want to know about New

England?"

She swallowed, trying to resume her composure. "Pardon?"

"You said you wanted to know everything."

She actually said she failed to fit in, but if he wanted to teach her, she was ready to learn.

"What's 'Down East' mean?"

Colin smiled, making his laugh lines appear. "Maine stretches over the Atlantic in the middle and then straight up to Canada. Down East is the area that's down from the northern part of the state and over to the east. Make sense?"

Maggie peered down at the map and noticed how Maine resembled a left-handed mitten and Down East the spot beneath the thumb. "Yeah, it makes sense."

"Next."

"What do natives mean by black fly season?"

Colin groaned a little. "Once the snow melts and it warms up, we are inundated with black flies. Horrible little pests."

"So it's a summer thing?"

"Well, we have a joke here in Maine. We have two seasons – winter and mud. Flies come with the mud."

Maggie gazed back out at the gorgeous scenery. "I hardly think you have two seasons."

"Wait until winter and you might change your mind."

That thought gave her pause. "Is it really cold until June?"

At this, the mischievous look returned. "I'm not saying."

They turned a corner and found a group of kids rolling in someone's mound of raked leaves. The children laughed as they threw leaves into the air and at each other.

"Anything else?" Colin asked as he spied the festive group off the side of the road.

"What does wicked mean?"

At this Colin laughed and pulled over. Maggie looked up at the sudden stop, but she didn't have to ask when he turned off the engine.

"That's one wicked pile of leaves," he said with a grin.

Tossing the map — and all worries — aside, Maggie hopped

out of the car and raced Colin to the virgin pile of leaves the children had yet to destroy.

Chapter Fourteen

FOR THE LIFE OF HIM, Colin never understood why he disliked Thanksgiving. There was plenty of good food and wine and later football to enjoy on TV. So why did he dread lounging around his mother's house all day, then indulging on fatty foods for hours?

Maybe because it took days to get his desk cleared to have one lousy eight hours of vacation — in the middle of the week, no less. Or perhaps because it was the same food served year after year, which might not have been an issue if his mother didn't serve the exact same thing every other Sunday at the "family dinners."

After his father had died, Bonnie had insisted on meeting every two weeks, serving heavy meals of ham and turkey while the entire family gathered around her table. The dinners were an effort to keep communication open, she had said, and to reassure everyone that the family was intact, that nothing had changed and that everyone was there for one another in their time of pain.

Truth was, each of them dealt with the grief in their own way, communication not being one of them. And Jake avoided the dinners nine out of ten.

As usual, Colin ended up being the male cornerstone of the events, running to the store for extra cans of cream of mushroom soup or making a packie run for more wine, helping cook and carve the massive bird or ham and cleaning up the endless pots and pans required to create such a meal. It wasn't that Colin didn't enjoy his family's company or the meals, he was tired of the same routine. On several occasions, he offered to change the menu or take the family out to a restaurant — his treat — but Bonnie insisted that routine was good, routine was what they needed.

Only, time had passed, and as far as Colin was concerned, the family routine was going to bore him into an early grave. He would never miss eating turkey or ham again.

When his mother placed the traditional ham on the table, along-side the regular candied yams, green bean casserole and mashed potatoes, a groan escaped his lips. She sent him a less-than-happy look. "Don't you have something you could do to help?"

Colin headed for the kitchen, but found Jude and Edith arguing over how to prepare the cranberries — Edith, as usual, bringing a can to slice up and Jude insisting on preparing the sauce fresh. The air was hot and sticky, steam rising from every pot on the stove, and Mark occupied the breakfast area, carving up the tur-key.

Colin headed for the living room to see how Kathy was making out with Frederick. Bonnie had hoped the Thanksgiving gather-ing would cheer her up now that her divorce was final, a good idea if Maggie wasn't expected. The two barely said boo to each other whenever they met and Kathy had yet to apologize. As far as Maggie was concerned, she wouldn't give the woman the time of day until an apology passed those designers lips. Yet, if he knew Maggie, she would be polite no matter what.

He smiled thinking of his roommate, coworker and in-law. Weeks had passed and they had spent hours working together and playing tourist. Colin had forgotten how fun it was to show others around Maine, to proudly exhibit his state and to enjoy its many attractions. They had hiked Acadia National Park, taken the ferry to Chebeague Island for a fireside crab dinner at the inn and revisited history at Old York Village.

And not once had he lost control.

Which, if he were honest with himself, was the real reason for his current foul mood. He wanted to be anywhere but here, doing anything but playing perfect son and brother in a jacket and tie. He simply couldn't bear another meal sitting across from Maggie, inching to touch her, to kiss her, to make love to irresistible Miss Georgia. And it was because of the folks inhabiting that very house that he wasn't able to do just that.

"This child is making me crazy." Kathy looked up from their game of Monopoly and pleaded for help with her eyes. She needed rescuing from the overactive child, but Colin dreaded doing that as well.

He slid into the foyer and leaned against the wall with a sigh. What was wrong with him tonight? It was Thanksgiving, a time of reflection, giving thanks, enjoying good company. But, he didn't feel up to playing patriarch. He wanted to be a normal thirty-three-year-old man full of lust, free to make love to the woman who was driving him insane.

His mother appeared in the hallway, carrying two coats. "Has Maggie arrived yet?"

"Not yet."

She nodded, then examined him as if wondering what the hell he was doing out in the hall. He wondered as much himself.

"I got a bill from that private detective you hired," she said, looking both ways to make sure no one could hear. "I thought you were done with that."

He took the coats and began hanging them up in the hall closet. "He's working on Jake now. The guy had a personal crisis so he was off the case for a while, but he's now back on track."

"Jake?"

"Yes, Jake," he answered a little too sarcastically. "My cousin who died mysteriously. The one you refuse to talk about."

Bonnie sighed, raising one eyebrow. "You're the one too stubborn to look at what's in front of you."

"Like what, mother?"

She wasn't in the mood to deal with him, he could tell. "Are you drunk?" she asked, leaning in close as if to smell his breath.

"No, but I'm contemplating it."

She shook her head. "Oh, Colin. You've been in a foul mood all week."

And well deserved, he thought to himself. He hadn't had sex in God knew how long and when finally a woman he likes appears in his life, she's off limits.

Colin gritted his teeth and tried to focus on his mother. "Where did you go last weekend, mom?"

He hadn't meant to ask; there were many times his mother took trips for business reasons and Colin never thought to inquire. If she didn't feel it was necessary to tell him, what business was it of his? But, Bonnie had mysteriously disappeared right before Jake had died and now she was doing it again. This time, curiosity got the best of him. This time, he had to know.

She stared at him a long time, and then sighed. "I went to Washington. My old college friend at the Smithsonian has been bugging me to come down and I finally took her up on it."

In the middle of their busiest time? This was hard to swallow.

Bonnie sensed what he was thinking, for she exhaled and looked away. "Okay, if you must know, I was there for another reason."

It all sounded so secret, so sinister. What on earth did his mother have to be secretive about? "Why, then?"

She fiddled with a button on her blouse. "Stewart asked me down for a state dinner. He was invited to a special function at the Pentagon and needed a date. There."

"Stewart Mallory?"

"Yes, Stewart Mallory."

Colin would have laughed if he knew his mother wouldn't be offended. It was all quite humorous. Here he was lusting after Maggie living in his own house and his mother and Maggie's father were enjoying each other's company in bliss in the Nation's Capital, alone, without the intrusive family around to cause problems.

"Why the big secret?"

"It's no secret," she said defensively. "There was nothing to it so I thought it best to keep it to myself."

"If there's nothing to it…"

He failed to finish his sentence for Maggie came bursting through the door, a swirl of leaves in her wake. "Wow, it's getting chilly out there."

Bonnie took the collection of pots from her hands while Colin helped her out of her L.L. Bean winter coat, the one they had picked out together at the flagship store in Freeport one late night. Colin recalled the fun he had showing her the store, open all year, twenty-four hours a day. It must have been midnight when they stumbled in, purchasing two winter coats – one for fancy occasions and one for outdoor wear. The sales clerks showed Maggie the trout pond in the men's department and gave her hiking boots to test out on the massive rock wall in the middle of the store. By the time they left at two-thirty a.m., they had signed up for ocean kayaking lessons and Maggie had bought a new wardrobe.

He couldn't remember having such fun at L.L. Bean, although he'd been in the famous store dozens and dozens of times. It was yet one moment of many when he had wanted to kiss Maggie madly, when they had stumbled home in the middle of the night and it was all too easy to stop at the bottom of the stairs and retire to one bed instead of two. How many nights had he fought down the urge, forced himself to walk up those lonely steps and resist the desire that was ripping him up inside?

"Hey," she said when she turned to face him.

Colin couldn't stand it anymore, couldn't wait another moment to have her, but his mother stood between them, reminding him yet again that personal desires had to wait.

"Hey," he said.

"What is that spicy smell?" his mother asked, peering into one of the pots.

"I made gumbo," Maggie said proudly. "I know you said to bring dessert and I made a pecan pie as well, but I saw this beautiful crabmeat and shrimp at the market — the one in Freeport with all that delicious homemade jam and maple syrup — and anyway with the weather turning chilly and all, I thought it would be a perfect night for gumbo." She paused when she realized Bonnie hadn't said a word. "Am I talking too much?"

"No dear, of course not." Bonnie rubbed her arms and smiled, but Colin wondered what his mom would think of Maggie's liberal use of her Cajun cousin's spices. "I'm going to bring these to the table," Bonnie said and hurried away.

Maggie pulled off her gloves and hat, turning her thoughts to Colin. "What's wrong?"

God, was his bad mood obvious with one simple greeting? "Nothing."

"Are you sure?"

Why was it that Maggie could read his thoughts and feelings when no one else could? Or maybe she was the only one paying attention long enough to see inside him. The idea that she cared enough gave him hope. If only they were alone, he'd find out for sure.

But they were alone. Most of the family was huddled in the kitchen and dining area while Kathy bought Boardwalk from Frederick in the living room. They stood inches apart, her lips within reach, and no one would be the wiser. He could steal one kiss, gather one semblance of assurance that they could become a couple before sitting through another insufferable meal as platonic in-laws.

Colin leaned down to brush his lips against hers, while Maggie sucked in a breath, her eyes stretching wide. They were one moment away from a kiss when Edith stuck her head into the foyer. "Dinner time," she announced, making them both jump.

Maggie gasped and smiled nervously. "Great, I'm starved."

She refused to look at him as she made her way into the dining room, greeting the rest of the family as if she had enjoyed Thanksgiving in Madison every year of her life. Colin followed, but what he really needed was fresh air, preferably a blast of the cold front blowing in.

As usual, Bonnie seated Maggie across from Colin, in perfect view and yet untouchable. As the rest of the family took their seats, Maggie avoided his gaze, arranging her napkin in her lap. Kathy, on the other hand, took the seat to Colin's left and had no trouble making eye contact and conversation. This caught Maggie's attention, and it heartened Colin that she might be jealous.

"There's a storm expected," Mark said, sitting next to Maggie. "Supposed to hit tomorrow afternoon. You might get your snow there, Maggie."

Miss Georgia greeted him with that sweet but ever so seductive smile, and Colin shifted in his seat. "That should give you good reason to stay inside, Mark, and finish that book."

At the mention of writing, Mark offered his own sly grin, but aimed it at his wife, who blushed profusely. "Oh, there's lots of great things to do inside when it snows."

"Don't be gross," Edith said, making the rounds pouring everyone a glass of wine.

"Your trip to New York isn't tomorrow, is it?" Kathy asked Colin. "I hope you're not traveling in such weather."

Bonnie paused tossing the salad and Maggie's gaze shot up.

"What's this about New York?" his mother asked.

Crap. He really shouldn't have mentioned it to Kathy but he needed information on the city's short-term corporate housing and her brother worked in commercial real estate. Maggie seemed truly concerned that he might take another job. Her whole demeanor changed and that playful smile disappeared.

"It's nothing," Colin began, as much to ease Maggie's worries as his family's. "The firm was interested in me working a couple of weeks before the holidays."

"It is the holidays, Colin," Jude pointed out.

It had been before the holidays several days ago when Colin actually contemplated working in New York. But he had to meet with clients tomorrow in Portland at a regional convention of one of the home improvement corporations. The timing hadn't worked.

"I thought you were going to Portland," his mother said. "And that you weren't going to work in New York for a while."

"I will be in Portland." Colin downed half of his wine with one sip. "And yes, mother, I've given up having a career of my own choosing."

"Oh dear, are we having a little whine with our Thanksgiving dinner, dear brother?" Edith said.

Colin gritted his teeth, wondering if he had any left. Why did Edith have to push his buttons tonight?

"You know, Colin," Jude piped in, "some people would love to have had a plume publishing job land in their laps. Am I right, Maggie?"

Everyone looked at Miss Georgia, who nearly choked on her wine. "I…ah…"

"If you remember correctly, Maggie did have a job land in her lap," Edith added a little too snidely. "Jake handed it to her."

"He handed Colin his, too, if you think about it."

Colin raised a hand, palm outward, to stop the insanity. "We don't need to discuss this, thank you."

A silence fell upon the table as everyone served themselves from the heaping bowls of food. Colin spooned out a couple of his favorites, in addition to a bowl of the spicy gumbo that sported an odd consistency, nothing he was used to on his trips down South. But he really wasn't hungry. Not for food, anyway. Especially with Maggie staring at him the way she was.

"What's up with this soup?" Edith asked.

"It's gumbo," Frederick announced proudly.

"The color's a bit odd, isn't it?" Bonnie asked politely.

"It's gluten free," Maggie said, gazing across the table. "I made it especially for you, Edith."

Edith was busy sliding her spoon through the soup, studying the dish intently. "I'm not gluten intolerant."

"But you told my father…"

"Is Uncle Teddy mad?" Frederick whispered, interrupting the conversation.

Maggie continued studying Colin, but she whispered back, "He's got his butt on his shoulders tonight."

Frederick snorted, milk coming out of his nose, followed by laughter that sounded as if it rose from the bottom of his gut. Maggie patted him on the back, but she didn't crack a smile. "I think someone jerked a knot in his tail," she added, which made the youngster laugh even harder.

"He's going to choke," Kathy admonished her.

"He's fine," Mark mumbled between bites of food. "It's a game they play."

"What game?" Colin asked. Anything involving laughter was preferable to the present horrid conversation.

"Maggie says these funny sayings to make Frederick laugh." Jude patted her son on the back and he began to calm down. "It's a Southern thing."

"Oh, is it?" Colin loved nothing better than a dare, and from the way Maggie was looking at him, she was egging him on.

"You wouldn't understand," she said. "It's above most Yankees' heads."

Kathy started to object until she realized Maggie was kidding. Colin, on the other hand, took the bait. "Bring it on, Reb."

Maggie wiped her mouth of turkey and placed the napkin in her lap gallantly. "Colin's so clumsy he'd trip over a cordless phone."

"That's it?" Colin asked. "That's the best you can do?"

She didn't falter a bit. "You're a little behind the times, Yank. I've been doing this for weeks and I'm not even halfway through my repertoire."

"Do the ugly tree," Frederick insisted.

"Colin fell out of the ugly tree and hit every branch on the way down," Maggie delivered, making Frederick burst into laughter again. "Then his granny beat him with an ugly stick."

Colin smirked. "That silly expression is about as useful as a trap door on a canoe."

She tilted her head slightly, as if she approved. "Colin's so tall he could hunt geese with a rake."

"Just because a cat has her kittens in the oven don't make them biscuits."

This stopped her cold. "What?"

"It's an old New England saying," Edith interjected with her own smirk. "Means that just because you live here doesn't make you a native."

Maggie's eyes narrowed, ready for a fight. "Bless Colin's heart, he thinks the sun comes up just to hear him crow."

Her eyes sparkled as she dared him in a comeback and Colin was too busy enjoying the sparkle in her eyes and that adorable grin as she tilted her head.

"Well, I'll just swaney!" Maggie finally said. "The tall drink of water can spit out expressions, but I do think I have bested the man."

Colin leaned across the table. "Even when I'm as nervous as a hound pissing peach pits."

At this, Bonnie's eyebrows raised, but Maggie burst into a full-fledge smile that made Colin's gut tighten.

"Sorry Mrs. Parnell," she said, even though she wasn't to blame for the expletive. Always polite, Colin thought fondly.

"That last one was good," Maggie whispered across the table. "You can't convince me that that's an old Yankee expression."

Damn, the woman looked so cute in her pinstriped shirt, matching sweater and strand of pearls. Colin wished he were sitting next to her so he could whisper back and take the opportunity to breathe in her heavenly scent. Hell, he wished they were back at his house and…

"So, what's up with New York?" Jude asked him, breaking the spell. "Are you still thinking about architecture?"

The atmosphere in the room shifted and Colin's bad mood returned.

"Can we change the subject please?" Suddenly, Colin lost his appetite. He pushed his plate away and leaned back in his chair.

"Don't you get enough satisfaction creating your *Yankee Living* buildings?" Edith asked. "Isn't that enough?"

"I hardly think that's architecture," Mark said.

"What?" Colin couldn't believe his ears. On one hand, they were sticking their sibling noses into his life again and on the other, Mark was insulting his creations.

"Hey, I'm on your side," Mark insisted. "You should be able to do what makes you happy."

"And working at the bottom for some unfeeling corporation is going to make him happy?" Bonnie asked.

"But it's New York," Kathy added.

"Where you pay a fortune for a closet to live in," Jude bit back.

While everyone debated the pros and cons of Colin's life, Maggie stared at him, concerned, their jovial bantering a far memory. "You're not happy at the magazine?"

He never meant to discuss this, never meant to have his feelings literally cast upon the table. He loved the magazine but it wasn't his career of choice. Architecture was his true calling, but he wasn't sure he would give one up for the other. Not to mention that Colin certainly didn't want to leave one particular woman sitting before him.

When he realized everyone was now staring at him, his blood boiled. "I don't want to discuss this."

Throwing his napkin in his chair, Colin headed for the back of the house, hoping to sneak out to the porch for air. A light rain was falling and a harsh wind blew in from the east, carrying the chill of the ocean with it. As nice as the cool air felt, the rain began to pick up, as if God, too, was throwing jabs his way. Colin quickly jumped inside, but he could still hear his family arguing his life — in front of the woman he wanted to make plans with. He decided to escape it all, descending into the depths of the dark, cool wine cellar.

Memories assaulted him instantly. He and his father used to retreat to the cellar on occasion, mainly so his father could sneak a smoke. If Colin searched hard enough, he was sure to find an old pack of Marlborough's hidden among the bricks and Cabernet Sauvignons. While his father damaged his health in private far from the scorn of Bonnie, they would discuss everything — careers, sports, girls.

And Jake.

Funny how everything always revolved around his cousin. Jake getting in trouble. Jake stealing Colin's girlfriends. Jake failing to show up for a family function or magazine assignment. Even now, Colin's life hung in limbo because of Jake and his adorable freckle-faced widow.

Colin leaned against the cool brick wall, closed his eyes and sighed. If only he could get her out of his mind. If only he could walk into his house and not spend every hour debating whether to make a move and lure her into his bed.

Maybe some work in New York was just the thing. Put a little distance between he and Miss Scarlet, not to mention his meddling family members. Perhaps he would call Amy Udall while he was in the city; they used to date a few years back. Perhaps they could take in a Broadway play, enjoy a fine meal in Manhattan.

Who was he kidding? He would only end up spending the entire evening thinking of another. One who spoke words like music. Vaudeville music, he thought with a grin, but music nevertheless.

Just then, Colin heard chairs moving on the floorboards above and feet heading for both the kitchen and the living room. He glanced at his watch. Six o'clock. Right on schedule. Time for dessert and football. His family was as predictable as Greenwich.

The cellar door squeaked open and soft footsteps descended the stairs. Colin leaned forward to see who the intruder was, his defenses rallying. Instead, he spotted the familiar Mary Janes and relaxed.

When Maggie saw him, she stopped abruptly, as if uncomfortable to be alone with him. "Sorry, your mom said we needed sweet wine for dessert."

Colin knew he should say something; Maggie was always commenting how quiet Mainers were, but for the life of him he stood there speechless, nervous as a schoolboy. She, too, appeared anxious, gazing around the cellar as if looking for a quick escape.

Some things are better left unspoken, Colin thought, noticing how her neck arched gracefully down to her shoulders, and the way her skirt hugged her full hips, curving into a small waistline. Sometimes words interfered.

Before she had time to object, and before he had time to change his mind, Colin strutted forward, placed one hand at her waist and the other on her cheek and lowered his lips to hers, kissing her madly.

Chapter Fifteen

MAGGIE RECOGNIZED THAT LOOK IN Colin's eyes, knew what was going to happen the minute her feet left the stairs and hit the brick floor of the wine cellar. Her brain demanded to make excuses and return upstairs, but her body had turned deaf. So many times the little voice inside her head warned her not to get so close to the fire, but tonight she wasn't listening. Tonight, she wanted to feel its heat. Tonight, she hoped to get burned.

When Colin placed a hand at her waist and pulled her close, Maggie tilted her head, letting his lips take hers, meeting his wild advances with a force of her own. She pulled a hand through his hair, relishing in the feel of the silky strands, as she opened her lips for more.

And Colin eagerly accepted the invitation, their tongues meeting in a wild dance as a groan sounded deep in his throat. He pulled her closer, deepening the kiss, and she rose on her toes to encircle her arms about his neck.

They couldn't get close enough, couldn't kiss enough. Colin nipped at her lower lip, then pulled it between his teeth and sucked until she moaned. He trailed kisses down her cheekbones to her neck and up beneath her earlobes. Their lips met again, forging deeper, pressing madly.

The fire burned out of control, its flames singing Maggie's skin, sending bolts of lightning roaring through her veins. She felt lightheaded and empowered at the same time, as giddy as a grade-schooler receiving her first kiss and as passionate as a woman at her sexual peak.

Maggie smiled, thinking how turning thirty wasn't such a bad thing, after all. Neither was being a late bloomer if this was how it felt to finally open on the vine. To have a man finally, really make love to her.

"What's so funny?" Colin asked, allowing them both a chance to breathe, their pulses raging out of control.

In that moment of pause, Maggie's logical mind piped in. What was she doing? Not only was she stepping over the line that she swore not to cross, but she was kissing Colin in the wine cellar of Bonnie's house! With the entire family upstairs.

Colin sensed her hesitation, so he kissed her again, this time sliding a hand between her sweater and blouse and caressing the length of her back. Leaning in to his chest that was twice the size of hers, Maggie allowed him to encompass her, like a snail fitting snugly into a shell. Everything felt so natural, as if they were meant for this moment. As if they were destined to be together since the instant Colin had slammed into her at the Pittsburgh airport.

He tugged at her blouse and pulled it free of its waistband, then slid his large, callused hand against her bare back. Maggie surrendered her defenses, moaned and arched against him as his hand moved forward and caressed a breast. He nibbled his way down her neck, sucking in the soft skin beneath her jawline, while his thumb reached up and circled a taunt nipple.

All dizziness subsided, replaced by a roaring thunder that echoed in her temples and reverberated throughout her body. As his thumb massaged, Maggie's knees grew weak and her insides glowed with bursts of fire.

It was all so wonderful, like she had imagined. There was no Vegas, no Jake. No awkward love making with men who didn't understand her. Just this wonderful man and his magical hands.

And kisses that set her soul aflame.

Just then, footsteps sounded from above. "Maggie," Jude called down. "Are you having trouble finding the wine?"

Cold water being thrown on them could not have been as startling. They both separated immediately, standing inches apart, trying to regain their breath.

"No problem," Maggie said a little too quickly. Her voice was edgy and anxious and she worried Jude might suspect.

"It's on the far wall. Do you want me to come show it to you?" Maggie closed her eyes briefly and exhaled, trying to force her heart to stop beating so rapidly. When she opened them again, she saw the frustration in Colin's gaze as he, too, attempted normalcy. "That's okay, I've got it."

"Okay."

When Jude's footsteps moved into the kitchen, Colin reached a hand up to touch her face, but Maggie slipped away, tucking her shirt into her skirt. "We can't do this."

Colin leaned an arm on the post behind Maggie's head, staring so intently she thought for sure he would kiss her again. God knew she wanted him to. She longed to taste that heady rush of wine and masculinity, breathe in his Old Spice and appreciate the way his body was steel beneath her touch.

Instead, Colin seemed to be absorbing her, leaning in close as if to take one last look. He closed his eyes as he buried his face into her hair, his breath warm on her ear. It took all Maggie's strength not to reach up and grab his shirt, to start the seduction all over again.

She almost did, couldn't bear not touching him again, but within an instant, Colin left her side, grabbing a bottle of wine from the far shelf, placing it into Maggie's hands and bolting up the stairs.

What had transpired? Maggie thought, placing a hand over her heart that was working overtime. It had all happened so quickly, so deliciously fast. And yet, she was glad of it. Touching her fingers to her lips swollen from an onslaught of passion, Maggie was relieved they had finally consummated their attraction, even if it was only kisses in a wine cellar.

"Oh, it was more than that," she said to herself, leaning against the post to try to tame her heavy breathing. "What am I going to do now?"

She knew what she wanted to do – follow Colin home and continue the lovemaking. Which made her heart race once again.

Maggie heard the front door slamming. She knew it was Colin leaving, knew he was having doubts about what had occurred and that he decided to make a getaway and not be questioned by his family. But did he regret it? Maggie hoped not, although they both desperately needed to dull their spurs — Jake was only three months gone.

"Shit," Maggie whispered. Jake.

She made her way up the stairs, handing Jude the bottle of wine without making eye contact and forcing herself to think about anything but Jake's demise and Colin's kisses. She stole out to the back porch for some air. She had to steady herself, had to think. As the screen door shut behind her, a blast of chilled air and light rain hit her hard, but the wake-up call was welcomed.

"You better not stay out too long. This rain is tricky."

Maggie nearly jumped at the voice coming from a shadow at the edge of the porch. If she hadn't seen the red tip of a glowing cigarette, she'd have thought she was hearing things. "Kathy, you scared me."

The red tip rose up and flared as Kathy the ghost inhaled. "No kidding," she said, releasing the smoke. "I thought you were going to jump off the porch."

"Did Colin leave?" Damn, she really didn't want to talk about Colin to her.

"I was going to ask you the same thing. Well, was going to ask you why he left."

Maggie leaned against the porch wall and sighed. "I don't know," she lied.

"Are you sure?"

She couldn't make out Kathy's face, but the last question seemed innocent enough. Still, she couldn't trust the New Yorker, so she refrained from answering.

Kathy seemed to sense her thoughts, for she moved closer and into the light. "You know, Maggie, I've been meaning to apologize to you."

Now here was a first. Maggie leaned forward to get a better look at her nemesis's eyes, and again, she appeared sincere.

"Right before Jake died, my husband left me." She smirked as she took another drag. "My second husband, I might add. For another woman, for the second time, too. And, well, I kinda went unglued. Didn't take my meds like a bad girl. And then, when my Jake died…"

God, Maggie couldn't bear hearing about Jake. Not now. "What's wrong that you need meds?"

"Didn't Colin tell you? I'm crazy."

Maggie might have agreed a few weeks earlier, but the woman before her seemed perfectly normal. Even nice.

"Manic depressive is the term," Kathy continued. "I do okay if I'm on my meds, but sometimes I get this insane idea that I'll be alright without them."

"I can certainly understand that, especially if you're feeling good."

Kathy looked at Maggie as if discovering a friend, her face lighting up. The difference was startling. "Exactly."

"So, you're feeling good now?"

She threw the cigarette on to the porch floor and stubbed it with her toe. "Yeah, thanks to my parents and Colin. He's been such a wonderful friend."

Something tightened in her gut thinking about the nights Colin disappeared, especially the one particular evening he didn't come home and he gave Maggie that ridiculous excuse. Here she was making love to the man and for all she knew, he still carried a torch for his prom queen. Somehow, though, Maggie doubted he loved Kathy.

"That's what I wanted to talk to you about," Kathy said, lighting up another cigarette. "Colin." She pointed to the pack, "Do you mind? I'm hopelessly addicted."

Maggie shook her head. "What about Colin?"

"Haven't you noticed how weird he's been acting lately?"

The question stopped her cold. Colin had been acting plenty weird since Jake's death and the reading of the will and Maggie was positive she was the cause of it all. But weird lately? Outside of his foul mood that evening, she wasn't sure what Kathy meant. Over the past few weeks, she'd never seen him happier.

"He's preoccupied all the time," Kathy answered. "He seems scattered."

"He's busy," Maggie inserted. "It's a tough time at the magazine with the holidays and all."

Kathy considered this as she took a long drag. "I guess so."

Now, her curiosity was up. Was Colin falling in love with her, exhibiting anxiety to the rest of the world? Just the thought of it made the little voice act up again, warning her not to take things out of context. A kiss might only be a kiss. She doubted Colin was that kind of man, certainly not like his cousin. And the other voice — the one of hope — sent a flurry of butterflies through her stomach.

Still, he did visit Kathy one night and didn't return home and told Maggie there had been nothing to it.

"You and Colin are really close," Maggie offered, hoping to get answers. "Surely he would have told you if there were any problems."

Kathy blew smoke straight up in the air and the smoke did a little dance about their heads as the wind wiped up. "We're just friends, and even then it's more on my part than his. He listens to my endless problems and doesn't tell me much in return."

Maggie realized she had been holding her breath, so she tried to relax, leaning back against the cold, damp boards. Usually about this time her teeth started chattering and her knees began knocking. She must be getting used to Maine.

"I'll give you an example of what I mean," Kathy said, leaning closer. "One night he came over after I called, but it took him a while and we had all gone to bed. The house was dark so he didn't want to disturb anyone. Well, the fool shuts his eyes for a second and falls asleep. Sleeps through the dawn. I found him in his car the next morning." She leaned so close Maggie could make out that her eyes were a deep, almost artificial shade of blue. "Can you imagine? The man slept in his car in my driveway all night."

Now, Maggie really did exhale, and her jaw dropped wide open. Kathy, on the other hand, took her reaction to be shock at Colin's action. "Yeah, see, I told you. He's acting strange."

Bonnie opened the back door and peered outside. Kathy quickly threw her cigarette into the mud. "What on earth are you two doing out in the rain?"

"Nothing, Bonnie," Kathy said, moving to the edge of the porch and exhaling smoke into the darkness.

"You told me to tell you when it's seven," Bonnie said to Kathy. "It's seven."

Kathy perked up, offering a brilliant smile to Maggie, which shocked her even more. "I've got a date," she said. "With my law-yer, if you can believe it. Gorgeous man. Who'd have thought?"

Kathy sauntered into the house, passing Bonnie at the door.

"Are you going to sit out here all alone in the dark?" Bonnie asked Maggie.

"Do you need help cleaning up?" Maggie made her way back inside, grateful for the heat greeting her on the threshold.

"Nope. All done." Bonnie paused at her purse and pulled out her cell phone. "I have to make some phone calls, though. Jude and Mark left because Frederick, believe it or not, fell asleep. But Edith is watching TV in the living room and I'm sure she'll love the company."

"Don't worry about me," Maggie assured her. "I'm going to find some dessert."

"Your pecan pie was to die for." Bonnie headed for the stairs. "I'll be done in a few."

Maggie looked around the now sadly vacant kitchen, but she really wasn't hungry. Not for pie, anyway. She ventured into the living room where Edith was riveted to the annual airing of *The Sound of Music*. At least it wasn't a documentary.

Maybe it was the wine cellar lovemaking. Maybe it was the frus-tration of longing to be back in Colin's arms and not being able to. Maybe she wasn't up to family socializing. But the last thing Maggie was going to do on Thanksgiving evening was watch a Julie Andrews musical, even if the film was one of her favorites.

She slipped into the hall and found her own purse and cell phone, then quickly made a call. Then she entered the living room and took Edith by the hand, yanking her to her feet.

"What are you doing?"

Maggie handed her the down parka she loved to wear on every occasion. "We're going out."

"What?"

"You heard me." She handed Edith her gloves and a knit hat with some hockey team logo on it. "It's time for some fun."

Edith planted her hands on her hips. "Where are we going?"

Maggie took the parka out of her hands and held it out for her. Amazingly, the woman did as she was told, pulling her arms through. "You'll see. It's a surprise."

Edith wasn't thrilled about being led away into the night without a clue, but she followed. As they drove past Madison on to the highway leading into Freeport, Edith was twenty questions. In contrast, Maggie drove in silence. First the familiarity with the cold, now a lack of conversation. If Maggie stayed in Maine any longer, she was going to turn into a Yankee.

"You're not going to make me eat more of that spicy food, are you?"

Maggie looked at Edith, studying her frumpy clothes and lack of hair styling. Maggie was the last person to suggest a makeover to someone — she had always been the recipient of such advice — but Edith needed help. "Girl, you have got to get out. You have got to sample life more often, spicy and otherwise."

Edith folded her arms. "I like my solitude."

"You like no such thing."

"And how would you know?"

They paused at a red light, so Maggie turned to face Edith directly. "Because I lost my mother at sixteen and I know exactly what you're doing."

She shouldn't have been so direct; Maggie needed to keep her big, fat, Southern mouth shut. But she couldn't help herself. She hated seeing Edith throwing her life away. It was like looking into an old mirror.

"I had a life once," Maggie told her. "Friends and everything. When my mother died, I retreated into my room and my studies and food. I gained twenty pounds that didn't come off until Jake…I mean, until recently. First it was school, then graduate school, then my career. I woke up one morning and realized I was going to turn thirty and it scared me to death. Because what would my mother, a woman so full of life and passion, who lived every moment to the fullest, think about me holed up inside myself all these years?"

The light turned green but Maggie sat frozen, thinking about what she had divulged. So many years hiding from life, hiding from facing the pain, ashamed of whom she'd become. Maybe being laid off was God's way of forcing her to face her demons. Maybe it all led to Vegas and then Madison, to Colin, to some sort of healing. Heaven knew, the last few weeks had been glorious.

They sat there for several seconds until the light turned red again. Maggie stared down into her lap to gather her thoughts, wondering what stoic Edith thought of her forwardness. "I don't want to see you make the same mistakes."

Edith sighed. "The only mistake I'm making is letting you take me bowling."

"How did you know?" Maggie looked up and caught the bowling lanes sign in the next block. She glanced over at Edith to see how she was absorbing this news, and found the woman grinning, shaking her head. "What's this, some weird Southern tradition? Bowling on Thanksgiving?"

"Actually, my dad and I used to go to the movies."

"Great idea. We could be watching *The Sound of Music* right now." Despite her protestations, Edith continued to smile, which gave Maggie hope.

The light turned green and they headed forward, pulling into the parking lot that sported three cars, one with a Greenpeace bumper sticker and a MIT decal.

"That looks like Malick's car," Edith said.

Maggie cringed, wondering how this was going to go down. "Well, now that you mentioned it, I asked him to join us."

Edith's face turned pale, which gave Maggie hope that the attraction was mutual. "What?"

"He spent the day with family in Bangor, but had to come back tonight. We have some web work that needs working on tomorrow. Anyway, I thought he could use the company so I invited him." Maggie studied Edith, hoping she wouldn't insist on going home. "He said he loved to bowl."

At this, Edith's demeanor shifted. She straightened her shirt and smoothed out her sweater. "I guess I can endure this," she said, although the usual sarcasm and snideness was absent in her tone. "Do I look okay?"

Maggie pulled out a brush and combed her kinky hair away from her face, fastening the curls above her cheekbones with a beret.

"What are you doing?" Edith glanced in the rear view mirror but didn't mind the adjustments once she spotted them.

"You have a beautiful face." Maggie threw her equipment into her purse. "Stop hiding it."

Edith touched a gentle hand to her hair, but her gaze was frightful and anxious. "My hair is unmanageable."

"So tame it."

Not wanting to give Edith any reason to back out, Maggie jumped out of the car and headed toward the bowling lanes. She heard the car door open and shut behind her, but was afraid to look back for fear Edith would change her mind.

Once inside, Maggie spotted Malick by the counter. "Hey Maggie," he said, coming alive when he saw Edith. "Wow, I didn't know you were coming too."

Realization dawned on Edith and she sent Maggie a killing look, but she joined Malick at the counter, who instantly began discussing the weather and what he had for dinner. Maggie rolled her eyes, knowing he was as nervous as Edith, but it was a start. And so far, Edith's feet were still planted inside the building.

The pair ordered shoes while Maggie paid — she insisted it was her treat — and then Malick led Edith to the bowling balls to pick out the proper one for a beginner. Edith absorbed it all as if bowling was the most fascinating sport on earth. Funny, how intellectuals adjust their thinking when men are involved, Maggie thought.

"What about you?" the counter man asked. "What size?"

Maggie paused, watching Malick explain the importance of a ball's weight and the size of the holes for thumbs. She really wasn't needed anymore. Three only made a crowd.

"I'm not bowling," she said.

She gave them a few minutes, and then made up some high-falutin story about a phone call and needing to rush home and call her father. They both took it well, having no objections to being alone. Within seconds, they had completely forgotten she was there.

Maggie headed home, happy her plan had worked but feeling a sharp stab of loneliness. She longed for Colin, wished there was no Jake memory hanging between them so they, too, could act like normal dating couples. Right now, they'd be bowling, drinking beer and laughing like Edith and Malick.

Or heading back to Colin's home, but not to separate bedrooms.

She sighed, thinking of that delicious scenario, trying to swallow the intense desire rising in her chest. The Yank was destroying what little sanity she owned.

She wondered if Colin was home, wondered where he had been all this time. When she passed the magazine and saw his car out front, her hopes fell.

"This is what you insisted on," she commanded herself. "You can't go around sleeping with the cousin of your deceased husband, now, can you?"

Maggie knew it was the right thing to do, knew they had to keep their distance, but the irony was killing her. "Why did it have to be Jake?" she asked no one. "Why couldn't he have said no and let Colin go to Vegas to recruit new staff?"

Somehow, somewhere deep in the recesses of her soul, Maggie knew it had all happened this way for a reason. But, with desire pulsing in her veins, she had yet to understand the grand universal plan.

She stumbled into the house, grabbed her latest historical romance and headed for bed. Despite the exciting sword play and the fact that the hero wore breeches and knee-length boots, her mind kept wondering back to the feel of Colin's hand on her back, the way his lips took complete control of hers. Finally, after twenty minutes of reading the same page, Maggie threw the book across the room and turned off the light.

Just then, Maggie heard Colin's car arrive, then the opening of the front door. Her heart stopped beating as she listened to him perform his nightly routine: keys on the secretary, locking of the door, the turning off of the porch light.

Then, suddenly, he paused and all became silent. Maggie held her breath as she imagined him standing before her door, as conflicted as she over what to do next. Moments passed and Maggie heard the ticking of the clock above the mantle in the living room, its repetitive sound mocking them with its "What…will…you…do?"

She peered over her toes to see the light pouring in beneath the door. Colin was there; she knew he was. Otherwise, he would have turned off the hall light by now. But would he knock? Should she feign sleep or rush into his arms? Maggie closed her eyes, wanting with all her soul to do one thing and knowing with all her mind that she shouldn't.

When she opened her eyes again, the light had been extinguished and footsteps were heading up the stairs. Maggie let out her breath, but she felt anything but relieved. Instead, the ache that had been growing inside her for the past few weeks now blossomed into one intense, relentless pain. She doubted she would sleep at all that night.

She had to do something. This couldn't go on. As Scarlet always said, tomorrow was another day. Colin was heading to Portland in the morning and she had work at the magazine.

Somewhere in those plans, she was going to seduce her cranberry professor.

Chapter Sixteen

MAGGIE STARRED AT THE COMPUTER screen and the development of the Spring Design Home page, but her mind was elsewhere. Portland, to be exact. Ever since she had vowed to seduce Colin, her brain focused on one thing only, reeling through the possibilities and searching for a discreet way to make it happen.

"We're finished, you know?" Malick picked up the Diet Coke on her desk and shook it. "I'm going to the kitchen, want me to put this in recycling?"

Malick had said something, but Maggie wasn't sure what it was. "Huh?"

He waved a hand in front of her eyes. "Hello?"

Giving up, Maggie turned and met his gaze head-on. "I'm sorry. Have a lot on my mind."

"Then go home. It's late."

She glanced at her watch. Four forty-five. Where had the time gone? And she was no more closer to reaching her objective than when she arose that morning and found Colin gone.

"Better get home, anyway," Malick continued. "Big storm is coming and it's going to hit soon."

Maggie laughed. "Malick, I live five minutes away."

He shook his head, and then typed a URL on his computer

screen, which brought up a weather site. With one click he set the Doppler screen into motion and Maggie saw bands of a weather system moving onshore.

"These storms can be pretty brutal, like a hurricane with snow. It's best not to be on any road when it sneaks up on you. You can get stuck pulling out of the parking lot."

Always the horror stories, these Mainers. They had been warning her about winter for the past two months, as if they doubted she could handle the season due to being born below the Mason-Dixon Line. She started to argue that it wasn't snowing yet and she doubted that even if a few flakes fell, she'd be home before they hit the ground, when suddenly a thought came crashing through.

Heavy snow coming. One could get stuck.

Bingo!

Maggie grabbed her coat and keys. "Gotta go, then."

She passed a startled Malick. "Well, I didn't mean right this second."

Maggie paused at the doorway, grabbing a stack of web page prototypes and throwing them into a folder. "You said to get going." And with those final words, she hurried out the room.

She stopped at Bonnie's office to make sure everything was in place. "Everything's fine. Go home," Bonnie said, looking up and over her glasses. "You'll be home tomorrow, right? In case I need you?"

"Yeah." God, she sure hoped not. "I'm going over to Portland to drop off some things to Colin," she added, just in case Bonnie really did come looking for her.

"Storm's coming, you know."

Maggie tried to offer up an innocent smile. "I'll be back before it hits."

"I don't know. It looks bad."

Maggie waved her hand as if snow was something she conquered every day. "I learned how to drive in Germany, and Europe had nasty snow storms." The worst had been three inches, but she left that fact out. "I'll be fine."

Bonnie, however, wasn't quite convinced. "If it gets bad, don't attempt to come home. Tell Colin to set you up at the hotel and wait it out."

It took everything in Maggie's power not to grin with giddy apprehension. Instead, she bit the inside of her cheek and nodded.

"I mean it," Bonnie said, like the concerned mother she was. In that instant, Maggie caught a glimmer of maternal fear, that oppressive motherly worry that's so annoying to kids but so comforting as well — that aura of protectiveness knowing that someone in the world worries about your every move. It had been years since Maggie had seen it, and it felt good to witness it now.

She'd hugged Bonnie before, shown her polite but sincere affection. But today, she leaned down and gave her an appreciative kiss on the cheek while wrapping her arms about her shoulders, the kind of attention she bestowed on her openly affectionate relatives down South. Before Bonnie's New England stoicism could kick in, Maggie straightened, waved and headed out the door.

She stopped first at the house, gathering her toothbrush, clean underwear and a change of clothes and stuffed them into a tote bag that could double as a purse. She didn't want to look too conspicuous, even though she was knocking on Colin's hotel room asking for sex.

"Holy crap," she said, pulling her hand through her hair. "What am I doing?"

The wave of apprehension failed to deter her, however. She grabbed some bottled water and a blanket, in case she got stuck in the car, then headed out for Portland into the face of an oncoming storm.

Malick had been right, the snow and wind came fast and furious, glazing the roads like an ice skating rink and making her windshield fog up. Maggie took it slow and careful, while her heartbeat raced at both what she was driving through and what lay at the end of the road.

Finally, she made it to the Westin, grateful to hand over the wheel to the valet attendant.

"Are you checking in," he yelled over the noise of the wind.

She shook her head, grabbed her tote and folder and ran for the comfort of the hotel's lobby. Shaking off the snow that had pummeled her in those few seconds of exposure, she approached the concierge. "Colin Parnell's room, please."

While the concierge looked up Colin's room number, Maggie noticed the group of suits laughing in the lobby, name stickers on their lapels. Suddenly, she wondered if Colin was meeting with clients, if she was interrupting important plans.

"Room Eight Seventeen in the Concierge Club level," the well-dressed man said. "Shall I ring him and tell him you're here?"

"No," she answered a bit too hastily. Heavens, but she was nervous. "I just need to drop something off."

What was she going to do if he wasn't in his room, she thought as she headed toward the elevator. What was she going to do if he was and had a client?

"I'll hand him the folder and leave."

"Excuse me?"

Maggie looked up to see an elevator attendant waiting for her to step inside. Was she talking out loud? "Club Concierge, please."

They rode in silence as the floors binged by. Several seconds for her neurosis to take control. If Colin wasn't there and the snow intensified, where would she stay? She could hang out in the lounge and wait for him to show, but how lame was that? If anyone asked, she would say she was waiting for her cousin-in-law to arrive so they could have secret, sordid sex. Only he didn't know it yet.

The elevator binged for the last time and Maggie closed her eyes, attempting to slow the rapid beating of her heart. If only she'd had more experience with men, if only she knew what was waiting behind door Eight Seventeen.

"Madame?"

Maggie realized with horror that the elevator door had been open for some time. "Thanks," she said to the attendant and stepped into the hallway, thankful to hear the elevator door — along with the attendant's curious gaze — close behind her.

Eight Seventeen. The arrow pointed to the left toward the waterfront, no doubt lovely rooms with views to mirror the gracious hallway she now stood in. Just walk down the hall and knock on the door, she instructed herself.

Maggie took a deep breath and planted herself in front of Colin's door. She straightened her clothes and smoothed back her hair, then raised her knuckles and knocked. Several moments passed and then the door flew open, as if Colin had been busy with some business and was irritated to be interrupted. She gasped absorbing the man before her, one hand still holding the doorknob, his tie eschew and his shirt halfway unbuttoned. His hair was uncombed and ruffled and his clothes slightly wrinkled, which gave Maggie hope Colin was alone.

"Uh." Maggie raised the folder gripped tightly in her right hand. "I have some work you need to go over."

Colin said nothing, then opened the door wider and stood back for her to enter. She strode as confidently as she was able to the middle of the suite, gazing around for signs of clients and finding none. She exhaled, realizing the tightness in her chest was cutting off her air, and placed the folder and tote on to a chair. Before she turned to explain why she had come, she noticed the tote bag unzipped, her panties displayed for all to see.

Maggie turned when she heard the door closing, but she quickly removed her coat and scarf and threw it over the bag. "I've got web page prototypes."

"Great." He approached stealthily, like a cat on the prowl. "I couldn't have made it through the weekend without seeing those."

Maggie didn't have time to contemplate his words or to ponder whether he was being sarcastic, for in a flash Colin pulled her into his arms, his lips hot upon hers.

She wasted no time doing the same, snaking her arms about his neck and rising on her toes so her body nestled against the hardness of his. He placed a hand at the small of her back and pressed her closer, moaning as his body reacted to her touch.

She grabbed his shirt and pulled it free of his waistband, slipping her hand underneath, hungry for the feel of bare skin. Her other hand slipped up the side of his face as he devoured her lips, her fingers resting in the strands of his dark, silky hair.

Colin moved his lips down her neckline, unbuttoning her blouse as he went, anxious to feel bare flesh as she. When he reached the last button, she pulled the blouse off and flung it to the floor, eagerly meeting his lips once again while trying to finish the last buttons of his shirt.

Soon, both garments were discarded and Maggie reached for Colin's belt buckle. Instead, he wrapped his arms about her waist and raised her, then headed for the bed, dropping her gently on top of the elegant bedspread. Before she had time to think, Colin removed her slacks, occupying her lips and the top of her breasts with kisses all the while. And they say only women can multi-task, Maggie thought with a smile.

Soon, they were facing one another again, Colin stretched out on the bed beside her, his hands exploring the reaches of her body — sliding over her belly and bottom, skimming up between her thighs — and causing a rash of shivers.

"Why do I always make you cold?" he whispered, his breath hot on her ear, which only brought about another round of goosebumps.

"I'm not cold," she whispered, wondering if steam was rising from her skin.

He paused in the caresses, studying her with eyes glazed over with desire. "Are you nervous?"

Maggie kissed him, nibbling on his lower lip and sucking it between her teeth. "No, just disappointed."

Colin pulled back slightly and gazed at her with a frown. "Disappointed?"

She slid a hand down his back and as far as she was able into the top of his trousers. "I was really hoping you'd look at those web pages. But you had to want to make love."

Colin stifled a smile as he reached back and undid her bra. He quickly rid her of the undergarment, then teased her nipple between his thumb and forefinger. "I could stop."

Maggie swallowed as the caress brought on a rush of sensations.

"Don't you dare."

He pulled her body tight against him, moving his kisses down her neck, his lips replacing his fingers at her breast. As his tongue danced upon her nipples and his hands relished the soft folds of her breasts, Maggie moaned, arching her back and wrapping a leg over his.

She couldn't get enough of him, wanted to be closer, and longed for his hands to touch her everywhere. And her feminine core exploded with new sensations as his tongue massaged her swollen nub and his teeth teased the sensitive spot.

Colin slid a hand between her thighs, slipping a finger inside her. Lightning bolted through her as his finger moved back and forth, then around the entrance, then back inside with greater force. Her breath came in shallow gulps when his thumb found the point of sexual origin and set off a series of fireworks that electrified her all the way to her toes.

It didn't take long before the fireworks reached a crescendo, wild energy bursting through her like the Fourth of July. Maggie had never felt anything like it before, waves and waves of pleasure skittering across her skin, rolling along her spine. The world stopped spinning. Problems about wills and absent fake husbands faded away. She arched her back and pressed her body against his hand as the most intense pleasure gripped her and held her hostage.

"Oh my god," she finally yelled out, wondering if the earth would split open at any minute.

"Hold that thought," Colin whispered when the hurricane subsided and the white spots began to clear from her vision. He left her for a minute, his warm body replaced by a whiff of cold air and Maggie shivered again. This time she really was cold.

"Hurry back," she whispered.

He did as he was told, arriving back on the bed sans clothes and pulling her back into his warm enfold. The kisses began again, then the caresses, then the teasing. It didn't take long for Maggie's senses to regain their immediacy and she began aching for more.

When she started moaning at his touches, Colin complied,

pressing inside. First he was tentative, gauging her reaction as if she were a virgin. Hell, Maggie thought, he did know everything about her, including her pathetic love life.

Feeling both empowered by the earlier rush of seductive energy and embarrassed that he may be worried about her inexperience, Maggie wrapped both legs around his bottom and tightened her hold.

This time, Colin moaned and pushed deep inside. Kissing her madly, he began a steady rhythm that rocked Maggie to her core. The sensations began to build again as he slid his hands to her bottom and pushed deeper. Suddenly, the hurricane sounded, this time tenfold in intensity and deeper in origin, and Maggie leaned her head back to let the waves pour wild over her. Within moments, she heard Colin following suit. Then he held her tightly as they rocked with the lingering pleasure.

They lay entwined for what seemed like an eternity, then Colin raised his head and began kissing every inch of her face.

"That was a nice ice breaker," he whispered. "Now, we can get on to the real lovemaking."

Maggie giggled, wondering how that was possible considering her entire body was limp as a noodle. But, somehow she'd manage.

"Did I interrupt anything?" she asked sleepily. "I was worried you might have a client in here."

Colin raised his head on an elbow, but his fingers of his right hand traced the outline of her body, following the curve of her back and the rounded shape of her breasts.

"I met all the clients I need to see today." He leaned forward, kissing her shoulder blade, letting his lips brush the inside of her neck. "There's a dinner tonight but I don't need to go. Until tomorrow morning, Miss Scarlet, it's just you and me."

Maggie leaned her head back, giving him ample room to work his magic. "Then ravish me, Yankee. The silver's underneath the bed."

At this, Colin laughed and it felt good to hear it. They had always felt so comfortable in each other's presence and now, even in the most intimate of circumstances, the familiarity remained.

Colin must have felt the connection too, for he snaked an arm about her and pulled her close, burying his head in her hair. Maggie hugged him tight as she breathed in that heady mixture of masculinity and her favorite aftershave, wishing the night would never end.

As she peered over his shoulder, she spied the clock. Six-thirty and fifty-two seconds. It was still November twenty-ninth. "Thank you," she whispered to the heavens.

Colin released her, his smoky brown eyes pondering what she had said.

"That wasn't meant for your ears."

He moved tendrils of hair off her face, and then used his palm to caress her cheek. But a sly twinkle glittered in his eyes. "Who were you thanking then?"

She laughed again. "I guess I forgot to add you."

He waited for an explanation, his look evolving into a little boy who didn't get a present for Christmas, which made her laugh again. "Tomorrow's my birthday. I was thanking the divine for not letting me turn thirty without having a…well, you know."

"Crap!" He rose to a sitting position. "It's your birthday?"

Maggie didn't want to go there, wanted the whole world to ignore her sliding downhill into her thirties. She figured living in a new place with new people, no one would be the wiser. "It's no big deal. This is one birthday I'd rather forget."

"Yeah, right, it's no big deal." He paused, soaking in what she had said. "Wait, that was the first time you had an org…?"

"Yes." She cringed, hoping he wouldn't actually say the word. "Didn't you find all this out in that report you had done on me? Didn't the private detective tell you what a lousy love life I had?"

"It didn't offer that many details, Maggie."

She felt deflated, exposed, and began tracing the bedspread pattern with her finger, suddenly embarrassed to be lying naked on the bed with a man. Even this man.

Colin placed a finger under her chin and raised her gaze to his, the big brother persona now taking control. "We have a lot of catching up to do then, don't we?"

He kissed her gently, but with a force that literally made her toes curl. She reached up to encircle his neck and pull him close, to start the cycle all over again, when a knock sounded on the door, making them both bolt to attention. Colin rose, grabbed a hotel bathrobe and threw it at Maggie, hitting her in the face.

"Sorry," he said, laughing, pulling on one of his own.

She pulled the overlarge terrycloth from her face. "Sure you are."

He looped the robe's belt tight and headed for the door. For a second, Maggie held her breath, worried it might be Bonnie, a client or someone from the magazine. But then she heard a hotel worker announcing cocktail hour and a cart being wheeled inside.

"Wait a moment," Colin said, heading back into the room and searching for his pants.

Maggie pulled them off the floor and threw them, hitting him smack in the face. "Sorry."

He sent her a sly glance, then removed his wallet, and disappeared again. Maggie heard the hotel worker thanking Colin for the tip, then the closing of the door.

She slid a bare leg free from the bathrobe and grinned seductively when he turned the corner, hoping to pull that hard Yankee body back into bed, but his face turned pale. He stood before her, wallet still in hand, looking as if he had seen a ghost in the hallway.

"Crap."

Maggie's smile faded. Was reality sinking in? Did he regret what happened? "What's wrong?"

Colin closed his eyes and cringed. "Didn't you notice we forgot something?"

Forgot what, she thought madly, then focused on the wallet. The lovemaking had happened so furious, did they forget to take precautions?

"Crap," Colin repeated.

"It's okay." She sat up, trying to reassure herself as much as him. "I was tested last time and, well, I haven't done this in a very long time."

Colin pulled a nervous hand through his hair. "I'm clean, too, Maggie. That's not the problem."

Realization dawned. How on earth would she explain that one to the Parnells? Maggie thought. It had only been three months, tops, since Jake passed away. What would they think if she got pregnant with Colin?

And yet, Colin didn't seem half as worried. He sat on the edge of the bed, grabbing her toe, lost in thought as his hand massaged her foot. He almost appeared at peace, as if a child might force the issue and push the family into accepting them as a couple.

"You're not thinking what I think you're thinking?"

When Colin looked up, he seemed to come out of a trance. "What am I thinking?"

Maybe she was reading him wrong. Maybe she was seeing more into this than there was. Was she hoping for a declaration of love, of commitment? Or was she praying he'd forget all about it. "Nothing."

A deadly silence descended between them, until Colin let his hand slide up the bathrobe all the way to her thigh. "Maggie, whatever happens, I'm here for you."

She wasn't sure what that meant, but she nodded. "I'm sure it's fine, Colin. I'm sure it's nothing."

"Well, if it is." He paused, his gaze serious and loving, which unnerved Maggie more than a brush-off. "I'll rectify things. You can count on that."

Where had the room's air gone? Suddenly, Maggie broke out in a sweat. And why had they suddenly moved to speaking of marriage — or at least something like it? Love she could have handled — even hoped for — but not that.

"Look." She pointed to the window overlooking the waterfront. "It's snowing."

She jumped out of bed, running to the scene. It was the first snow of the season and her first witnessed in years. In all her longing to get to Portland, Maggie had completely missed that fact, driving through the winter wonderland without even realizing what was going on around her.

She stood at the glass watching the flakes flood the street as the lamplights below painted the scene with an iridescent glow. Somewhere in the black distance of Casco Bay a foghorn sounded and the ferry returned to port.

Colin met her there, wrapping his arms about her shoulders. "What just happened?"

She met his eyes in the window's reflection. "I don't want to get married," she whispered. "And I'm not ready to tell your family. I don't know where this is leading but I'm not..."

Colin turned her around and kissed her protestations. Then he cupped her cheeks with his hands and rested his forehead against hers. "Maggie, I'm crazy about you," he whispered so seductively she felt it all the way to the tip of her toes. "I want you in my bed every night. I want to kiss you every minute of every day. But if I can't have that..." He slipped his hands behind her knees and raised her in the air, causing her breath to skip. "...then I'll take you any way I can."

And with those final words, they headed back to bed.

Chapter Seventeen

S OMEONE WAS RINGING A BELL. A loud one. But it wasn't any sound Colin recognized.

He managed to open an eye, realizing it was morning and somewhere brighter than home. When he spotted the cart of empty wine bottles and room service, he knew he was at the Westin. And if his memory served him correctly…

Colin reached down and felt the soft, delicious curves that made up Maggie, who was fast asleep on his chest, one arm stretched across his body. Colin smiled, recalling their endless lovemaking until dawn and how he sent his Southern belle into the stratosphere several times that night. Not to mention that she hadn't traveled alone.

He still glowed from that peaceful, sated feeling, but there was a buzzing that wouldn't stop.

Colin opened both eyes, realizing the phone was ringing. He reached out a hand and pulled the receiver to his ear. "Yeah?"

"Colin? Are you still asleep?"

Not anymore, Colin thought, as his mother's voice brought him to full attention. "Busy night, Mom. What's up?"

Maggie stirred, no doubt reacting to who was on the phone. Without making a sound, Colin kissed her forehead.

"I'm looking for Maggie."

Now he was fully awake. "Oh? How come?"

"Today's her birthday." Bonnie paused to talk to someone else, someone standing close who demanded to know what was going on. "Her father decided to surprise her and he flew in this morning, but she's not answering her phone."

Colin rose to a sitting position and Maggie shifted, rising on an elbow and studying him with droopy eyes. "Where are you?"

"Downstairs." He could hear Bonnie relaying information to Stewart.

"You're in the lobby?"

Suddenly, Maggie was sitting up as well.

"Yes, shall we come up?"

"We?" Colin glanced at Maggie. "Stewart's with you?"

Maggie wasted no time. She jumped out of bed and headed for the bathroom, grabbing the bathrobe and her tote bag in the process. Within a heartbeat, Colin heard the shower start.

"What's that?" Bonnie asked.

"The maid. Are you telling me you two are sitting in the lobby right now?"

"Yes, dear." She sounded impatient. "I picked Stewart up at the airport and we came straight here. Now, do you know where Maggie is or not."

"Yeah." Colin rubbed the sleep from his eyes, feeling as if he'd been drinking all night. "She came by with some papers yesterday and the snow got bad. I made her stay the night."

"Good girl. I warned her about the weather."

Colin smiled, thinking how ingenuous his Southern belle had been. "She's fine. Safe and sound."

"Then give us her room number and we'll go up and surprise her."

That would be a surprise, all right, he thought. "Ah, I have it here somewhere, not sure what the number is." He tried to force his eyes open further, tried to come up with a plan. "I tell you what, Mom, I know where she is. I'll go knock on her door and tell her you're here. Then we'll meet you in the restaurant. I need a few minutes to jump in the shower, but I won't be long."

"Colin, it's eleven o'clock."

Crap. He missed his meeting with a client. "So, tell them to hold breakfast for us."

"I'm sure Maggie's been up by now. Just because you're sleeping late…"

He really didn't want to have this conversation anymore. He needed time to wake up, time to think. "Mom, I'll see you downstairs in five." Colin placed the phone back on the cradle, then joined Maggie in the bathroom, coming out of the shower.

"Don't tell me, your mom and my dad are in the lobby."

Colin nodded, still trying to rub the sleep away. "They're heading to the restaurant and are going to wait for us. I told them five minutes."

Her hair stood in a million directions and her towel was wrapped haphazardly about her glistening body. Still groggy from lack of sleep, Maggie dripped water everywhere. But to Colin, she was the most gorgeous woman he had ever met.

"God, I love you."

He wasn't sure where that came from, but was glad to have said it. He couldn't bear more months like the last three, couldn't stand wanting this woman with such an exhaustive desire while having to keep at a distance for the sake of Jake and his family.

But, how did Maggie feel? Her face drained of color and she stood motionless before him, water falling into a puddle at her feet.

"God help me, I love you, too."

Colin wasted no time taking her in his arms, but her hands held fast to the towel about her. When he realized she wasn't hugging back, he released her and she stepped away.

"You want to tell them, don't you?" she asked.

"It's the perfect chance. They're alone in the restaurant. We can explain."

Maggie shook her head, anxiety showing in her face. "What will they think?"

"Who cares what they think?" Colin sighed, knowing he had raised his voice. But, he was sick of letting Jake run his life. Even from his grave, his cousin held an iron fist over his future.

He felt Maggie's hand on his arm. "We have to give it some time."

Not caring that she was soaking wet, Colin pulled her into his chest and held her tight. She smelled of roses again. He breathed it in, branding it to memory, praying it wouldn't be the last time he'd be able to hold her like this. "I've been waiting my whole life, Maggie. Time is not something I'm good at."

She nodded into his shoulder and Colin sensed she understood. "Then we'll tell them?" he asked.

She pushed away, but this time headed for the bedroom. He found her hurriedly pulling on her clothes. "If you said five minutes, we better hurry."

"Maggie, they'll understand."

"Understand?" Now, her voice was rising. "Bonnie thinks I'm a grieving widow. How is this going to look?"

"Like two people who met and fell in love."

She searched for her shoes. "Sure, Colin, I met and married your womanizing, non-committal cousin within hours, inherited his wealth, including the magazine, and now I'm snagging you. And you think this is going to go down well with your family."

"Well, if you put it that way." He offered a smile, anything to dispel the tension between them, but Maggie remained stiff and uncompromising.

Having pulled on her shoes, she turned her focus to the mirror and her hair, but her gaze starred at him through the reflection. "Colin, I married a man on a lark and regretted it for the past few months. Please don't rush me into anything."

Her last words wounded him to the core, even though her request was perfectly reasonable. There was so much history to deal with, so much pain from years of betrayal. After all this time, Jake continued having the last laugh.

And now he was being unfairly compared to the brute.

Colin drew nearer and starred at the chocolate brown eyes that had been his undoing from the moment he first spied them in Pittsburgh.

"I'm not Jake," he said with such conviction that he felt his skin prickle with the anger.

Then he turned and headed for his own shower. Preferably a cold one.

"So?" Stewart asked, anxious to hear if their suspicions had been correct. "What's going on?"

Bonnie giggled and Stewart swore he could hear the New England cadence in it. God, he loved this woman, loved every inch of her, including her adorable smile and laugh.

"He was fast asleep. Sounded surprised when he heard it was me." She giggled again. "But shocked when he heard you were in the lobby."

"And Maggie?"

Bonnie waved a playful hand. "Gave me some story about not remembering her room number and that he'd go knock on her door. I swore I heard the shower running."

Stewart leaned back in the booth and a waitress arrived, pouring them both a cup of coffee. He wasn't sure how to react to his daughter making love to his girlfriend's son. He approved, of course. Colin was a fine man and would make an excellent son-in-law; Stewart realized that from the moment they'd first met. Yet, thinking about his daughter being intimate was not a road Stewart wanted to travel.

Bonnie touched his hand with a knowing smile. The woman seemed to know every thought in his brain. "She's thirty, Stewart, more than a grown woman. And those two are made for each other. You should have seen their silly banter at Thanksgiving. I've never seen two people so much alike."

Except for the fact that they both owned two distinctly separate, extremely strong, regional accents. Stewart wondered what his grandchildren would sound like.

Heavens, did he just think grandchildren? "I'm not ready for this."

"You're not ready for what?"

Bonnie's smile disappeared and Stewart knew what she was thinking. Their relationship had catapulted to a new level within weeks of the funeral. Their discretion had been fine at the start, but the sneaking around and making excuses was wearing thin. Stewart was ready to drop on one knee, but he had the family to consider. "What will the kids think?"

"They'll understand. We're not dead, you know."

The waitress returned with two glasses of water. "All set here?"

The question stopped Stewart cold. He was, in fact, very ready. He had grieved enough, suffered in solitude far too long. He wanted to be with this woman with all his heart and soul.

"We have two more people coming," Bonnie told the woman with hair a bright artificial shade of auburn and an accent thick as maple syrup. "I'd suspect they'd like coffee too."

The waitress headed toward the kitchen, allowing Stewart time enough to explain himself. He took Bonnie's hand and pressed his lips to the inside of her palm. "Give me a little more time. Let me spend some time with Maggie, talk to her alone."

Bonnie nodded. "I need to talk to Colin myself."

"You need to explain what happened."

She exhaled and looked away, the weight of a great secret hanging heavy on her shoulders. "I know."

"You need to put this to rest, Bonnie, before we can move on. You owe it to them." He kissed the other palm. "How do you expect them to come to us and admit their attraction when they still don't understand how Jake died."

Bonnie straightened with a purpose. "Let me do it, then. This is my mess, let me clean it up."

He wished they weren't sitting across from each other, for he wanted to pull her into his arms. "However you think is best."

Maggie sauntered into the restaurant, her clothes mussed and her hair damp from a shower. Bonnie glanced at Stewart and gave him a wink.

"Hey baby." Stewart rose, grabbing his daughter and twirling her into the air as was his custom. Maggie laughed, causing everyone in the restaurant to stop talking and stare. "It's her birthday," he announced to the audience, and one of the patrons wished her well.

"How old are you, sweetie?" Bonnie asked.

Maggie fell into the booth beside her dad and stole his coffee, adding cream and sugar. "I'm going to be twenty-nine for the rest of my life starting today."

Bonnie smiled, but Stewart recognized that knowing look beneath its veneer, the one observing youth agonizing over a milestone that will become insignificant over time. Maggie had yet to cross the bridges he and Bonnie had traversed. Wait until she hit fifty.

Ouch, he thought. He didn't need to remind himself of that fact. The way he was feeling these days, age didn't matter. He felt like a schoolboy heading for the prom. Stewart stole a glance at Bonnie and watched the blush steal up her cheeks. If only they were alone.

"So what's up with you rising so late?" he said, trying to get his mind on to something else. "Usually you greet the dawn."

Maggie gulped her coffee like a Mardi Gras reveler nursing a hangover. "No thanks to you. If I had been a normal child, I could have learned to sleep later."

"If you'd been a normal child, you wouldn't have seen the world."

Maggie added more cream to her cup, giving Bonnie a "do you believe this guy?" look. "Dad's standard answer to everything."

"It's true," Stewart insisted. "Thirteen countries and counting."

"You're right, as always."

Maggie kissed him on the cheek and gave him a tight squeeze, the way she did as a child. One thing about this Jake ordeal, he found love again and he got his baby back.

"Is Colin coming down?" Bonnie asked. "He sounded like he slept in as well."

Maggie blushed, which confirmed Stewart's suspicions.

"I'm right here." Colin approached the table, trying to tame his equally damp hair. He looked as disheveled as Maggie.

"What on earth did you two do last night?" Leave it to Bonnie to get right to the heart of the matter. Beneath her serious façade, Stewart saw the semblance of a grin.

"Oh, you know. There was a convention dinner." Colin stole a glance at his cohort, but Maggie looked away, drawing circles on the tablecloth with her spoon. "We had some wine. Time got away from us."

Brilliant, Stewart thought. Totally non-committal. He reached out a hand when Colin's attention made his way around the table. "Good to see you again, son."

"You, too, sir."

Colin sat next to his mother and avoided looking at Maggie, who did the same, which struck Stewart as odd. The waitress brought two fresh cups of coffee and placed them on the table, pencil in hand.

"Are we too late for breakfast?" Maggie asked, looking at the menu. "I'm starving."

For a split second, Maggie glanced up at Colin and something familiar passed between them. Stewart swore they almost smiled. Then, the frost settled again.

"I can talk Frank into keeping the grill heated, but you gotta hurry," Auburn answered.

"I'll have the country breakfast," Maggie said. "With the bacon and the home fries and the wheat toast. Oh, and a glass of orange juice please."

Heading around the table, the waitress glanced at Stewart. "Nothing for me. I already ate."

"Me too," Bonnie offered, blushing again, which made Colin and Maggie look up inquisitively.

Colin handed the waitress his menu. "Just coffee." To Stewart, he added, "I can't stay long. I'm sure you and Maggie have a lot to talk about. She and I have talked enough."

Maggie studied Colin above the edge of her coffee cup. An uneasy silence fell between them, tension so thick it heated up the room.

"We have a surprise for you," Bonnie said, trying to dispel the uneasiness.

Maggie seemed grateful for the interruption. "For me?"

"Of course, for you, Magpie." Stewart laid an arm about his daughter's shoulders. "No one else here has a birthday today."

Maggie glanced back at Colin who shrugged. "I had nothing to do with it."

"A friend of mine has a guest house," Bonnie began. "And after some renovations that we both worked on, she's letting me rent it out for you."

Stewart tried to read Maggie's reaction; her reply was polite and pleasantly surprised but not genuine, unusual for her. When Bonnie explained how they had purchased some furniture — also part of the birthday present — Maggie displayed happiness and gratitude, yet something was missing. When he noticed Colin's frown and agitation, Stewart realized the problem.

They were taking Maggie away. She and Colin would no longer be together without careful planning and secrecy. Something Stewart knew all too well.

"Are you okay with this?" he asked her. "We wanted you to have your own place, since you've spent years living with roommates and…"

"It's fine." She said it too fast, with too much conviction. "I'm sure I'm going to love it."

If only Stewart could be sure. As soon as they were alone, he would pry the truth out.

"We thought we'd stop in town and let you pick out some dishes and towels, then head up to Madison and show you the place," Bonnie continued enthusiastically. "If that's okay with you."

"Yes, that would be lovely." Again, the frosty politeness. This wasn't like Maggie at all. If she was truly happy for gaining her own place, she'd be kissing and hugging everyone present.

"Well." Colin stood, smoothing out his clothes that desperately needed a good iron. "I have a client to see about."

"Bye dear." Bonnie reached up and kissed him on the cheek. "Do stop by later."

"Will do."

Colin turned toward Maggie and a strange look passed over his features. It reminded Stewart of how he felt every time Maggie waved and drove away in that poor excuse of a car — to college, to her many jobs, to her new homes. And his stomach ached as if someone had punched him and left a gaping hole. What were he and Bonnie doing? In their attempt to find Maggie a place of her own, were they ruining her chance at happiness? Colin's happiness as well?

Stewart reached out his hand. "Don't worry, Colin. Your women are in good hands."

Colin's face lightened as he shook. "I'm sure they are." Before he moved to leave, he looked at Maggie one last time, touching her chin with two fingers. "Happy Birthday, Reb."

Colin hadn't made it to the lobby before Bonnie began describing everything from curtains in the bathroom to the paint of the outside window trim. Maggie smiled and nodded, but Stewart doubted she heard one word.

"So do you really like it?"

It was the fourth time her father had asked her that since they arrived at the darling cottage. What wasn't there to like? The place resembled something out of a Brother's Grimm fairy tale: a sloping roof with gables, flowerboxes beneath rounded windows, a vegetable garden out back that was now covered in snow.

"It's lovely, Dad. Truly. It was very thoughtful of you and Bonnie to do this."

"But?"

She honestly didn't where he was going with this. "But what?"

Stewart sat next to her on the beige couch, so new it smelled like the furniture section of a department store. Even the pillows sported tags that warned of some sort of justice if you yanked them off, which everyone always did. Maggie let one rip. "Are these for real?"

"You're avoiding the question."

Maggie sighed. "What was the question?"

Stewart rose and pulled on his coat. "I'm getting nowhere with you. I thought we had torn down the walls between us, but you seem to have built new ones overnight."

He headed for the door and a panic rose in Maggie's chest. She wasn't ready to be alone, even if she now lived in Snow White's cottage.

"Colin and I made love last night."

He paused at the threshold and Maggie wondered how a father would absorb such news. Surprisingly, Stewart smiled as if he got what he wanted. "I know."

"You know?"

He moved back to the couch and wrapped an arm about her shoulders and kissed the top of her head. "You never sleep until eleven in the morning. And you both looked as if you just crawled out of bed." She started to object, to argue that even army brats slept in once and a while, but what difference did it make? She already admitted their tryst. And her father knew how much she cared for Colin. Plus, he was right. They had bridged the silence gap two months before and there was no turning back.

"I love him, Daddy."

He hugged her close. "I know you do."

"I don't know what to do about it."

"For one, you could have politely said no to the house."

Maggie sent her dad a get-real look.

"Okay, maybe it would have been hard to have turned Bonnie down. She did spend weeks fixing this place up, but that's what she does, Maggie. Eventually, she would have understood, could have passed it on to someone else. Sooner or later you're going to have to tell them about you and Colin."

Maggie broke away, shaking her head. "I'll tell you what, Dad. You come clean about you and Bonnie and I'll tell the family about me and Colin."

She shouldn't have said it; he really needed to speak of it when he was good and ready. But he surprised her again. "You're right."

He exhaled and then leaned his forehead against hers. "I'll make a deal with you. If I do, will you tell them about Jake and how you feel about Colin?"

Fear gripped her throat; she wasn't ready for this. So, she nodded instead.

"Good." He tapped her chin, much the way Colin had done earlier. "Then if it's okay with you, I'm going to go see about a lady."

Maggie hugged him tight, grateful that her father had found love again. "I'm so happy for you, Dad. I love Bonnie dearly."

He leaned a chin on top of her head, making her feel like she was ten years old. "I'm glad, sweetpea. Your approval means the world to me."

Stewart straightened. "You know, it's your birthday. Let's go do something fun. Or watch a movie. Maybe we can get pizza delivered here."

Maggie said nothing, simply turned her father around and pushed him toward the door. "You have to see about a lady."

"I'm sorry, baby. For a moment, I forgot it was your birthday."

"Bye Dad."

She opened the door and waited for him to pass. He resigned to leave, buttoned his coat and gave her a kiss. "Go back to Colin," he whispered. "He's waiting for you."

She gave him a final hug and waved as he walked down the pathway leading to the main house and the driveway. When his car faded from her view, she retreated inside her storybook cottage, the loneliness biting into her soul like the bitter wind howling outside. Colin, no doubt, was back at work or at the sprawling Colonial she had come to cherish over the past three months. And, no doubt as well, Colin was still fuming over their earlier argument.

"What did I do?" Maggie couldn't believe she had compared Colin to Jake. "What was I thinking?"

Yet, as hard as she tried, fear held her from grabbing the phone and asking him over.

She fell on to the beautiful couch that reeked of newness and fought back tears. The cell phone buzzed beside her.

"Hey darlin'," Stacy's voice boomed. "Happy birthday!"

That did it. The dam broke and Maggie struggled to speak as sobs threatened.

"What did that damn Yankee do now?"

She wanted to explain that it was she who did the damage this time, unfairly comparing a wonderful man whom she loved dearly to that rascal Jake, but she couldn't get the words past her emotions.

"Maggie?"

She was just about to whisper something — anything — to keep Stacy from calling 911 when she heard the front door opening and saw a bottle of scotch being placed before her, a red bow tied around its neck. Then a gentle hand pried the phone away from her.

"Stacy?"

Her roommate's response was so loud, Maggie could hear her from the couch. "Okay, Yank, what did you do to my Maggie this time?"

When she glanced up at Colin, he winked, not minding the reprimand at all. "I asked her to marry me and she turned me down. Somehow she's gun-shy with Parnell men. Can you believe that?"

At this, Stacy turned silent, making Maggie laugh through the tears. Stacy at a loss for words? It was going to snow in Atlanta.

"I'll tell you what, darlin'," Colin attempted in a Southern drawl. "I'm going to show this woman a good time for her birthday and then she can call you back in the morning. Does that work for you?"

"I got a better idea," Stacy replied. "How about you call me back and you and I will talk."

Colin laughed. "Fair enough. But I want to meet you one day. Ever find your way up north?"

"Well, if you're as good as Maggie's says you are, maybe she'll make me the maid of honor."

Maggie headed for the kitchen to avoid hearing her roommate embarrass her yet again. But Colin laughed, ended the conversation and followed her, grabbing her hand and pulling her tight into his chest. His breath was warm against her cheek. "I thought we could christen your new place," he said soft and deep, sending shivers up her spine.

His kiss said he wouldn't take no for an answer, not that Maggie had any intention of sending him away. "I thought you were mad at me," she whispered when he came up for air.

Colin pulled her close, enveloping her like a cocoon. "I figured if I had to choose between meeting you on the sly and not seeing you at all, then sneaking around won." He pulled back to gaze into her eyes, making her realize how much she missed him, even though they were apart mere hours. "I can't live without you, Reb. And I don't want to try."

How long after Vegas had she forgotten Jake, even though she reeled over the ordeal? Days had passed and she couldn't recall his face. Yet, she remembered every inch of Colin — the laugh lines about his eyes when he smiled, the sparkle in his eyes when he teased her, the way his callused hands, worn from creating new projects, covered hers completely. There was no comparison and she knew it.

She slipped a hand down to his and urged him along the long hallway.

"I vote we start in the bedroom."

Colin wasn't ready to leave a warm bed with Maggie inside and be greeted by an empty house, but he promised his mother they would visit for lunch and he needed to shower, read his mail and check messages. The silence of his home made the loneliness that much more acute. For once, he wished Frosty was around, his annoying barking and growling would be a welcome distraction to the fact that he lived alone. Again.

Refusing to let the malaise set in, Colin headed for the kitchen for some coffee, noticing two messages on his answering machine. He punched the button as he began loading up the coffee maker.

"Colin, Steve Bradshaw here in New York," the first one announced. "Everyone at the firm was disappointed you couldn't come down last month. All I keep hearing is 'Why didn't we get Parnell on that project?' "

Colin paused, measuring spoon in hand, forgetting how many scoops of coffee he had put into the filter.

"It made me think — made all of us think — why don't we hire this guy?"

Colin gave up on the coffee, heading to the answering machine to make sure he heard right.

"In other words, Parnell, we want to offer you a job. You said things were stabilizing at the magazine, so give me a call and let's talk. Let's see if we can come up with a plan that will work for all of us." A pause followed and Colin swore he could hear his heart beating. "Call me."

He had to sit down for this one. After all this time and his earlier rejection because of Jake, the firm of Turley, Bradshaw and Hunn were offering him a job? Before he had time to contemplate what that meant, the answering machine buzzed for the second message.

"Parnell, David here."

Crap, he'd forgotten about David and his investigation of Jake.

"I'm sorry, pal, for all the delays. My father passed away a few days ago after a long bout in the hospital. I apologize for not getting back to you, but I've been useless trying to keep my family together and arrange this funeral."

Colin wished they were actually speaking so he could dispel David's worries. Right now, the last thing he wanted to think about was Jake and he certainly understood how debilitating a father's death could be to a son.

"But I'm back on track and I got some news on your cousin."

Crap. Could things get any more complicated? Colin thought.

"You're not going to like this," David said with an ominous tone. "Looks like our girl knew more than we thought."

Now, Colin definitely heard his heart pounding through his chest.

"Your cousin, Jake, died in a hospital in Houston, Texas. And from everyone I've spoken to at M.D. Anderson, there was a woman by his side to the very end."

Chapter Eighteen

G RIPPING HIS COFFEE LIKE A lifeline, Colin stared at the enormous chest before him, the one still sitting in the same spot of the living room as the day it arrived. Then he pulled out the key and slipped it into the rusty lock. After a light snap, the lock pulled back and he lifted the lid.

As expected, all Jake's worldly goods lay before him — his letter jackets, his journalism awards, the silly trophy he won in college for downing the most Jell-o shots within ten minutes. And on top sat a letter addressed to Colin in Jake's shaky handwriting.

Colin picked up the letter, ignoring the rest, but fear stilled his hand.

"For God sakes, Colin, just open it."

He had heard the familiar car in the driveway, the accustomed steps in the foyer, yet Colin's focus remained on Jake's chest. But when his mother spoke, frustration and hurt lacing her words, he knew this story ended with her explanation and the letter he held in his hands.

"Why?" He turned to look at the woman who never kept a secret from him in his life. The woman who was his partner in business, his closest ally against the world.

She gingerly sat down in the Queen Anne chair, guilt and remorse facing him from across the room. "I can explain."

"Explain? My cousin is dead from leukemia and you knew all along? He died in a Houston cancer hospital and you never told a soul, not even me or Maggie?"

"He insisted, Colin. He made it a condition when I did the bone marrow transplant last year, that I never tell anyone about the disease." She paused to gather her emotions, tears threatening. "I seriously thought he was going to get better afterwards; he certainly improved. He didn't tell me the disease had returned until he was on death's door. And he wouldn't tell me the name of the hospital unless I promised to come alone and not tell anyone how he died."

Colin shook his head trying to make sense of it all. That tidbit at least explained where she was last year and in early September, but still, it was all so baffling. "You went through all the trouble to give him a bone marrow transplant but you couldn't tell the rest of us about it?"

Bonnie moved to the edge of the coffee table and attempted to touch his hands, but Colin pulled away. "Please, Colin. You know Jake. Always so vain, never wanting help from anyone. This was exactly how he would have wanted it."

"No." He couldn't comprehend why anyone — even Jake — would want to die alone. Colin stood and began pacing the room, the letter still gripped between his fingers. There had to be a better explanation.

"It took him months to get up the nerve to ask me for the transplant. He was so relieved I was a match. He thought for sure, you'd be the one."

This stabbed Colin to the core and he struggled to catch his breath. Bonnie quickly stood and placed her hands on his shoulders. "Darling, you know how he was. He thought the world of you, but he would never let you know."

As always, all logic about Jake escaped Colin. "So much so he was worried I'd have to save his life?"

Bonnie rubbed her hands up and down his arms empathetically like she used to when he was a child and Jake would steal his toys, then best him at sports and lure away his girlfriends. "He adored you. He was always so jealous of you, always admired what you had."

Colin didn't want to hear this. How could a person adore someone and make their life miserable? It never made sense and it made even less sense now. "He could have had what I had, Mom. I begged him to take over the magazine…"

"Jake? In charge of *Yankee Living*? Over my dead body." Bonnie sighed, falling into her chair as if the weight of Jake hung too heavy on her shoulders to stand. "I loved that boy, you know I did. But he was an irresponsible, unreliable child."

Colin dropped on to the opposite couch. "I know."

"You were my rock."

The pain in his chest intensified. Colin began pacing again. "I'm a little weary of being everyone's savior, Mom."

"I said rock, not savior. We don't expect you to move mountains, but you are so wonderful at running this magazine."

"I love the magazine, that's not the point."

"What is the point, then?"

Colin paused halfway across the room and glanced back. What was the point? Was it because he earned an architecture degree and never used it, although he put his talents to use every month on the magazine projects? Was it because his father and uncle had left him the patriarch of the family and he tired of being the Parnell handyman? Or was it because his life always dictated his actions?

"I don't know," he finally answered. "But I've been offered a job in New York."

Bonnie absorbed this news silently, a frown playing her forehead. This would certainly screw things up at the magazine, Colin thought, although having Maggie there would help.

Maggie.

Colin closed his eyes, thinking of how delectable waking up to her lovemaking had been that morning. How could he leave Maggie now?

"How does Maggie fit into all of this?"

Bonnie held a hand to her mouth as she leaned on an elbow

and stared out the window. The snow had ceased and the sun shone brightly, but a cold wind wiped around the house, howling in bursts as if mirroring their heated conversation.

"Maybe that's something I should ask you?" Bonnie looked back at Colin. "How are you going to leave her and go to New York?"

Colin stopped pacing and fell back on the couch, gazing out the same window that rattled with the chill. "I don't know." He sighed, knowing it was now or never. "I'm in love with her, Mom."

To his surprise, Bonnie smiled. Then she reached over and took his hand in hers. "I know you are, sweetheart. The question is, what are you going to do about it?"

Colin looked down at their enjoined hands, the letter still tight within his grip. There were still important questions to be answered. "How did Jake…?"

Bonnie released him and stood, placing a warm hand on his shoulder. "Read the letter, sweetheart. He wrote it before he died, insisted he explain this all to you. I think all the answers are in that letter."

He felt her squeeze, but Colin hated to see her go. Suddenly, he was back in grade school, thrust into some family activity with Jake where everything was a competition. He looked up at his mother as he did then, silently begging her the question, "Do I have to?"

And, as usual, his mother read his mind. "Yes, you do."

She grabbed her purse and headed for the door. While she pulled on her coat, she added, "See you at noon, right? And Maggie's coming?"

Give it to his mother to always think of turkey and cranberries, even in the most trying of times. "Yes. But it's time we told the rest of the family what happened."

She straightened her red beret over her hair. "Yes, it's time."

When the door closed behind her, the morning's revelation fell heavy on his heart. He pulled the letter out of his grip and stared at it before opening the flap and pulling out several pages containing Jake's shaky writing. He wasn't sure what he'd find there, wasn't sure what fresh pain Jake would inflict, but he had to know.

> *Dear Cuz,*
> *You probably hate me at this moment and I don't blame you.*
> *Knowing you, my big brother cuz, you're just as mad I died on*
> *you without an explanation. Bonnie's furious with me, too, so*
> *you're in good company.*
> *To tell you the truth, this is better. It's like performing in a*
> *play, taking a nice, short and sweet bow and retreating off stage.*
> *Who needs the people waiting at the stage door, fawning all*
> *over you? And you know how I am. I can't stand any fuss*
> *unless it's a woman telling me how smart I am. Ha, ha.*
> *But you deserve an explanation. I promised you I would*
> *take over the magazine and recruit staff and I let you down. I*
> *was really going to do it, Colin, I swear. After the last bouts of*
> *chemo and the transplant, things were starting to look as if I*
> *was in the clear. I found out the cancer returned days before I*
> *was to leave for Vegas.*
> *I decided to go, find some prospective writers and editors I*
> *could steal from other publications and then head to Mexico.*
> *They have an alternative medicine program I wanted to try,*
> *which, as you can now imagine, didn't work. But, Vegas turned*
> *out differently. I met Maggie.*

There it was, that horrible, stabbing pain that only Jake could deliver. Colin gazed to the ceiling to steady the beating of his heart, anxious to know the truth but dreading it just as much.

> *You must have met her by now. Isn't she a hoot? (That's*
> *how Maggie would have put it.) I met her at the ice breaker*
> *and something told me she was familiar – of course, that seems*
> *crazy since I didn't see her name tag until I got closer. But I*
> *felt like I knew her, you know? I'd seen her resumés, writing*
> *samples and Christmas cards. All those years of Uncle Gavin*
> *telling me about this adorable girl from Georgia and her won-*
> *derful thesis and it didn't do her justice. I mean, this girl rocks.*

She must have thought I was nuts coming on to her, although I have to admit, she had that look most girls get around me so maybe it was simple attraction. I hope not. Yeah, yeah, I know what you're thinking. A man who played around as much as I did would only be stupid enough to fall in love with a girl at first sight. And a mousy one, at that. The kind you go for. Go figure.

Crap. Colin rubbed his eyes, trying to will away the image of Jake falling in love with his girl. All this time, he had hoped it was some cruel joke he had played on Maggie, a way to get out of his obligation. Not love.

To tell you the truth, Colin, Maggie reminded me of you. All that optimism you used to have before Uncle Gavin died, your dry sense of humor, the way you take charge of any situation and put all chaos into order. Maybe I was homesick. Maybe I was finally realizing what a great family I have and what a jerk I've been all this time. Or how lucky I was to know someone as smart and together as you.

Jake's penmanship began to blur. Colin rubbed his eyes again, this time to wipe away the emotions. Damn his cousin. So much time and energy wasted competing when they could have been good friends.

Anyway, I got her drunk and convinced her to marry me. Thought it would be a good reason not to come home and I wouldn't have to explain this dreadful, boring disease to any-one. But, for a bright moment, I actually thought I could have her. For one tiny moment in my life, I thought I could be nor-mal, have a real relationship, maybe even be happy for a little while – like you. But I had a plane to catch for Mexico and I left her in Vegas. I left her my part in the magazine as well.

Now, she's probably with you. Do take care of my Maggie, keep her happy. You might be appalled I gave her the stake in

the magazine, but she's like the sister you never had, really. I
have no doubt you two will be the best of friends. And I've read
her work. She's damn good.

   As for us, please forgive me cuz. I'm slipping away and all I
can think about is you and what a horrible cousin I've been all
these years. If I could do it over, I'd do it differently, although
little good that does us now, right?

   Shit, can't even die right.

The pain in Colin's chest gripped him tenfold, but this time it
had nothing to do with betrayal.

   I'm having a hard time writing so am going to sign off.
   Have a good life, cuz. Remember me well.
   Your bratty relation,
   Jake

The wind took the house by storm, howling down the chim-
ney fluke like a ghost demanding entrance. One of the shutters
broke loose on the porch and rattled against a window. Inside,
Colin's coffee grew cold and a chill permeated the room. Colin
acknowledged none of it, the paper still held tightly in his hand.

"Where've you been?" Edith gazed at her watch as Colin
walked through the door. "Mom said noon."

He pulled off his coat and scarf, trying to figure out what was
different about his sister. "Been a little busy. What did you do to
your hair?"

Just then, his Webmaster turned the corner into the foyer. "You
remember Malick," Edith said, blushing profusely.

Colin shook his hand. "Of course, I do. I stole him from an
Austin start-up."

"Savemyassfromdebt.com," Malick answered with a laugh. "Boy
did that one go down bad. Right after acquiring a load of debt."

"Hope you're happy here."

Edith began fidgeting with a curl. What did she do to her hair? She seemed to have tamed the wild curls with combs and trimmed the back into a bouncy, smart haircut that accented her face, which, Colin noticed, glowed when she smiled. And was she wearing a dress? More like a jumper, turtleneck and tights, but still a dress.

"I plan on hanging around," Malick said, stealing a glance at his sister, who blushed again. The day was full of surprises.

Colin pulled off his coat and hung it in the hall closet, his heart still heavy from the morning's revelations. As much as they drove him crazy, he was thankful to be around family today. "Is everyone here?"

"Everyone except you."

"I like to make a grand entrance."

"Yeah, well, tell that to Mom."

Colin headed for the dining room, nearly stumbling upon Jude and Mark necking in the shadows of the hallway. "Oh, sorry, Colin," Jude said when she spotted her brother. "We were taking an opportunity away from the little one."

"No problem." He certainly wasn't one to object to any chance at secretive lovemaking, but since when did Jude and Mark get so affectionate? It wasn't like them. Hell, it wasn't like anyone in his family.

Except for Maggie.

"Is Maggie here?"

Jude took the change in conversation to smooth her hair and brush out her shirt. "In the kitchen, with Mom and Stewart."

"So Stewart's here, too." Guess everyone was going to learn about Jake's last months on earth.

"He made the gumbo," Mark said, before grabbing his wife again. "And this one has gluten, although I have to say, I liked the pale one Maggie made."

Colin decided to leave the lovebirds alone, so he entered the empty dining room and poured himself a scotch. Seemed only fittin', as Maggie would say, considering the day, the circumstances and how New York had come calling with a job.

"Crap," he said aloud. The more the year progressed, the more complicated things became. He closed his eyes and leaned back against the buffet. Every day seemed a new dragon to slay. Now he had Jake's demise to ponder and a hot architecture position waiting for his answer.

"You said a naughty word, Uncle Teddy."

A warmth like wildfire spread through him as he gazed down at the cherub face silently berating him for using such language. "I did, didn't I Frederick? I promise it will not happen again."

"You always say that." Frederick planted his hands on his hips and pouted.

"I'll give you my slice of pie if you don't tell grandma."

His face brightened instantly. "Deal."

Colin pulled his nephew into his arms, raising him high in the air. He couldn't imagine not seeing his buddy every week. "You smell like alcohol," he said, when he brought Frederick's face to his.

"I had a tough morning," Colin answered.

"Maggie's here."

"Funny you should mention her."

"She likes you."

At this, Colin couldn't help but smile. "What makes you say that?"

"We were driving once and she was telling her dad about Uncle Jake and she said she really liked you."

Colin adjusted the boy so he fit comfortably on his hip. "When was this?"

"The first time Stewart came to town."

Colin ran through his memory like skimming a hard drive. The weekend Stewart installed the water heater. October. Just before the peak of foliage. "What did she say exactly?" He couldn't believe it. He was digging for information like a junior high school student.

Frederick began playing with one of Colin's buttons. "She said she flirted with you at the airport and she really liked you but it was all kinda crazy."

He didn't know why, but finding out Maggie was attractive to him long before the holidays gave him a little kick. He'd assumed as much in Pittsburgh, but there was so much baggage between them since, not to mention him yelling at her at the reading of the will.

Colin cringed, remembering that weekend and the three weeks that followed. Would they ever get past the pain Jake inflicted? Would Maggie ever be able to confront the family with the strange, awful truth and allow them to live a normal life?

Frederick grew impatient and asked to be let down, just as Bonnie entered with a large pot of something smelling wonderful. Stewart and Maggie followed, she looking every bit as adorable as when they collided at Gate Seventeen. It took everything in Colin's power not to pull her into his chest and devour those lips.

"Bonnie said you were offered a job in New York," she whispered anxiously, bringing food to the table. "Is this true?"

He leaned in close, breathing in her fresh scent of flowers. "Give me a reason to stay."

She looked at him surprised, as if he missed something gravely important. "What about the magazine?"

"Not good enough."

"*Yankee Living* isn't good enough?"

He wanted to laugh. The magazine was their life, yet somehow this crazy Georgian had made it hers as well. He could see her as chairman of the board one day, her Southern accent rising above the rest. "Yes, it's good enough but it's not the reason I'm looking for."

"Your family?"

Malick, Edith, Jude and Mark entered the room while Frederick danced around the table in glee. All great reasons to say no to New York. "Try again."

Maggie turned away from the table and leaned in close, so that her words would be for his ears only. "You're going to give up your dream career for me?"

Colin leaned forward so close, their noses almost touched.

"Bingo."

Her eyes grew as large as walnuts and Colin couldn't read if she was frightened with the thought of spending her life with him or overcome with emotion. He was about to inquire which when Bonnie called the room to order, Jude and Mark sitting down at the massive table while Edith and Malick stood in the back.

"I've asked you all here for a reason today."

"Did Mom just say 'you all?'" Edith stole a sly glance at Stewart, who winked.

Bonnie ignored her. "There is something I have to tell you about Jake."

He had to hand it to her, his mother was a master diplomat. Like a doctor skilled in bedside manner, she explained Jake's battle with leukemia, his insistence on keeping it a secret, the bone marrow transplant and the experimental treatments in Mexico that failed. She answered questions from the astonished family members, silently reaching over and taking Maggie's hand when she noticed the blood drain from her face.

"I don't understand," Mark finally said. "Why didn't you tell us before and why tell us this now?"

Bonnie gazed down at her lap, tears creeping down her cheeks. "I thought if I could promise him this one thing, to not speak of his disease, I could go to him and convince him to come home. But Jake was a solitary man. Despite his social life, he forced people away. I couldn't change him mind and he ended his days solitary as well."

"You were there." The words nearly choked Maggie. Colin reached over and squeezed her shoulder and she reached up and met his hand.

"Yes, I was there," his mother answered, hoping that would at least relieve Maggie's fears that Jake hadn't died alone.

"What about Maggie?" Edith asked, looking her way. "Surely you knew about all this."

"No," Bonnie answered. "Jake left for Mexico after they were married in Vegas."

The explanation was as unsubstantial as chicken broth, but

everyone seemed to drink it up. Perhaps in the shock of it all, no one thought how odd it would be to marry one night and disappear. Colin shifted nervously. If only Maggie would tell them the truth and be done with it all. If only they could learn how little her marriage to Jake had been.

"He didn't sleep with Maggie."

Every head turned toward Frederick, who looked pleased with himself for knowing so much. "Maggie said so."

"Said what, Frederick?" Jude asked.

He stood up in his chair so he had everyone's attention. "She said they got married and Jake left and they never slept together."

"Out of the mouth of babes...," Edith mumbled, while everyone stared at Maggie.

"Ah, we had a quickie marriage," she said.

"In front of Elvis," Frederick added.

"What?" Mark asked, smiling.

"We went out to dinner and had too much champagne." Maggie began twirling a strand of hair and Colin wondered if he should come to her aid. He was about to ask, when she added, "He talked me into this crazy chapel where Elvis performed the ceremonies. I thought it was all a joke, but you know Jake, he could talk Eskimos into buying ice cream. Especially drunk Eskimos."

Colin couldn't help wondering how much convincing Jake did that night.

"We went back to the hotel, he said he'd meet me later in my room, but it appears now he was actually catching a plane for Mexico. I never saw him again."

A stunned silence descended upon the group. Even Edith stared with her mouth open, at a loss for words.

"She was only after my magazine."

Maggie turned and sent him a reproachful glare and Colin took the opportunity to explain how Jake knew who Maggie was from her years of articles to their father. How one effort to recruit their Georgia fan had turned into admiration and love on his cousin's part. At the last piece of news, Maggie blanched.

"Love? Me? You've got to be kidding?"

Colin sighed, hoping that didn't mean what he feared it meant, that love was exactly what Maggie wanted from Jake. "I have his letter to prove it."

"Why didn't he write me a letter?" Jude asked, trying to extinguish the anxiety in the room.

"He left you his Jag," Edith answered.

The two sisters began discussing the items Jake had left behind and what they might have meant, when Bonnie called the family back to order. "There's something else I have to tell you."

Edith pulled out a chair at the table and sat down. "I can't take any more of this standing up."

At the head of the table Bonnie stood, taking Stewart's hand and grinning like a teenager. "Stewart has asked me to marry him."

Jude gasped, covering her mouth while her eyes stretched wide and Mark appeared equally surprised. Malick grinned and Edith smiled knowingly. "I knew it," she said.

"I'm retiring from the army next month," Stewart said, "and looking to move to Madison."

"We're considering a summer wedding," Bonnie added, gazing up at her fiancé with love.

The room burst into action, everyone jumping up and offer congratulations. Whatever fears Bonnie had over the family not accepting her happiness or Stewart into the family, were relieved instantly. Hugs and kisses abounded.

Colin glanced over at Maggie, who, no doubt, had a hand in all this revelry. He had never seen so much affection before; clearly her Southern touchy-feely stuff was contagious. She smiled at the happy couple, but he sensed an anguish inside. Maggie had received a Jake ambush and he knew that pain well, had experienced it only hours before.

Colin moved to go to her, not caring what the others thought or said, when Jude waved a hand in the air, silencing everyone. "Since this is come clean day, we have something to announce as well."

"We don't want details of your sordid love life," Edith mumbled. Jude sent her sister a reprimanding look. "Mark has finished his novel and his publisher said he's eager to look at it."

Congratulations went around again, Mark beaming at the accomplishment. "But that's not all," he added.

Everyone turned silent as he and Jude exchanged happy glances. "We're going to have another child," she announced.

Another uproar ensued, more hugging and kissing. Colin swore they could have picked up and dropped his family smack dab in the middle of Georgia and no one would have been the wiser. Ironically, the only person not genuinely enjoying all the personal contact was Maggie.

"What about you?" Bonnie asked Edith. "I know you brought Malick here for a reason."

Whatever blood existed in Edith's face disappeared instantly. Colin worried his sister might pass out from embarrassment. How could his mother do such a thing? "He's my…uh…"

Malick didn't waste a beat. He took Edith's hand and kissed it, then proudly wrapped an arm about her shoulder. "We're together."

Jude punched her sister in the arm, the equivalent of a congratulations and Edith took it for what it was, smiling broadly.

"Wait." Mark held up his hand. "I'm still lost here. We're all full of good news and yet I can't get the image of Maggie drunk before an altar, then waiting at a hotel room for a man who never showed up."

Maggie sighed and offered a brave smile. "It's okay, Mark. I got over it a long time ago."

"But Jake married you and deserted you on your wedding night."

She shook her head. "It wasn't a real wedding. We were many sheets to the wind. If anything, I need to apologize to you all for pretending it was something else all this time. I didn't know what else to do, considering I was still his wife when he died."

Bonnie took her hand and squeezed. "You did what you thought was right."

"I told you, she was after the magazine."

Now, it was Maggie's turn to punch Colin in the arm, but he grabbed her hand and pulled her into an embrace, kissing the top of her head.

"She likes Uncle Teddy."

All heads turned back toward the impetuous five-year-old who glowed with excitement over spreading more news.

"She said so," Frederick reiterated. "She said she really liked Uncle Teddy."

Edith grinned mischievously. "Is this true?"

Maggie slipped an arm about Colin's waist and leaned into his chest. As God was his witness, Colin was never going to relinquish his hold.

"No." Maggie said, which made him look down at her grinning face. "It's more than that, Frederick. I'm in *love* with Uncle Teddy."

"Oh. My. God." Jude looked like she was going to explode with the news. If the dining room table had been a clothesline, they had enough gossip to last a century.

But all Colin could comprehend at the moment was the sweet Georgia peach in his arms.

"Are you going to take that job in New York?"

She gazed up at him so beseechingly, he almost laughed. As far as he was concerned, Madison and the woman in his arms were the center of his universe and nothing was going to change that. "Never crossed my mind."

The old Maggie returned, her smile lighting up the room. Colin leaned down to kiss her waiting lips when he realized everyone was staring.

"If you all will excuse us…"

He led her past a half dozen grins, and then slipped into the kitchen, kissing her the instant they were alone. It took several minutes before he let her breathe, relishing every inch of those delectable lips.

"Colin," she said, when he moved to her neck. "My head may have been turned by Jake but in the end it meant nothing."

He sighed, leaning his forehead against hers. "It's okay, Maggie.

I knew what Jake was like. You don't have to..."

"It was only a handsome man showing me attention, nothing else."

He cupped her cheek, letting his thumb dance across her bottom lip. "Prove it."

She smiled nervously. "You want to make love in the kitchen?"

"No, I want you to marry me."

A flash of fear passed over her face.

"I'm not Jake," he repeated.

She slipped her arms about his waist, pulling him even tighter against her and nuzzling her face against his. "No, you're not."

"Then that's a yes."

Maggie kissed the inside of his neck, making her way up to his lips, rising on her toes to give him the full effect. "That's a yes."

Colin savored the kiss, and then pulled her high in the air while twirling her around. Maggie laughed, but placed a hand on his chest to return her back to earth. "There is one condition."

"You want my share in the magazine, too."

She punched him again and he feigned pain.

"No child of mine is going to say 'you guys.'"

Colin laughed, knowing damn well that any child growing up in New England wouldn't be caught dead using the Southern expression, but he nodded. "For you, Miss Scarlet, anything."

She seemed pleased with herself, hugging him tight. "And they said the South would never rise again."

Right now, it sure felt as if the north had won. When he got her back home that afternoon, he was going to dissolve the Mason-Dixon line forever.

"Are you two teenagers going to join us or what?" they heard Bonnie call from the dining room. "The gumbo is getting cold."

As Colin held her tight, he thought about all the changes that had happened since Maggie had come into their lives. She didn't realize it, but they had all transformed for the better, breaking out of a long darkness since their father's death. And now he was eating gumbo at the family dinner.

Colin took Maggie's hand and they joined the family, who

instantly offered more congratulations and hugs. He thought about Jake, who should have been there. Jake, who Colin always admired for breaking the cord, but who missed out on so much warmth and affection. As he gazed around at his family, basking in newfound love, settling on Maggie still wrapped inside his arms, he knew that nothing could replace any of this.

And that for once in his life, Jake had done something right.

Bonnie poured champagne and they all rose their glasses in a toast, first to Bonnie and Stewart's marriage, then the new baby and then to Edith and Malick. When they turned to Colin and Maggie, Colin raised his glass. "To Jake. For sending Maggie to Madison."

They sipped in silence, the loss of their cousin still fresh in their hearts. And for a moment, Colin sensed Jake was there with them, enjoying the camaraderie. No doubt, also rolling his eyes.

Maggie slipped an arm about his waist, raising her glass in one final toast.

"To damn Yankees," she said, her brown eyes twinkling with merriment. "God love 'em."

Maggie's Gluten-Free Seafood Gumbo

1 8-ounce jar of gluten-free roux such as Your Way sorghum roux
2 large yellow onions, chopped
1 green bell pepper, chopped
1 yellow bell pepper, chopped
1 red bell pepper, chopped
1/2 cup celery, chopped
1/2 garlic clove, chopped (optional)
2 (32-ounce) boxes seafood stock
1 pound shrimp (about 30-35 shrimp), preferably wild Louisiana shrimp
1 pound crabmeat
Salt, pepper and/or Cajun/Creole seasoning to taste
2 cups cooked Louisiana rice
Green onions, chopped, for garnish

Directions: Pour roux in a large stock pot and heat over medium heat. Add to the pot the chopped onions, bell peppers and celery, known as the "Cajun Trinity," and stir. Cook over medium-high heat until the vegetables are tender or until the onions are translucent, about 5 minutes. Add the seafood stock (you can adjust the amount to your preferred thickness) and bring to a gentle boil, then simmer, uncovered for about 10 minutes. Add the shrimp and cook for 5 minutes. Add the crabmeat and cook for 5 minutes. Add additional salt, pepper or Cajun seasoning to taste. Remove from heat, serve gumbo over rice and garnish with chopped green onions.

About the Author

Cherie Claire lives in South Louisiana where she works as a travel and food writer and pens several blogs about her unique culture. For Cherie, a bowl of gumbo really does ease most pains.

To learn more about her Cajun novels, upcoming events, Louisiana recipes and to sign up for her newsletter, visit her website **www.CherieClaire.net**.

Write to Cherie at
CajunRomances@Yahoo.com.

ALSO BY CHERIE CLAIRE

The Cajun Embassy
Ticket to Paradise
Damn Yankees
Gone Pecan

The Cajun Series historical saga
Emilie
Rose
Gabrielle
Delphine
A Cajun Dream
The Letter

www.ingramcontent.com/pod-product-compliance
Lightning Source LLC
Chambersburg PA
CBHW050025180626
46810CB00002B/581